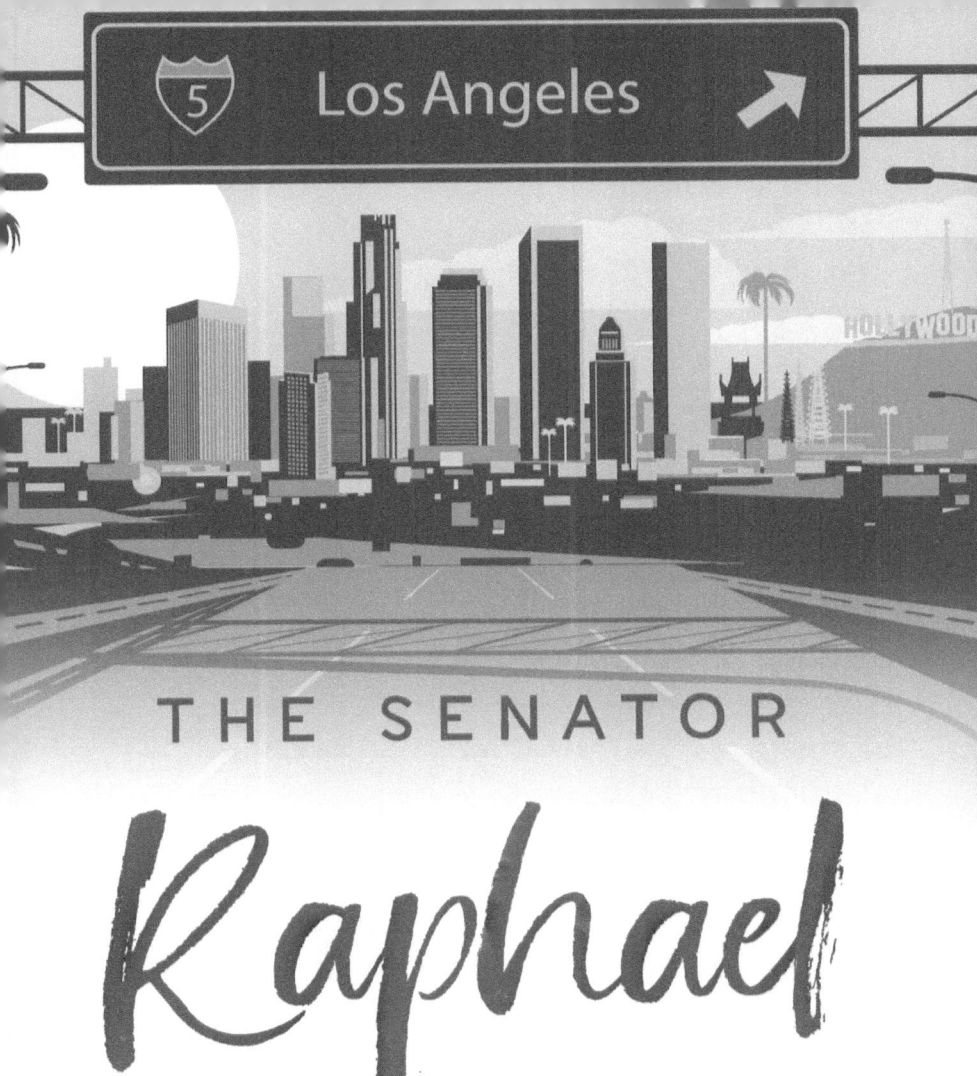

THE SENATOR

Raphael

ERIKA VANZIN

Want to get more FREE from Erika?

Sign up for the author's New Releases mailing list and get "Backstage" for free! You will periodically receive news and offers.

Click here to get started:
https://hello.erikavanzin.com/welcome/

To you, who carry the weight
of the world on your shoulders
and yet never falter in your
determination to make a difference,
I offer my deepest gratitude.

CHAPTER 1
Raphael

"Why aren't you married yet?" Sandra, the president of the women's association I'm having lunch with, asks me with a knowing smile.

She seems confident of the answer to her question, but she's trying to put me on the spot in front of the other members of the association and the few journalists invited to this event. It's sort of her job. I asked to meet with them for lunch as part of my campaign strategy, now I have to try to convince them to vote for me and not one of my opponents.

It should be easy, considering I'm running for senator against misogynist pricks, but I'm also running as an independent, a third party. There's no big party having my back when it comes to scrapping a few votes. We're running really close right now.

I sweep my gaze over the thirty or so faces waiting for my answer, seated at the table in this Malibu villa facing the ocean.

"Because I haven't found my better half yet," is the publicist-approved answer. Apparently, *Marriage is a farce and every woman I've known disappeared from my life* doesn't sound so good when you're running for senator of California.

She nods, curves her lips in a composed smile, looks down at the hors d'oeuvres laid out on the fine China in front of her, then looks back at me with a renewed challenge. She represents Los Angeles high society well, with her conservative pantsuit, pearl necklace, and modest makeup. She's playing her part, and right now she has to challenge me to determine if I'm worth the vote.

"You haven't found her *yet*, or you found someone of the wrong gender for a candidate aiming at the White House?" A few small gasps pierce the silence. It's considered borderline offensive asking these kinds of questions to a virtual stranger during a public lunch. But then again, there's no privacy for me. Not if I want to run the country. I'll always be under public scrutiny.

I smile. If she only knew how many times someone's asked if I was gay, she would realize her probing question is not as original or scandalous as she thinks.

"Why would I hide a male partner? It would be a bit hypocritical given it's an issue I'm fighting for. When I say that everyone should have the right to fall in love and spend their lives with whomever they want, that's not just campaign jargon." I let my smile fade a bit to give a serious tone to my reply. I look around the table and see a few heads nod approvingly.

"So, you're just picky and haven't found anyone yet?" Her tone seems almost to imply an offer to join me at my side.

I let a calculated laugh escape my lips to lift the heaviness of the conversation. "I've never found someone who would willingly jump into this life. I choose this life, I've worked for it since I was twenty years old, but I can't ask someone to give up their life to follow mine. That's not love, that's coercion, and last I checked it was illegal."

Everyone laughs at the table, including Sandra, who seems to relax a bit. I look up at Cindy, the only one of my staff invited to this lunch, and she tilts her head and smiles softly, inviting me to move on. It's time to steer the conversation in a more useful direction than my personal life. They got their chance to scratch the curiosity itch, now it's back to business.

"But we're not here to talk about me. I want to hear what I can do for *you*," I state firmly. I want to be clear that they are the center of this conversation, not me.

"Shouldn't it be the other way around? You try to win our favor with big promises and your winning smile?" Bridget, one of the older women seated at this table, gets straight to the point. I like her.

"Sure, I can come here with a fancy speech to win you over, big smiles for the camera," I wave at the woman taking pictures of this event, and she blushes but keeps doing her job, "eat a good meal and then go home. But that won't solve *your* problems. I'm a white male who's spent most of my life surrounded by other white males trying to overpower women. They can't teach me what you *really* need. I need you to tell me what your struggles are, and let me figure out how to help you." And I really mean it. Unlike my other opponents, I choose my fights based on what I believe, not what's most convenient for my career.

Bridget arches her black eyebrows in surprise and a few murmurs arise from the table. I'm not always this straightforward when I meet someone who could support my career, but these women deserve my respect and my honesty. They are a small representation of this association that helps thousands of women struggling in this country. When I say I want to help them, it's because I genuinely want to. I'm not running for senator because I want power, I'm running because I want to change things.

I look at Cindy and she nods in response with a discrete smile on her face. I broke the ice. Now I can relax a bit and maybe enjoy this hundreds-of-dollars-a-plate meal, and try not to throw up the caviar waiting on my plate. I *really* hate caviar.

***

I wave at Sandra and the other women as my driver opens the car door for me, and I ease into the black leather seat. When I close the door with its tinted windows, I finally relax.

"Cindy tells me it was a success!" Matthew's smiling face greets me.

He's my campaign manager and best friend since college. I would have wanted him with me today, but we agreed that Cindy was a better fit, giving the women the freedom to share their thoughts without a man there taking notes.

"I'm quite confident they will support us. Did Cindy give you some insight about what we have to work on?"

His blue eyes seem to light up at my question. "Even better. She told me Sandra will email her a detailed list of their concerns," he says nodding. Some unruly brown curls fall over his forehead.

"Good. Make sure we have consultants addressing specific topics. I want to work on a program that solves their problems."

He nods. "Already on it."

"Good. So why are you in this car, if you have everything running smoothly?" I pin him with my gaze on his, sitting across from me.

I take off my tie, fold it, and put it next to my computer on the seat next to me. I watch the smile fade from his face and brace for the bad news while we navigate the slow Los Angeles traffic.

"You've dropped another point five percent since last week," he states without beating around the bush.

Shit. I was already in trouble fifteen days ago, now I'm basically drowning. There's still a long run until midterms, but now is the time to consolidate my pace and get ready for the final push. Losing too many voters now means I can't even think about competing for the final leg of the campaign.

"You know why, right?" he asks without hesitation. I chose Matthew as my campaign manager because he doesn't hold back when it comes to telling me the truth.

"I'm not going to fake a relationship for some bigots who think I should be married because I'm thirty-five." I stand my ground. We have had this discussion a hundred times and I'm not giving in.

"It's not some bigots. They're your voters. They want stability, and a married man is the poster child for stability. Today they asked you for the umpteenth time if you're gay, and it wasn't some closed-minded old grandpa," he points out.

"And I handled it well, didn't I?" I start to simmer with anger.

I can't understand losing voters because I'm not in a relationship. Would they prefer one of those fake marriages where everyone cheats and hides it under the rug? Or would they rather just be lied to and pretend everything is fine? It doesn't make sense.

"They want commitment from you—if you want them to trust you with their lives. And a married man shows exactly that. You can learn to love whatever woman you choose, but you have to settle down at some point." His voice softens along with his features and I'm glad the car stops in front of the Hunting Club, because it's hard to swallow the lump growing in my throat.

"My answer will always be a no. I won't fake a relationship for the sake of a bunch of votes," I say before opening the door and getting out of the car.

I quicken my pace and walk to the desk where the young man we hired recently greets me with a smile. I sign in and walk around the counter toward the bar. Technically, this is a hunting club, hated by every environmentalist in Los Angeles because of what it represents. But in reality, no one here has ever hunted, at least not the people I know personally. It's just a cover for a men's club where the most powerful public figures in this city meet privately. It's on an invitation-only basis, discrete, and we can relax and be ourselves without being under public scrutiny all the time. It's a breath of fresh air when you need to vent your frustrations without ending up in the gossip magazines.

I walk to the bar and sit next to Harrison Bates, one of the people I consider a friend outside of this place. He's a Hollywood star, an Oscar-winning, panties-dropping kind of guy, and right now he seems to need alcohol even more than I do.

"Do you want to talk about it?" I ask.

He briefly glances at me before turning his attention to the sparkling water in front of him. He's currently filming a movie where ninety percent of the time he's half-naked, so he's on a forced diet: no alcohol or anything caloric for him. I have no idea how he endures that life.

"Not here."

I look around and see people I would prefer to not have eavesdropping on our conversation. I stand up and beckon him to follow me.

After we change out of our clothes, we reach one of the small saunas and sit inside, towels knotted at our waist. Harrison sits in front of me, and I have to admit the hours he spends in the gym are not wasted. The guy is ripped.

"Are you done checking me out?" He smirks.

"Honestly, no. How can you look like that twenty-four seven?"

He chuckles. "It's a nightmare, trust me. I can't eat anything, drink only water and those protein shakes I hate, and I hit the gym seven days a week plus film the movie. I can't wait for this torture to end."

I shake my head, admiring his resilience in his job. "So, that's why you're wearing this face?" I prod.

"No, I have this face because I'm almost sure this movie will flop." He smiles sadly, resignation showing in his eyes.

"Any particular reason or just a gut feeling?" He's been in this industry long enough to know how far a movie will go even before it hits the theatres.

"The director is a freak, not in a good way, and the chemistry with Agatha, my love interest in the movie, is about the same as with a tree trunk."

"Ouch." I smile.

He shrugs. "She's hot, I'm hot, but we don't hit it off."

"And humble too!" I bark out a laugh.

He smirks again. He is so damn confident, which is why he's so successful in Hollywood. "You were the one checking me out a few minutes ago."

"Well, I can't deny that," I admit. "Have you talked with Aaron about it? I know he's not producing the movie, but maybe he has some suggestions."

Aaron is a member of this club, a successful movie producer, and someone who dictates the rules in the Hollywood Hills. He's also our friend and someone we can count on.

"No. I turned down one of his TV shows to film this movie. He'll kick my ass and say, 'Told you so,'" he grumbles.

I smile. There's always been this dance between those two. One trying to convince the other to work on a project together, the other too busy to consider it. I think Harrison is scared that if the movie flops like this one it will ruin their relationship, and he doesn't want to lose a friend.

"So, suck it up and make things with Agatha less awkward."

"I can't. I really can't. She's a diva, and I can't deal with her attitude. And I can tell she doesn't like mine because she can't leave the set fast enough between takes."

"Maybe it's a stupid suggestion, but have you tried going out with her outside the set? Maybe knowing each other better will help."

He frowns. "Oh, no. We slept together and it was a total disaster." He says it like it's no big deal. And for him it probably isn't.

I snort, trying not to laugh. "So, maybe *that's* the problem, huh?"

"Probably, but knowing it doesn't change the fact that the movie will flop, and I'll have to deal with the consequences."

I nod, not knowing how to help him. I close my eyes and enjoy the sweat running down my body, feeling my muscles relax a bit.

"So, are you going to tell me why *you* have that face or are we going to pretend everything is normal with you?" he asks after a while.

I knew this question was coming. He can read my moods better than anyone else.

"The campaign is sinking faster than I expected," I admit.

I open my eyes and land my gaze on his frowning one. "Are there really people that don't like you? I thought you were the one dropping panties with that dazzling smile." He jokes but I notice the slight concern in his tone. He's one of the few people who knows how important this campaign is to me. He was there years ago to pick up the pieces.

"Apparently, not being married is keeping some people from voting for me," I sigh, tired of having this conversation.

"Really? Why do they care?" He rests his hands behind his head, showing off his muscled arms.

"Gods only knows. They think a man who commits to a woman is more reliable than a single one. Never mind that most weddings end up in flames in the first few years. Or that so many cheat behind their significant other's back."

He nods and seems to think about it. "What does your team say about it?"

I sigh, already knowing where this conversation is going to end up. "They want me to find someone to marry, or at least have a serious relationship. An arranged thing, like a hundred years ago."

He frowns. "So why are you worried? You have a solution, just go with it."

I look at him with a disapproving stare. "Am I the only one who thinks marriage should be between two people who love each other? And meaningful? Why are you all so careless about it? I know most marriages these days are a farce, but that doesn't mean I want to join in the destruction of it."

"So, find someone you love and marry her," he states simply.

"Okay, sure. Let me take a look at my contacts and see if I can find the love of my life."

Harrison rolls his eyes. "Actors do it all the time. Our publicist usually sets up the relationship for us. You just have to choose someone you like, then get on with it. Sometimes it's strictly platonic, other times we hook up. It helps our careers. It can be just a few dates or a longer period and more commitment, but the public appreciates it, so why not? Just try to choose someone you admire. It's not that big of a deal."

A marriage in Hollywood can last a few hours—no joke, I saw an actor marry a fan in Vegas and end up in court a few hours later to end the thing, the signatures weren't even dry yet—to several years, but nobody cares whether it's spur-of-the moment or they love each other. They're celebrities, everyone expects them to have an eccentric life. I can't marry someone and divorce her a month later.

"You make it sound easy."

He scoffs. "Because it *is* easy."

"You're not helping, you know that?"

He shrugs, closes his eyes, and enjoys the heat, leaving me to overthink our conversation.

***

I walk into my living room that is already dark. The lights from the swimming pool are filtering through the windows, giving a warm glow to the earth tones of the walls and furniture. The thing I loved most about this house was the Mediterranean vibe it had the first time I saw it. On sunny days, it feels like it belongs in a little Spanish town.

I inhale deeply and the faint smell of bleach reminds me that I'm not on vacation in some foreign country. This is my house, one my staff keeps meticulously clean, but that I never have the chance to enjoy.

My phone buzzes in my pocket. I grab it and see my father's name, then let it go straight to voicemail. He probably saw the news Matthew gave me today and wants to rant about it. I'm honestly too tired to deal with him right now.

I walk into my home office and turn on the table lamp, sitting at my desk. Noticing a yellow folder with Cindy's curly handwriting on a post-it that reads 'Keep an open mind,' I open it and a dozen women's headshots stare back at me. Pictures and information ranging from where they went to school to what their careers are. Potential wives lined up like it's a cattle call. I hate it. I hate all of this but I'm sinking and apparently this is what people expect from me.

Closing the folder, I decide to deal with it tomorrow. I open the last drawer of my desk and pick up my senior yearbook. I've opened it so many times since I graduated, the pages are almost falling out. I don't have to search for her. The book opens exactly to the page where I see her staring back at me with a smile. She was the one I was supposed to spend my life with. She was *The One*. Period.

How can they demand I walk down the aisle with someone I don't even love? And for what? To give another woman a chance to leave me? Not a single woman in my life sticks around long enough for me to savor the happiness. Sure, it wasn't always their fault, but I resigned myself years ago to the fact that there will never be a happily ever after for me. So, why bother? Why put my heart out there, even if am just faking it?

CHAPTER 2
Raphael

I breathe once, twice, three times. I stare at my father's home office door for a long moment before grabbing the handle and opening it. I know this will be a difficult conversation. After I ignored his calls yesterday, after the lunch with the women's association, I don't expect this will be a walk in the park. My father is like that. You do what he says, when he tells you to do it, and the way he wants it. No exceptions.

"Finally, you decide to show your face around here," he sneers.

I struggle not to roll my eyes. I learned not to when I was a kid and my father made me pay for my insolence. Just once. It took just one punishment to not do it ever again. But sometimes I just can't resist challenging him, even if the consequences are brutal. God only knows how many times I ended up with bruises when I was a teenager.

"I was working on a plan after yesterday's meeting, and I put my phone away. I needed to focus," I lie.

I sit down on the brown leather couch next to his desk. This house hasn't changed since I was a kid. Arches and stuccos give this place the Mediterranean feel I've always loved. It's why I bought a similar style for myself. Growing up with my father wasn't easy, but I still have good memories of my childhood here.

"Don't you pay someone to do that?" His cold stare pins me to the couch.

My father gives me chills sometimes. Physically we are very similar. Same brown hair—at least until the gray overtook him a few years ago—green eyes, height. He's a bit bigger than me, but he's still fit, considering his almost seventy years. The stark difference between us is the coldness in his eyes. I can't be that detached when I talk to someone I care about.

"Yes, but some things I want to process personally before talking to my staff. I want to be sure to tell them exactly what I want. Saves me the headaches later." I try to keep my composure. Showing nervousness in front of him is like waving a raw steak in front of a shark. You will end up in pieces.

He stares at me for a couple of long moments, but then he lets me breathe. I'm not off the hook yet, but at least this part is over. Still, I'm sure the worst is yet to come.

"You lost another zero-point five percent this week." His stern voice is like a punch in the gut.

Here we go. He lays out the reason why he was calling me last night.

"I know. I'm working on that. I have the endorsement from Jeff Johnson. Keep it quiet. We haven't gone public with that yet." I try my best to downplay this achievement.

Jeff Johnson is a former vice president of the United States. It was hard to get him on my side, especially because I'm running as an independent and his old party is far from thrilled to get involved with a wild card, but I played that card well. It took me years of nurturing the relationship to be able to cash in on all the favors I did for him. I'm proud of this endorsement, but I can't show my father. I don't want to give him an opening to say I should have divided my efforts on a wider strategy, not played all my cards on that hand.

I never divert my eyes from his face. If I had, I would have missed the slight widening of his eyes. It was just a flash before regaining his composure, but I saw it. He's impressed. Pride inflates my chest, but again, I can't show it.

"Is he willing to support you in the next steps of your career too?" he asks after a long silence that I don't dare to break.

Becoming the president of the United States of America. I know where my father is aiming to place me. I've known he was playing the long game since he suggested years ago I become a politician. He can't do it himself, so he's counting on me. My father has an "honest job" as a contractor. He deals with big projects like malls and airports around the world.

His company is thriving, but it's just a cover. If you dig deeper—and trust me, the FBI has been trying to for forty years now—his business is not so transparent and legal. He's never involved me in this work and there's a reason for that. He has other plans for me, and he wants me clean. He wants me to lead one of the most powerful countries in the world. Why? He hasn't told me yet.

"Like I said, he's supporting me as a senator. The next step is a mere formality. I'm playing this right. I'm not leaving anything to chance." I try to sound confident without bordering on arrogant.

"I hope this boosts your ratings because right now, your campaign strategy sucks."

Too much to hope for a pat on the back and a *Good job, son.* "Well, unless there are more surprises in the immediate future, this endorsement should do the trick." I start to feel annoyed.

"There is always a surprise," he states grumpily and his tone gets my attention. He never complains, and his gruffness means something's happened that he couldn't stop.

"Spit it out, Dad. Keeping secrets is not going to help me." My stomach clenches in a painful vise.

"The dinner with the investor next week is cancelled. I got tipped off that the FBI is digging into one of their companies and it doesn't look good. They're going to confiscate a bunch of stuff and I don't want you involved in this shit. Especially if the FBI can track the money to your campaign."

Now I understand his concern. "Shit," I whisper. It's beyond me how my father can get a tip-off from a government agency, but this sounds like one of his unofficial businesses.

I really needed that money for my campaign. One of the problems of running without a party is that you are always short of cash compared to your opponents. You need connections with rich people who see you as good investment. My father is a good source of those connections.

"Which one did you choose to marry?" he asks me out of the blue.

I snap my head in his direction. "What?"

"I sent Cindy a list of women to choose from, to marry and boost your credibility. Which one did you pick?" His voice is firm, and I know this is not a simple question, it's an order.

I should have known my father was behind this farce. "I didn't choose anyone because it's not necessary. I'm fine just how I am," I snap and immediately regret it. The fury simmering in my father's eyes makes me uncomfortable. I'm not scared he's going to hit me—he stopped doing that a long time ago—but there's a lot of other things he can do to make my life a living hell.

"Are you arrogant and stupid enough to you think you can run for president without a wife? You will sink and I'm not going to feed your ambition without the certainty that you can pull this off. You want to run without a party and a wife? You won't see another penny from me. Get your shit together and grow up. It's time for you to put this before everything else in your life," he hisses with a coldness that freezes my bones.

I clench my fists and let my anger bubble to the surface, fighting back. "I've been doing this since I was twenty-one years old. I *have* put this before everything else! Don't bullshit me! You know I don't have a private life. I dedicate every second of my day to this job. How can I put a woman through that?"

"Nobody gives a shit what your wife thinks. That's her problem. When she marries you, she knows what she's signing up for, and trust me, she will benefit from that life. She will not be a poor little girl neglected by her husband. She will be powerful and rich. That's all it takes to convince them. I put together that list because I know those women would do anything to get to you. All you have to do is choose. Marry one of them or you won't see a penny from me." He ends the discussion.

Considering he's the major investor in my campaign, I realize I don't have much of a choice. I hate him. I hate how he can control my life just by threatening to shut his wallet. And I can't do anything about it. I *need* his money. I tried to do it without him, but in the end, I had to go back to my old man.

I stand up and storm out of his office, slamming the door behind me. I cross the huge living room to the patio doors before taking a deep breath in front of the swimming pool.

"Do you want to talk about it?" Marianne's worried voice comes from a deck chair next to me. I didn't notice her stretched out there, enjoying the sun in a navy-blue bikini. She is my father's second wife and the sweetest woman I know.

"About what? Your husband being an asshole?"

There's always been good rapport between the two of us. Maybe because I was an adult when my parents got divorced, but I never had hard feelings for her. She takes care of my father and I appreciate that.

"Tell me something I don't know." She laughs, teasing me, then pats the deck chair next to her for me to sit.

I take the spot and rub a hand over my face. "He wants me to marry. Sent me a list like I'm selecting groceries."

She nods. "I heard about that. He told me."

I glance at her expectantly. "And?" I ask when she doesn't say anything more.

"And while it's an unusual way to get married, all those women are willing and consenting. You're a good man, Raphael. They'll be fine with you."

I don't know the details of her marriage with my father, but she's the daughter of my father's biggest competitor. A few months after he married her, the companies merged into a huge conglomerate nobody can take down. I'd always suspected love wasn't involved when they got married.

"God, this is so wrong," I whisper, rubbing my forehead. "How can I marry someone I have zero interest in? How can I endure a life with a woman I feel nothing for?" I look her straight in the eye.

Her gaze softens and a sweet smile crosses her lips. "She'll never come back, Raphael. You will never find a woman you love in the same way, but you can learn to live with the one you choose. You can't think of living a life alone; your heart can't heal that way. You'll become a grumpy, sad man who hates everyone, and you don't deserve to end up like that. You have a good heart, too good for the tank of sharks you're jumping into, but you can change the world with it. If marrying is a way to do good for millions of people, do it with a smile on your face."

The lump in my throat is almost painful. She always has the right words to inspire me to be better. Unlike my mother, who turned her back on me when I needed her most.

"So I have to plan a wedding, huh?" A small smile arches my lips.

She grins, her brown eyes lighting up. "If you need a hand with that, count me in. I loved planning mine!" She beams and I can't keep from chuckling.

"I'll call you when I pick someone from the list. God, that sounds gross. Like a mail-order bride or something." I rub my face again.

She chuckles. "It's not like that. Your father organized every-thing into a folder, yes, but the reality is those women are not forced into this. They're not desperate to flee from their country to a man they don't know. They're women who know exactly what they want and that happens to be you."

"Gee, thanks. I feel so much better now," I tease. I look at my watch and realize I'm almost late for my meeting this afternoon. "I have to go, but thanks for the chat." I pat her hand, kiss her cheek and stand up. She waves and sips her cucumber and lemon water.

I get into the car and grab my phone while my driver takes off from the gated Malibu community where my father lives.

"Hey, Matthew. Are you free tonight? I have to choose a wife," I reluctantly say to my best friend.

I don't like it. Scratch that, I *hate* it. But Marianne is right. If marrying someone gives me the chance to change the world, I have to give this thing a try. I'll deal later with the sense of un-ease and betrayal that grips my stomach.

"What do you think about this one?" Lola waves a sheer, black lace bra in front of my eyes that looks two sizes smaller than what I need.

"Does it even cover my nipples?" I raise my eyebrow, annoyed.

"Barely, but you'll get higher tips." She winks at me.

Buying lingerie with Lola is always an experience. While I don't enjoy it particularly, since I have to wear it for work, buying it with my roommate is always fun. We both work in an exclusive nightclub where we get insanely high tips to serve drinks while squeezed into sequined shorts and a bra. We're just bartenders, not dancers in golden cages like some sort of exotic birds, but we do have requirements for what to wear: lingerie. Hence, our monthly raid at the store of one of the most expensive brands available. She makes our monthly visit to Rodeo Drive less painful, especially when we grab food and enjoy our day off.

I met Lola when I first moved to Los Angeles seven years ago and was looking for an apartment. We instantly connected, and when I told her it was difficult to find a job that paid enough, she introduced me to the club. I wasn't thrilled to serve drinks in lingerie, but the tips were insanely high. Not my ideal career, but it pays well and thanks to the tips, I'm saving a ton of money. The nightclub has no sign outside, only the most influential people know about it, and you can access it only if you're with the right crowd. Discretion is the key for working in that place, and it's perfect for someone like me who doesn't want to be in the spotlight.

"God, how can they charge five hundred dollars for a bra that doesn't even cover your tits?" she asks, showing me a tiny piece of clothing that is definitely not a bra. It's three strips of black fabric sewn in a triangle shape where your boobs basically hang out. Shouldn't this be sold in a sex shop? It's part of the "daring collection"— the only daring thing about it is the price tag. How did they even find a place to put the tag?

I chuckle and check out the bustier in front of me. It's black lace with feathers on the bra cup. It's elegant and covers more than that thing Lola showed me. "I don't know, this one is twelve hundred dollars." I show her the garment and she seems to appreciate it. I think we have a winner.

"At least your boobs are covered! Not that it would stay on for long if I wore it," she giggles.

I admire how casual she is about the side gig of our job. I'm not brave enough for something like that. She's one of the girls who offers extra services to clients in exchange for a higher tip or a particularly expensive present. Not exactly a prostitute, but she can make some extra cash sleeping with guys willing to pay her. Our boss knows about it, and he closes one eye to keep his clients satisfied. That and other things like the drugs consumed not so subtly at the tables.

I was a bit skeptical in the beginning about spending the night with virtual strangers, but working there I discovered they're not regular "Johns," they're well-known public figures and we definitely know their names. Men so out of our league we don't stand a chance of even breathing the same air outside that place. If only their girlfriends and wives knew where they were during the day, they wouldn't be smiling so brightly at the cameras. Or maybe they know and don't care; it's not my place to judge.

"Are you coming for lunch?" Lola asks after we pay way too much for our lingerie. Her blond waves shine in the California sun as we walk out of the shop.

"Not today, I have to go home and answer some emails before my shift tonight."

She pouts. "You're always studying and working on papers. When will you start enjoying your life?"

I stopped doing that eight years ago, when I made a decision that completely changed my life. I knew it was the right thing to do, but it doesn't make my life suck less now.

"I'm enjoying my life plenty!" I lie.

I'd like to go out, travel, see places, have a job I love, and a family, but I'm stuck in this limbo where I can't go back to my past and I don't have a future. I'm just getting by, day in and day out, without a purpose or goal. Surviving on autopilot. And I'm okay with that.

"No, you're living like a ninety-year-old lady in sexy lingerie," she points out.

"God, that is the worst thing my mind could conjure. Thank you for searing my brain with the image of an old lady in a sexy outfit!" I jokingly push her as she laughs.

"So, see you at home?" She kisses me on the cheek.

"Yes. Are we carpooling tonight?" We normally use her car when we work on the same night.

"Not this time. I have breakfast with a cute doctor tomorrow morning." She winks at me, and I feel my heart squeeze.

She's a nightclub bartender with a side gig of paid sex, and she somehow manages to have a perfectly balanced life—with relationships and everything in between. I can't even think of being with someone for more than a hookup.

"I want every detail when you come back," I say before opening the door of my Uber.

"Do you want a video? I can record our performance." She laughs winking at me.

"Please, don't. I don't need that kind of detail." I wave at her as I close my door.

I watch her move toward the restaurant with a smile on her face. She's happy and I envy her a bit. I wish I could be that carefree.

I walk into our shared apartment and head straight for my room to change into a pair of shorts and a tank top, grabbing my computer from my desk. I sit outside on the deck chair in our tiny garden and check my email. I don't have many, mostly spam or newsletters I subscribed to, but no real human interaction.

The only genuine thread of email I exchange is with a New York University professor, Hans Gruber, who helps me out by sending me material for different courses I want to take. He teaches Criminal Law, something I was interested in pursuing in my previous life. A dream I can't stay away from, even if I know I'll never follow that career. Still, it's fun to have something to dedicate my time to without the pressure of tests, finals, or failing courses.

I open Gruber's email and a lump forms in my throat.

Dear Ms. Argent,

I had the pleasure of reading your last assignment this week-end and personally graded it. I wish I had more students with your passion, dedication, and sensitive intelligence. Attached you can find the paper with my grade and some notes in the margins.

I know we already discussed this topic, but I always hope you'll reconsider your decision not to pursue a college career. We can work together to find a solution for your peculiar situation. It's a shame that a curious mind and a kind heart like yours can't help other people in obtaining justice.

I wish you my best,

Professor Hans Gruber.

I reread the email three times before my heart finally slows down. This is one of the moments when my heart says, *Fuck it, let's do this!* and I almost believe that another future is possible for me. But then I remember it's not just my life on the line, and the dread sinking in my stomach makes me want to scream.

I open the attachment the professor sent and find a scan of my paper with a circled red A+ at the top and notes about books I should read to dig deeper into the topic. I write down the titles and hope to find some student online willing to sell me a copy.

I type and delete my answer five times before stopping and closing my laptop. What I want to say I can't write in an email. It's not even a conversation I could have in person in a public place. It would have to be confessed in a whisper in the privacy of someone's home, and even there it wouldn't be safe.

I move into the living room and grab some grapes to eat while I watch TV. There's nothing much on, but I catch the end of a special about the upcoming elections showing Raphael Wyden shaking hands with the president of a women's charity organization. I have mixed feeling about that guy. He seems genuinely committed to helping people, the only politician who doesn't give me the creeps. But I always see him coming and going at the nightclub, conversing and leaving with a redhead who Lola says is an escort. At least he doesn't have a girlfriend or a wife. I give him credit for not cheating on some poor woman like most of the guys who frequent the club.

***

I walk into the changing room at the nightclub and put on my latest purchase. The bustier looks good on my slim waist and the sequined shorts are sexy but still cover me adequately.

"You look gorgeous. Are you trying to steal all our men?" Sabrina, one of the baristas, slaps my butt jokingly.

"Oh, no. They're all yours!" I smile as I put my phone in my locker and walk out with her.

"One day you'll realize how much more money you'd make if you gave them more of your time, and then we'll all be screwed." She winks at me before entering the main room where the lights are dim, making the place look more luxurious.

The girls always make fun of me for being one of the few that don't go out with clients. All the bartenders here, men and women, top up their wages at the end of their shift by meeting some client's expectation. I'm not comfortable doing that.

I walk behind the bar and let Elvira know she can take off. She smiles at me, blows a kiss in my direction and sways her way toward a tall man in his mid-forties that I know has a wife waiting for him at home. I saw pictures of them online on vacation at some Aruba resort not even two weeks ago.

I put some ice in the container in front of me and busy myself rearranging the bottles behind the bar. This place is strange. It's a nightclub, so people spend most of their time in the main area where the bar is, but we're in the VIP restricted area upstairs, where people come not to dance but to relax a bit on the couches before going back to the main area to dance or somewhere more private with the girl they choose. There's music coming from downstairs but it's not so loud you can't talk.

Basically, this is where everyone comes to chill and relax. I'm okay with this because it means I don't have to rush with the orders. The bar is never crowded, and people don't complain much if you take too long to prepare a drink. They're usually fine with ogling our outfits and dumping a load of cash for our tips. More money, less work. The girls downstairs have it much worse.

"Sweetie, when do you finish working tonight?" A slurry voice I unfortunately recognize makes me turn around.

One of the usual clients, a man in his fifties with a small beer belly and a big wallet, sits on the stool in front of me. He's drunk, and I don't know why Seb, the bouncer at the VIP door tonight, let him in. One of the rules about this place is we don't serve alcohol to someone who seems tipsy. They don't want to deal with drunk asses harassing other clients. Which is why I'm perplexed about the bouncer sending up someone who's already drunk.

"What can I get you, honey?" I ask him with a smile, cringing inside.

"You can start by giving me head, as a warm up." He smirks and I have difficulty refraining from rolling my eyes.

"I'm just a bartender. I can only give you a cocktail." Every time he comes, he asks me for sex.

It's useless explaining I'm just a bartender, not an escort. He completely dismisses my explanation, always proposes more money, and I tell him every time that I wouldn't do it for even a million bucks. Usually, he laughs it off and comes back again the next time he sets foot in this place.

I start to prepare a non-alcoholic drink for him, shaking and make a scene preparing it, so he doesn't ask what it is.

I place it in front of him and he sips, making a face. "Fuck, you should stick to sucking dicks because this thing sucks," he slurs loudly, attracting some of the other clients' attention.

My heart starts pounding in my chest, partly because I don't want to deal with his drunk ass, partly because I want to punch him in the face. I hate my job sometimes.

"Feel free to leave it here if you don't like it. It's on the house." I try to smooth out the situation.

"Or, you could let me fuck you to make up for this shitty cocktail." He's more angry than drunk now.

"I told you, I'm just a bartender here." My voice is resolute, but I'm starting to think it might be better if I call security.

We don't have bouncers inside the VIP area, but we do have security guys ready to intervene as soon as we press a button under the counter. We don't need to use it often, but sometimes we can't deescalate a situation and we have to kick someone out. Once he's out, he can't come back again, and his name gets put on the blacklist. Which is why clients usually don't make a fuss.

He pushes the drink toward me roughly and topples the glass over, and I have to jump back to avoid getting splashed. Elvira, the bartender who just ended her shift and had been chatting with a client, looks at me, worried. I smile at her, hoping she won't call security. One thing about getting help is that you alert Ice, the owner of the place. He doesn't care if you're in danger, it's the clients who are more important to him, and you don't want to find yourself on the receiving end of his angry tirade.

"You're just a whore like the others in here. You're just too stupid to admit it," he rants, and I don't even have time to respond because Elvira is at his side, clinging to him.

"Hi, sweetheart. Do you want some company?" she coyly asks. "I can show you a good time."

He switches his glassy eyes from me to the brunette with long legs at his side and smirks. "Sure, you can."

"Wait for me on the couch over there and I'll take care of you." She gestures at one of the sofas in the main area. The man wobbles to the couch but finally sits down.

"Give me some straight vodka." She winks at me.

"Are you sure? I can call security, he's drunk," I suggest. I don't want her to get hurt.

She waves a hand at me and smiles. "Don't worry about it. I'll give him some vodka, he'll pass out drunk and when I wake him up in his car after he's sobered up, I'll tell him it was the best sex of my life. Works every time." She winks at me, and I smile.

"Thank you." I push the glass in front of her.

"Don't thank me. You gave me easy money tonight." She grins and strolls to the couch where the guy is waiting for her, then they disappear down the stairs.

I look around to check if anyone called security, but nothing seems out of the ordinary, and I sigh with relief.

***

I change back into my comfy leggings and t-shirt and put the lingerie in my bag.

"Was it okay with the drunk asshole?" I ask Elvira when she come into the dressing room and takes off her high heels.

She smiles at me and nods. "Like I told you, I gave him some vodka, he passed out, and when I woke him up an hour later, I thanked him for the best ride of my life. He was so drunk he paid me double for my services."

I chuckle. "God, he is so dumb. I wonder why Seb let him in? He was really out of his mind tonight."

Elvira shrugs. "I heard he's Ice's friend and he lets him get away with way too much. Seb just didn't want to piss off the big boss."

"That explains a lot."

Elvira is about to reply when the door swings open and Ice furiously storms in. "Out!" he shouts toward the barista and the girl scurries out, shrinking a bit.

I freeze on the bench where I'm seated. This is why I didn't call security, but it's obvious someone did, or at least they told Ice what happened. Now I'm in a lot of trouble.

"When a client asks you to do something, you shut your mouth and do it!"

I flinch slightly and I hate myself for that. I don't want to give him the impression he can intimidate me. "I am a bartender and he asked for sex. I don't do that," I counter firmly.

He scoffs. "I think we can change that. What do you think?"

"You want to force me into prostitution? Every girl in here is willingly doing this job. Do you really want to cross that thin line with me?" I hiss and see that it shocks him.

Ice is a big, sturdy man in his sixties with salt-and-pepper hair and a scar across his tanned face. He is terrifying and he knows he can get what he wants.

"Don't push your luck, sweetheart. You don't want me to start digging around in what you're hiding. Do you really think I don't know you came out of nowhere, with no past, no relationship, no family? There's no information anywhere about you prior to seven years ago. How do you explain that?"

His threat makes my stomach quiver. I have to go away, leave Los Angeles and start new somewhere else. But I need money, lots of it, because I won't be able to get a well-paid job in the future so I need to save as much as I can now while I can count on my body to earn big tips.

I stand up, facing him, though he towers above me. "Remember that we call the people that come to this place 'sweetheart' or 'honey,' but we know their real names. To be precise, I have a list ready to send to every single newspaper in the country, with every extra service they require of your baristas, every kink they have, and every drug they take, if anything happens to me or one of the girls. Sure, you can fire us, or even hurt us, but you won't survive long enough to see another day. Do you think those clients will be happy to see their faces all over the news? Think carefully about every single one of them, and then think even more deeply about what every one of them can do to you."

"Don't threaten me," he spits.

"Or what? Are you willing to find out what happen if those newspapers get a tip-off about what's really happening in here? About the escorts you let in to offer extra fun for the customers, or the drugs you let your men sell here? Yes, I know that some of your bouncers have a side hustle." I grab my bag and shoulder him while I walk past him and out of the dressing room.

My heart is hammering in my chest as I make my way out of this place. Sure, I desperately need this job, but I don't know if it's worth going up against a man who runs a shady business that's no doubt darker and deeper than I even know.

CHAPTER 4
Silver

The sun kisses my skin. I close my eyes and enjoy the warmth on my face. It's still the end of February, but Los Angeles weather is nothing like the freezing temperatures of the Midwest where I grew up. I take in the peace of this place, the sound of the waves crashing on the rocks of the cliff I'm standing on. A slight breeze carries with it the scent of the surrounding greenery.

"I don't know what you're going through, but I'm here to listen to you, if you want." A soft female voice comes from behind me.

I open my eyes, turn around, and study her. She's approaching cautiously, like I'm some sort of wild animal. "What?"

She points to the cliff. "I know sometimes life seems difficult, but I'm here to listen, if you want to talk."

I frown, look back at the ocean, then at her. "Oh, shoot! I'm not jumping. I swear. I was just enjoying the sun," I hurry to explain when I understand what she means. "God, I'm not trying to kill myself." I step away from the steep rocky ground and reach her.

"Thank God. I thought you were going to jump." She half-laughs, shaking her head.

"I swear I'm not." I mean, life sucks right now, especially after last night with Ice barking and threatening me, but I'm not *that* desperate.

I take a good look at her. She is in her mid-fifties, in hiking clothes, with long blond hair gathered in a messy bun on her head.

"Are you hiking up to the stables?" I know there is a ranch open to the public not far from here.

She shakes her head. "No, I'm just taking my daily hike, and when I saw you, I wasn't sure if I should talk to you or tackle you to the ground," she laughs.

"Do I look that desperate that I'd jump off a cliff?" I smile at her.

"No, but you look sad," she admits.

I nod. "Just a bad night. That's all."

"If he makes you so gloomy, dump him. Life is too short to chase after an asshole. I made that mistake three times. Trust me, I know what I'm talking about." She nods knowingly while she starts to walk toward the trail.

I chuckle. "Thank you for the advice. I'll keep it in mind."

She winks at me, waves, and then goes on with her hike. I look at her back until she disappears from sight. She has no idea how far from the truth she is.

I gave up on relationships a long time ago, when I realized that I can't get into anything serious if I can't talk about my past. At some point in every relationship, you want to know the other person on a deeper level. You're curious about their childhood, family, girlfriends or boyfriends in high school.

I can't go there. When they ask about the first twenty-one years of my life, I have to lie. I'm twenty-nine and I can only talk about the last eight years. And they're not exciting or memorable. Far from it. I tried to date a sweet guy once, but when things got serious, I started to avoid answering his questions for fear of tripping over my lies. He suspected something was off and dumped me. I couldn't blame him. Something *is* off about my life.

***

I walk into the living room of the apartment I share with Lola and find my roommate trying to fit into a latex corset that I'm sure is at least a couple of sizes too small.

"Can you even breathe?" I ask, helping her zip it up.

"Sort of," she whispers, clearly not enough air in her lungs to speak like a normal person.

She tries to bend to put on her high-heeled boots, but she can't even reach them before the corset's zipper gives up and explodes, exposing her back.

"Shit!" she curses, turning her head trying to take a look at the damage.

"It's beyond saving," I announce, and her shoulders drop, followed by her head.

"I hoped I still could fit into this," she pouts.

"When was the last time you tried it on?" I arch my eyebrow.

"Ten years ago. I was fifteen. But I didn't gain that much weight!" She seems almost offended by my face as I try to hold back a laugh.

"No, but you probably have more boobs than when you were a teenager!" I chuckle.

I help her take off the culprit and she sighs. "Change of plans. The red top or the green lace one?" She points to two pieces of fabric on the couch.

They're both sexy and daring, exactly like she is. I've never known someone more confident than her, and I love that about her. She doesn't like drama; she knows what she wants and she definitely doesn't throw a fit when something doesn't go her way. I need someone like that making my life easier.

"The red one," I say without a doubt as I sit on the couch.

She removes her bra and puts on the top. I like how she doesn't care if she flashes her boobs at me. I do envy her carefree spirit.

She swirls around a couple of times. "What do you think?" she asks expectantly.

"You will definitely get laid." I chuckle and she squeals excitedly.

"Yes!" She beams. "Now it's your turn. What are you wearing?"

I frown, tilt my head, and try to find a response to her question. "Pajamas and face mask?"

She crosses her arms over her chest. I don't like where this conversation is heading. Her intentions are written all over her face, and when she speaks, my suspicions are proven true.

"No, you are not. It's our day off and you are not spending it in here like a nun. You are putting on something sexy and getting laid too." She points her perfectly manicured finger at me.

"No, please. I need to sleep and rest. I don't want to go to some club." My voice is pleading, but her arching brow tells me I'm not convincing her.

"You can sleep and rest tomorrow. The good thing about working in a nightclub is that we don't have to go to work until night and we can sleep in in the morning," she points out logically.

I know she's right. I should go out and enjoy my day off like a normal person, but I keep replaying the conversation I had with Ice last night in my head, wondering if he knows something more. I can't get it out of my mind that he pointed out my exact fear: my nonexistent past. Maybe he's just good at reading people and he's noticed how I tense up when someone brings it up. Or maybe he noticed that I never talk about it with my colleagues, but there's something nagging me about the fact that he thought about that and pointed it out.

"I'm not in the mood," I whine and she growls at my response.

"This is exactly why you have to come out. You're moping around more than usual these days and I'm tired of seeing your pouty face. I heard about Ice's tirade, and you can't stay here thinking about it. He is an asshole; we all know it. Don't let him get inside your head," she scolds.

"I don't have a pouty face!" I chuckle.

"Oh, yes, you do!"

"You're not giving up, are you?" I sigh, knowing she can be relentless when she makes up her mind.

Her arched eyebrow is answer enough. I sigh, stand up, and walk to my room with Lola hot on my heels. I don't want to go out, but maybe she's right, all I need is some fun to get Ice out of my head.

"I hate you," I grumble, opening my dresser.

"I know, but you'll be thanking me tonight when you come home with some hot guy." She shrugs and starts to go through my things to find an outfit for our night out. At least I don't have to worry about what to wear—we both know Lola will have the final word on that.

***

The club we pick is one of those where you wait in line for hours if you don't know the right people. Approaching the entrance, we smile brightly.

"Hi, Cameron!" Lola chirps, leaning on our ex-colleague's arm. He was one of the bouncers working at our nightclub until a few months ago.

"Hello, sweetheart! How are you doing?" He is genuinely happy to see us.

Lola gives him a languid onceover. He is tall with wide shoulders, buzzed brown hair, and dark brown eyes. His button-down shirt is so tight over his muscles it almost rips when he flexes his arms. He is exactly Lola's type and I think they hooked up a couple of times when he worked with us.

"I'm doing great, but Silver needs to cheer up. Ice was an asshole with her last night. Do you think you can get us in?" she pouts.

I roll my eyes. I should have known she would use my misfortune to skip the line. "It's not like he fired me, he was just... Ice," I explain.

Cameron chuckles and Lola turns to glare at me.

"Don't worry, sweetheart. I got you covered," he says, lifting the black velvet rope and letting us in.

"Thank you!" we answer in chorus and kiss his cheek on our way in.

"Hey! We've been in line for hours, that's not fair!" a guy shouts.

I turn around to see a sandy-blonde, blue-eyed surfer staring at us. He's with a couple of friends just as gorgeous as he is. He doesn't seem angry, just tired of waiting in line.

I smile sheepishly at him. "Sorry, when you get in, find me and I'll buy you a drink!" I wink at him, and he grins. The loveliest dimples appear on his cheeks.

"Good call, I like him. And his friends too." Lola grabs my hand and drags me toward the entrance.

I chuckle and shake my head. "Are you taking advantage of the lights out here to scope out the hottest guys?"

"Off course I am. Have you noticed how dark these places are? You can't tell if someone is really your type until the morning after when it's way too late to discover you don't like them."

She's right. Every nightclub is so dark you can't see anything except what's right next to you. Everything seems perfect and beautiful, but when the lights go on, you see whatever anyone's trying to hide, guys included.

We make our way inside and are immediately overwhelmed by the loud music, the thick air, and bodies waving and sweating to the beat. While I don't mind working in a place like this, being on the other side of the bar is not something I crave on my nights off.

"Drink or dance?" Lola shouts.

"Drink!" I need alcohol if I don't want to punch someone in the face for grinding against my ass.

We head to the bar and push our way to grab the bartender's attention. Lola spilling her tits over the bar usually does the trick. We order a couple of margaritas and lean against the counter watching people dance. The music is louder and it's more packed here, but the view is always the same: a bunch of people trying to impress their companion of choice for the night. Some are already making out, others are grinding against a stranger's ass, but most of them are just hoping to get lucky and get laid tonight.

I sip the margarita the bartender hands us as Lola leans closer. "I'm going to take a look around. See you around or at home?" she asks, and I know she means she's going to walk around until she finds someone to hook up with.

"See you in the morning!" I smirk at her. If she finds someone, she'll be too lost in the chase to remember to tell me she's leaving, so I just go ahead and say goodbye now.

"Call me if you need a ride back, but I hope you find someone to do the honor." She winks before taking off and scouring this place.

I watch her being sucked in by the crowd, and then go back to people watching.

"I'm here for my drink."

I turn to where the voice is coming from and find the guy from the line. I smile and beckon him to the bar. "What do you want?"

He grins. "A beer is fine."

I wave down the bartender, put in our orders, and then hand him my credit card.

"Are you really paying? I didn't find you to take advantage of your proposal." He seems genuinely surprised by my gesture.

"I'm not one of those girls who just assumes the guy will pay. I told you I was buying you a drink and I meant it."

He nods, smiling. "I'm Brad." He offers his hand and I shake it.

"Silver."

"What are you doing here, Silver? Besides buying beer to make up for cutting in line." He smiles again, and those lovely dimples make an appearance. Seeing him up close, he's even better looking than I remember.

I laugh. "My friend dragged me and then ditched me as soon as we stepped foot in here."

He chuckles and shakes his head. "Same here. I hate these places, but my friends wanted to come, and I was in the car so I had no choice," he confesses.

"Why don't you like it here?" I'm curious. He doesn't seem that out of place in a club like this.

"I prefer outdoor activities. And you? Why don't you like it?" He leans closer and the air seems to ignite with electricity around us.

"I work in a nightclub, so it's not where I want to go on my day off."

He barks out a laugh and shakes his head. "I can understand that."

I study him for a few seconds then look down at my margarita. He seems like the kind of guy who's not here to pick up someone, at least not in a pushy kind of way, and I appreciate his presence.

"What do you do when you're not forced by your friends to go club hopping?" I ask when the small talk dies down.

"I'm a marine biologist." He grins but not in a bragging way. Nothing about him gives me a show-off kind of vibe.

"That explains the surfer look." I wave a hand in front of him.

He smiles shyly. "Yeah, I get that a lot. Not many people take me seriously when I tell them I'm a biologist."

I frown, a bit confused. "Why is that?"

"Because they don't understand what my job really is. They think I hang out at the beach or on a boat doing nothing all day," he explains and I'm surprised.

"Well, they're idiots and sorry for the surfer comment. I didn't mean to disrespect you," I say seriously.

He shrugs and shakes his head. "No, I'm sorry. I wasn't trying to complain. Can we please start over?"

"You want me to buy you another beer?" I chuckle, bumping my shoulder against his.

He smirks. "Will you do it if I say yes?"

"No, but you can try!" I wink at him, and he smiles leaning closer.

"Is it too soon to ask for your number and then kiss you? Because I get the feeling that if I don't take this chance, I won't have another opportunity to meet you again. This isn't exactly my scene."

He seems vulnerable and sweet. I'm used to cocky bastards asking me to follow them into the bathroom, and here I am, with a cute guy asking if he can kiss me. This is why I don't like to pick up anyone at a club. It's just my luck to find the only sweet, genuine man who wants something other than sex.

"You don't want my number, trust me. And as for the kiss... there won't be more." My eyes never leave his as I say it.

He frowns, puzzled. "I'm not asking to have sex with you, I just want to know you better. That's it. You're gorgeous and funny. You seem smart and I'd like to know you outside this place," he rushes to explain.

And this is exactly the problem. Sex with someone sweet like him would be okay. But something more? A date or two? I can't afford that. Not knowing there will never be a happy ending for us.

"The problem is, I don't date." I scrunch my nose at his dumbfounded expression.

"Wait. Are you ditching me because I'm *not* asking for sex?" he asks in disbelief.

I chuckle. "Not exactly, but sort of. You seem like a good guy, someone who doesn't pick up a girl just to have sex with her in your car or in the back of the club, and I'm not the kind of girl who dates. I could give you my number and then ghost you in a week, but I don't want to do that. I like you. You're nice and sweet, and I don't do nice and sweet."

He laughs and shakes his head. "Damn! This is the first time I got rejected for being too nice. I'll have to work on my asshole skills."

I chuckle. "Don't. You're perfect as you are. Don't lower yourself to the level of most men. I'm just not your girl. My life is screwed up and I don't want to screw up yours too."

He relaxes his shoulders and looks at me. "Well, Silver, you're kind of a nice woman too, even if your life is messed up."

I smile. This is my life: being nice, trying to do the right thing, and paying for that with a miserable, lonely existence.

CHAPTER 5

Raphael

If she talks about her dogs again, I swear I will rip my ears off. She is beautiful, she come from one of the most influential families in the country, and she has so many bachelor's degrees I can't even count them, all from Ivy League schools. I can't understand why she keeps talking about her dogs all the time. Every anecdote, memory, or conversation is related to those two furry companions. I'm shocked she didn't bring them to this dinner.

She's the last of the women on my father's list. My last hope to find a partner because the other eleven were a no-go. In the fifteen days since my conversation with the old man, I've gone on twelve dates including this one, and I've never felt so miserable. Thinking about spending the rest of my life with one of them fills me with dread bordering on panic. I've always considered myself someone who's willing to do anything to reach my goals—at least as far as my morals allow. But in these two weeks I've discovered my limits.

"Are you listening?" Cassandra's shrill voice brings me back to reality.

"Yes. You were talking about your visit to DC with your best friend and how much you would like to live in the White House."

I point out her not-so-subtle suggestion that she be by my side when I become the president of the United States.

She huffs, pats my arm, and rolls her eyes as she smiles almost maniacally. "No, silly! I was talking about the matching outfit I bought for me and the boys."

Here we go again with the dogs.

"You have matching outfits?" I ask, puzzled about how that works. Do human outfits come in dog sizes? God, I never expected that question to pop into my head during a date. I mean, I love dogs and animals in general, but she's obsessed.

She brightens at my question. "Yes! I asked my designer friend if he could sew us different outfits for every occasion. We have some for formal occasions, some for the gym, and even matching pajamas."

That last part raises even more red flags. "Do they sleep in your bedroom?"

"Of course, silly! We sleep all together in my king-size bed." She answers like it's the most common thing in the world. I know a lot of people who let their pets sleep in the same room as them, but the thought of waking up in a bed populated with matching pajamas is going too far for me.

"Can I ask you something really personal? Fell free not to answer if you think it's inappropriate," I ask cautiously.

"Yes, sure!"

"What do you do with your dogs when you have a partner coming over? I mean, when there's intimacy in the bedroom." As soon as the question leaves my lips, I'm terrified of hearing the answer.

She smiles like this is a normal conversation topic. "Oh, it's not a problem. They move over to the nightstands and keep quiet. They like to watch."

And there it is. The last straw. I'm not going further than this. I discretely move my hands under the table and fire off a text to Matthew—a fat *SOS*. Not even two minutes later he's calling me.

"Sorry, it's my campaign manager, I have to take this." I excuse myself as I stand up and walk away from the table for some privacy.

"Please, come pick me up," I whisper-shout over the phone.

Matthew chuckles. "It can't be that bad."

"Trust me, it's worse. Send a car immediately." I don't like to play the boss voice card with him, but this is an emergency. "Please," I add more quietly.

"Okay, okay! Don't panic. I'm coming to pick you up. We need to talk anyway," he adds, chuckling.

"Thank you." I end the call and take a deep breath to calm down before going back to my date.

I look around, taking in the other tables. It's an upscale restaurant where only rich and famous people hang out. It's trendy but not tacky like most you see these days. A friend of mine, Sady, co-owns this place and is also the chef. I chose this place, calling in a favor and asking him for a private table in the back, just in case the date didn't go well. And thank God I did. If anyone eavesdropped on this conversation, I would have lost any chance at a career in politics.

"Sorry for the interruption. Something came up and I have to go." I look Cassandra straight in the eye. I want to be sure she understands that the night ends here.

"Oh." She pouts for a heartbeat, but then she recovers and puts on her cool expression. "We should continue this some other time. Maybe somewhere more private," she proposes coyly.

I shiver just thinking about it. "I'm swamped with the campaign, and I don't want you to wait for my call. Feel free to see other people, no hard feelings here." There is no other way to ditch someone. I'm not famous for gracefully dumping my dates. Far from it. I know how insensitive I come across, but I despise this whole dating thing. It's one of the many reasons I don't date. Sex without strings? Here for it. Dating? Not so comfortable with that.

"Did you already choose someone else from the list?" she asks. I can't tell if she's offended, and to be completely honest, I didn't get into the details about how my father picked these women. It never occurred to me that he may have asked them to date me. It's quite humiliating when I think of it like that.

She may sense my surprise because she adds gingerly, "It wasn't a secret, was it? I was contacted and asked if I wanted to date a politician, that it was an arranged relationship, and I thought it was something people knew about. Considering the number of women you've gone out with in the last two weeks, I just figured there's a list you're choosing from."

Damn! That sounds even worse than I imagined it would. I shake my head. "I don't shout it from the rooftops but yes, there is a list. Nothing personal, really. It's just this date didn't click. Does that make sense?"

She sighs and nod. "Yeah, I can relate. I agreed to go out with you only because if I tell my parents I'm a lesbian they'll disown me. I thought a fake relationship with a silent agreement to see other people would be better than ending up alone."

Yet another reason I wasn't on board with this charade. We would be two miserable people dragging along through life. The fact that you can learn how to love the person you live with is utter bullshit and this is proof.

"Trust me, I'm not the solution to your problems. On the contrary, you'd be under scrutiny twenty-four-seven and you couldn't have any other relationships even if you wanted to. You would be miserable, I would be miserable, and we would live the worst life ever." I suddenly feel more relaxed with Cassandra than I have with anyone else.

"Yeah, maybe you're right. I should probably choose someone more low profile." She shrugs and I understand that nothing will change her mind. She'll carry on without any intention of coming out to her parents. But who am I to judge? I'm doing exactly the same thing.

***

"Please, tell me you have good news," I ask Matthew as I sit across from him in the car he brings to pick me up.

He can't hide a smirk as he studies me like I'm some kind of strange phenomenon. He stays silent for a while, biting his lips to keep from laughing, but I can see in his eyes that he can't hold it in too much longer.

"Go ahead. Make fun of me." The corner of my lips curve in an amused smile.

He raises his hands and shakes his head. "I'm not making fun of you, but I'm curious to know why you ran out of that restaurant."

I sigh out loud and rub a hand over my face. "She's a lesbian and her dogs watch from the nightstands while she has sex," I blurt out.

He looks at me for a long moment, his mouth hanging open in disbelief. "She what?"

"Don't ask."

"How did that conversation even come up on a first date?" He is cackling and I'm not even annoyed by it. This situation is so messed up I can't begin to make sense of it.

"Well, there won't be a second date. That's for sure." I'm firm on this point. I don't want him to push in that direction.

"Yeah, I got that. Are we going back to any of the previous ones? Is there someone that you're at least comfortable with?" He tries to test the waters.

Matthew and I have been friends for years. He knows me well enough to understand that I won't compromise on something like this. I frown and study him to see where he's going with this conversation.

"Or," I counter, "we don't push our luck and we stop having this conversation. Maybe this is a sign that this whole dating thing is wrong, and we shouldn't go on."

"Shit, Raphael! Since when do you believe in signs?" he snaps, and I'm taken aback. It's not like Matthew to lose his cool like this.

I arch an eyebrow and pin him to his seat with a stern look.

"Sorry. It's just that the endorsement Johnson gave you was good. It was the push we needed to fight back. But it's not enough."

I nod. I know he's worried this campaign will tank, but I can't just decide to make a life with someone where there's not even the slightest connection. Growing old in a loveless marriage is an awfully long time. Even a year is too long for me.

"How's it going after that endorsement? I haven't had time yet to read the report you gave me today." My words come out less aggressive than before.

"Great, we're back in a comfortable zone. Not winning hands down, but fairly competitive for the final leg of the campaign." His shoulders relax and I let down too. If he's confident, I'm confident. I trust him with my life.

"So, why are you pushing this wife thing?"

He's calm but firm. "Because you need one if you want to climb this damn ladder. Do you want to reach the top or not?

Because if you don't, or if it's too much for you, just tell me now. I can't keep wasting your time, my time, and your resources on something that will never happen. It's not fair to anyone working for you."

I appreciate his frankness, it helps put everything in perspective, but sometimes people just ask way too much of me.

"I know that, and there is no doubt where I want to go. But it's *my* life. *I* am the one that has to wake up in the morning next to a person I feel nothing for. While you get to raise your kids with the woman you love, *I* have to fuck and impregnate someone I don't care about and who doesn't give a shit about me. Because they won't stop at my marriage, and you know it. They will *demand* kids, a dog, and a fucking house with a picket fence. So, excuse me if I don't pick one of the first twelve women they serve me on a silver platter. I'd prefer to look elsewhere if I can't find a connection with any of them."

Matthew has the decency to look embarrassed and lower his gaze to his hands folded in his lap. The silence that follows is almost deafening. "Sorry. We'll look for someone else. Forget I even suggested the other thing." He finally looks at me and his apology is sincere.

I look out the window and suddenly realize we're not heading home. "Where are we going?"

The grimace on Matthew's face is not reassuring. "Jen called. She asked to meet her at the nightclub."

"She called you?"

"You weren't picking up."

I rub a hand over my face and sigh. "I need caffeine if I have to go through this too. Can we stop at the café next to the nightclub?"

Every thought of our conversation disappears as soon as he mentions Jen's name. She's part of a past I want to forget but can't, even if it sometimes kills a part of my soul.

Five minutes later, we enter the café. There are few customers at ten in the night, but enough to attract a few insistent glances. I sweep my gaze over the faces seated at the tables. Someone recognizes me, or they're just surprised seeing someone in a suit and tie, or maybe they're staring at Dave, the massive bodyguard towering over everybody in here.

A loud conversation grabs my attention and I look toward the counter. A redhead I recognize as a bartender from the nightclub is waiting for the barista to make her order. She is gorgeous with her flaming red hair and pouty lips. Even in leggings and a sweatshirt, she's the sexiest person in here. Maybe it's because I always see her in lingerie, and I know what she's hiding under those clothes, but I can't take my eyes off her.

I don't recognize the man next to her, the loud one who attracted my attention. He is way closer to her than a normal acquaintance should be and the girl seems uncomfortable. She's staring ahead and flinches every time he taunts her with a question.

"Come on, give me your number, I promise we'll have a good time," he insists for the third time.

She closes her eyes and lets out a slow breath. When she opens them, she seems more determined. "I've told you a million times, I'm not interested. Not now, not ever."

She tries to keep her voice down, but we're close enough to hear everything. The kid behind the counter looks in their direction with a worried expression. No doubt comparing his size to the man bothering her and isn't sure if he can take him if it comes to that.

I look at Dave, then at Matthew. All of us assessing the situation, trying to determine if we need to intervene.

"Why? Your pussy is too good for someone like me?" he sneers.

My hands twitch. I want to grab him and take him out with a couple of punches to his ugly face, but I can't without getting in trouble. But God, it's really difficult not to slap him. I glance at Matthew and see he is just as annoyed as me. Dave moves in closer, I can see his massive body in my peripheral vision.

"No, because I really don't like you and I don't want anything to do with you," she snaps back, raising her voice.

"Bitch. Do you think you're better than the other whores you work with?"

"Enough!" My voice rings out loud and clear. The silence in the place is almost deafening. Both of their heads snap toward me. She is surprised, he is pissed off.

"She told you she's not interested. Back off."

He comes closer, his eyes alive with fury and an arrogant smirk on his face. Dave shifts to move in closer but he doesn't come between us. He knows it's not my habit to hide behind my bodyguards. I've made that very clear since the beginning. He will only intervene if there's a danger I can't handle. I'm not crazy enough to assume I have superpowers.

"Or what? What are you going to do, superman?" he taunts, and I struggle not to put my hands on him. I'm so close to making a scene here in public.

"You really don't want to find out," I state so coldly he's caught off guard for a second. Then he launches at me, throwing a punch. I dodge his fist, grab his wrist and push him against Dave who doesn't even budge. He grabs the man by his shoulders and holds him in place.

Everything happens so fast, the only sound I hear are gasps from the customers. He looks like an idiot, my face is safe, and she's free of that asshole. Situation under control. Dave is so huge compared to him that he doesn't even resist when he's walked out of the café. He just scurries out with his face an angry red.

"Thank you," she says, coming closer, not wanting the other customers to listen in. They're all looking curiously at us. "You didn't have to do that. I can handle him. It's not the first time he's harassed me, and I can kick his ass."

I smile at her. "I bet you can, but he was bothering me too."

When she looks up at me, I almost choke. I've never seen her outside the nightclub, and I've never realized how beautiful she is in normal light. Her eyes are a warm shade of brown, her lips pink and full, but the freckles peppering her small nose are her best feature. Without makeup, she looks a lot younger than when she's in the club.

She smiles at me, raises her coffee, and nods, blushing slightly. "Thank you for saving my coffee. I owe you a drink." She tiptoes and pecks my check.

This time I'm the one who's surprised. I inhale deeply and take in her sweet scent—strawberry and mango—and I have difficulty resisting the urge to close my eyes and breathe her in a second time. Matthew clears his throat next to me and I am brutally reminded of reality. I take a step back and put a reasonable space between us.

"May I escort you?" I surprise myself with the proposal.

She blushes again and I can see Matthew's amused face studying us intently.

"I'm just going around the block. I work tonight and I'm headed for the employee entrance in the back of the club," she explains in a puzzled tone but doesn't turn me down completely.

"I want to make sure that prick doesn't follow you when you're alone. Please, for my own peace of mind." I don't know why I'm insisting on walking with her. I look like the creep I just kicked out.

Around us people seem to hold their breath waiting for her reply. Or maybe it's just me.

She nods once and I let out a small sigh. "Okay."

I put my hand on the small of her back and follow her outside in silence, Matthew and Dave behind us. We don't talk, we just walk the short distance from the café to the back entrance of the nightclub, and when we come to a halt, I don't know what to say.

"Well, this is me. Thanks again for your help. I really appreciate it," she says before stepping forward and swiping a card to open the door.

I smile, say nothing, and watch her slip inside. I turn around to find Matthew handing me his jacket with a smirk on his face. Dave is trying to hide a smile too. I look at the coat and frown.

"I'd cover up down there if I were you." He waves at my crotch.

I look down and notice the massive erection straining my suit pants. "Shit!" I hiss and grab the jacket.

I've spent the last fifteen days dating women to find *that* spark, and it left me more bored than excited. But five minutes without even talking to this girl and I'm walking around with a massive erection between my legs. This is not good. Not good at all.

CHAPTER 6
Silver

Waiting in line to order my coffee, I notice the place is particularly packed tonight, and I feel the pain of the two girls behind the counter. They're rushing to make orders, but there's always someone complaining about been late for some appointment. Oh, the joy of serving customers!

I look around a bit concerned that I'll spot the prick who harassed me last night. That dude doesn't know boundaries, and the fact that he followed me into this café was creepy enough to make me worried today. I'm used to assholes like him, considering my work, but they usually stick to the nightclub rather than approach me in my daily life. That man is either sick or an entitled asshole who doesn't know the meaning of *no*. The most dangerous kind of idiot.

The only positive side to what happened last night is Raphael Wyden. Damn, that man has charisma for days. The way *"enough"* rolled off his lips, the firmness in his threats to the creep, the way he effortlessly dodged his fist—all of that is enough to send shivers of pleasure down my spine. And the intensity of those green eyes. Seriously? They should be considered weapons. I've never daydreamed about a man as much as I have in the last twenty-four hours about Raphael Wyden.

"Do you want to order?" The stern voice of the barista in front of me pulls me back to reality.

I spaced out, interrupting the already hiccupping flow of their shift. In my defense, it's insanely difficult to get the charming Raphael Wyden out of your mind after he's defended you with panty-melting intensity

"Cappuccino," I blurt out.

"What size?" She glares at me, and I can't blame her. She's having a really bad day and I'm not helping.

"Grande, please," I murmur, and she writes my name on the cup.

I'm a regular here since getting hired at the nightclub, but I'm that nightmare customer who changes her order every time. They know my name, but I don't have a usual drink and that throws them off every time.

I hurry to pay and move out of her way, apologizing and tipping her double. That makes her smile a bit, and I'm relieved while I wait for my order.

I grab my cup make my way to the front door. It's already dark outside and I don't notice the small crowd lingering in the small patio area.

The first flash just as I open the door surprises me. It blinds me and I freeze on the spot. There is a heartbeat where everything is still, like time stops somehow. Then the rattling of the cameras goes off and flashes blur my vision like a bomb exploding in my face.

"Are you Wyden's mistress?" someone asks.

"Are you two dating?" another one questions.

"Are you two lovers?"

The questions bombard me from every direction. The group pushes against the door trying to get in my face. My hand is still gripping the door handle keeping it open. I'm so stunned by the horror unfolding before my eyes that it takes me way too long to react, cover my face, and close the door. Fucking paparazzi. What the hell is going on?

I turn around and find people staring at me. I walk away from the door, knowing that the paparazzi won't follow me inside if they don't want someone to call the cops, but I'm still trapped.

Looking around for a way out, all I can see is the small corridor where the bathroom is located. Walking quickly in that direction, I avoid the curious glances customers are throwing my way. When I close the door behind me, I let out a shaky breath. What the hell is going on? Why are the paparazzi after me?

I can't even think. I have to get out of Los Angeles. I can't stay here any longer. If my face ends up in the magazines I'm screwed. But how did they find me? How did they know about...? Wyden. They asked me about Raphael Wyden.

I grab my phone from my pocket and Google the future senator's name. A bunch of articles come up with pictures of our interaction in this same café. Me with freaking adoring eyes, me kissing him on the cheek, and him with a massive erection in his pants. It's not a trick of the lights, where shadows make you see something that's not there, those pants are straining way too much against his crotch.

What the hell do I do now? I can't stay here much longer, if *he* finds me...

"Are you okay in there?" The barista's voice come from the other side of the door.

No. "Yes!"

"Do you want me to call the cops? I'm not sure they'll come because they're not doing anything wrong."

They're harassing me. They're putting me in danger, but I can't tell her that. I can't tell anyone. So, I open the door.

"No, don't call the cops. That'll make it worse, and they'll just follow me anyway."

She smiles sympathetically and nods. "Last night you and Wyden were quite the news in here. They probably got a whiff of that."

I nod because I don't know what to say. From the pictures online, I don't think it was an employee ratting us out. Chances are someone filmed the scuffle, me thanking him with a chaste peck on the cheek, and shared it on their social media. From there, magazines, gossip websites and paparazzies went wild.

"Is there another way out?" I plead, hoping she can help me.

She shakes her head, and my heart sinks a bit. "Not through a door, but there is a small window in our manager's office. It faces the back alley. I can show you if you think you can crawl out of it."

Well, it's better than being stuck here. "Yes, please." I follow her toward the office.

The escape is easier than I anticipated. The window is big enough for me to lower myself on the other side of the wall without breaking my leg. The alley is empty, and I can breathe a bit easier, even if I don't know what to do. I don't want to go home and pack my things, risking a paparazzo discovering where I live before I have the time to leave the city. The safest choice here is going to work and waiting until tomorrow before making a decision I'll regret.

My heart hammers in my chest while I slip the hoodie over my head and tuck my hair inside the sweater. The walk to the back entrance of the nightclub never seemed so long. Every person I meet, every glance in my direction is a reason to speed up my pace to get safely behind the closed door of the club.

"What happened to you?" Elvira asks as soon as I sit down on the bench of the changing room.

"Nothing, why?" I play dumb, but my shaky voice gives me away.

She raises an eyebrow, calling my bullshit. "Are you sure? Not even a kiss with one of the hottest men around?" she persists, a smug smile plastered on her face.

I was hoping my colleagues hadn't seen the pictures, but considering how gossipy they are, there's no chance of that. There are strangers out there who know where I grab my coffee, there is no way people who have known me for years would miss something major like me going viral on the internet. I silently curse my bad luck or bad judgement. Why did I kiss him? A thank you would have sufficed, but as usual, when I screw up, I do it royally.

"He just saved me from that prick who comes here every week and harasses me. He approached me outside the club."

That news is enough to divert her attention to the other topic. "Are you serious?" She is worried.

I nod. "He's becoming a problem. Showing up here drunk and slurring obscenities at me is one thing, but following me outside this place and making a scene in a public place is a completely different level of creepy," I tell her as I slip into my sequined shorts and bra.

She frowns and crosses her arms over her chest. "It's not just creepy, it's dangerous. Have you tried talking to Ice? I know he's his friend, but he's crossing a line."

I scoff. "Last time he handed me my ass because I didn't give the guy a blowjob. Do you think this time will be any different?"

She shakes her head and sighs. "At least here you can call security if he pulls something shady," she says as we walk out to our stations for tonight.

It's not much comfort but it's better than nothing.

Fortunately, it seems like everyone decided to go out tonight and order drinks at my station. I rush to make them, focusing on not screwing up my orders, which helps keep my mind off what's happened in the last twenty-four hours. Because if I go there, I'll panic. I'll go back to the night that changed everything eight years ago. I'll run out of here, pack my things, and jump on the first bus out of this city and state entirely.

But I can't do that. I need to think about it carefully, plan my disappearance, withdraw enough money to not use my debit card for a while. I need to think ahead and make my move accordingly. Even if I am terrified, and my instinct is to leave everything behind, I have to force myself to not bolt. I've built a life here. I worked in this not-so-great place to save money for my future. I can't just throw away what I've worked for so hard.

"We need to talk."

I look up and those green eyes I daydreamed all day are staring back at me. Raphael Wyden stands in front of me with a serious expression and a massive bodyguard behind him. The same guy who threw out the creep yesterday. My heart hammers in my chest, and not because I'm happy to see him.

"Well, I don't want to talk. I want you to disappear before someone takes a picture of us together again," I say as I finish the cocktail I'm preparing.

I move in front of the guy who ordered the drink and fortunately he doesn't even glance at me, too focused on the brunette who's looking at him like she wants to eat him alive. I hand him his cocktail, grab his money, give him the change and pocket the generous tip. I move to take another order, but Raphael cuts in.

"I'm serious. We need to talk," he hisses.

I pin him with a stern look and move closer so I don't have to shout over the music. It's not so loud in the VIP area, but I don't want anyone eavesdropping on this conversation.

"No. we don't. You have to tell your fucking PR team to do their magic and make the paparazzi disappear from my life. I don't want to talk to you, I don't want to be seen with you, and if you feel the urge to play hero, please, don't do it with me. Leave me alone," I spit.

I'm so close I can see the muscles of his perfectly shaven jaw snap with tension and his eyes squint a bit. He is furious, but I don't have time right now to think about his feelings. He's a grown man; he can deal with it.

I turn to the guy next to him who's waiting to order a drink and smile at him. "What can I get you?" I smile seductively even as I'm simmering with anger.

Who does he think he is? Just because he's a big shot in this city doesn't mean I have to do what he says. I'm not his entourage he can order around. I'm fuming but I have to keep a smile on my face.

"Vodka tonic." He glances at me briefly before continuing to scroll on his phone.

I turn to grab a new bottle of vodka from the counter behind me and when I turn back a redhead is gripping Raphael's arm. She smiles sweetly at him and bats her long eyelashes. She's wearing a midnight blue minidress that leaves nothing to the imagination. I peek at Raphael while I'm preparing the drink and he seems not so eager to see her, but he hides it well.

"Here you are," she purrs seductively at him.

He says nothing, puts a hand on her lower back, and guides her out of my sight. It's not the first time I've seen them together here.

"Well, at least we know he likes redheads." Elvira bumps her hip against mine while she shakes her cocktail.

I look at her and roll my eyes. "Yeah. The similarities end there. It's not even the same shade of red," I point out. The girl is a natural redhead, while I just dye my hair way too often to cover my blond roots.

"That's for sure. You have nothing else in common. She's an escort," she says before going back to her side of the counter.

A sense of discomfort settles in my stomach. Lola gossiped about that girl being a sex worker but having Elvira confirm it is unsettling. Yesterday, I got the impression he was a good man, someone who doesn't think twice about standing up for others, but maybe I'm just another redhead that caught his attention. The massive erection plastered all over the internet certainly gives away his preference. But the fact that he pays for sex doesn't sit right with me.

***

It's almost five in the morning before I can finally go home. I'm the last of the bartenders to walk out the back door, and when I step onto the alley's dirty concrete, my stomach drops. There's no one in sight, not many cars even on the main road. The usual cacophony of Los Angeles traffic is silent, and that's what is most unsettling. I usually have my earphones on when I walk out of here, but today I want to be alert. I want to hear every sound in case someone follows me.

It's the same feeling I had eight years ago, when I first moved away from my home. I was always checking my back and watching for anything that seemed off. Gradually, I became less paranoid and started to relax a bit more. But now it feels like I'm back to eight years ago, with fear gripping my gut every time I step outside.

I walk toward the main road, almost running from this dark alley. We've asked time and time again to have the lights fixed, at least the one over the employees' entrance, but Ice seems deaf to our requests. I let out the breath I was holding when I finally reach the end of the narrow passageway.

I take a couple of long strides before noticing the black SUV with tinted windows parked near the alleyway. The front door opens and a big guy with buzzed dark hair steps out, blocking my escape. I turn around, fear gripping my stomach in a vise that makes me almost throw up.

"Miss Argent, can you please come with me?" His deep thunderous voice is menacing enough to make me whimper.

I scurry away without looking back, but he reaches me effortlessly, gripping my elbow and making me turn around. I'm so terrified I can't even speak. This is it. This is how I'll die. He promised he would have me found and he did. After ten years, he succeeded.

"Please, Miss Argent, follow us," he repeats, guiding me toward the back door.

He opens it, gently helps me get into the empty back seat, and then closes the door. He makes his way to the driver seat and starts the car. I reach out and try to open the door next to me, but it's obviously locked. He glances at me to the rearview mirror and frowns.

"It won't take long," he tells me in a calm tone.

He seems almost wanting to reassure me, but why? My death will be fast? They're not going to torture me before ending my life?

I start to sob, and my stomach hurts as I watch the empty streets beyond the tinted glass. A few days. I just needed a few days to disappear again. And instead I walked straight into my own death. A kiss. It was just a fucking kiss on the cheek.

CHAPTER 7
Raphael

The black SUV enters the empty warehouse and a painful grip tightens my stomach.

"Are you nervous?" Matthew asks.

I glance at my friend and frown. He has an unreadable expression, but he seems more amused than pissed, like he was a few hours ago. When I told him I approached Silver at the nightclub, he almost punched me in the face and pointed out that someone could have filmed us and shared it online. I was there to get the name of the woman who turned my day upside down with a kiss, since he couldn't get it by talking with the girl who answered the phone. I know Ice, the piece of shit who runs that place, and it took me five minutes to know not only her name but also her phone number and address. I hate that guy.

"Why should I be?"

"I don't know, maybe because she almost clawed your eyes out when you tried to talk to her?" Now he's holding back a laugh.

I turn to Dave who shakes his head innocently. He's the one who told my best friend that. I certainly didn't share this information with him. I glare at him, but you can't intimidate the guy even if you point a gun at his face.

"I'm not nervous." I totally am. She freaked out when I approached her, and her reaction threw me off balance. I get being a private person who doesn't want to end up on the gossip sites, but she seemed to be overreacting a bit to a situation that can easily be solved by my staff.

When Jordan, one of my father's men, opens the back door of the SUV, nobody comes out. I glance at Matthew and his frown tells me he's puzzled too. Jordan reaches into the car and drags out Silver from the back seat. When my eyes meet her face, my heart sinks.

She's a mess. Puffy eyes, makeup running down her face, red nose.

"What the hell happened?" I march toward her terrified face.

"You? You're the fucking prick who kidnapped me?" she hisses angrily in my face.

"What? I didn't kidnap you, I just wanted to talk to you in a more private place, as you pointed out not even four hours ago. I offered you a ride," I answer, annoyed. I'm not used to this kind of dramatics.

She scoffs and crosses her arms over her chest, no longer fearful now. Considering the fury blazing in her eyes, I'm concerned for my safety.

"A ride? A fucking ride?" she shouts. "Your felon here approached me without any explanation, forced me into a car and drove for half an hour in total silence into a shitty neighborhood, ending the joyride in this decrepit warehouse. And you're telling me you were giving me a fucking ride? I thought I was going to die, you dumbass!"

I'm speechless. Utterly speechless. What she's describing sounds right out of a nightmare. I chose this place because a friend of my father owns it and I knew nobody would bother us here.

I turn to Jordan. "You didn't tell her anything? I asked you to pick her up because I had other things to do, not to terrorize her like we're mafia mobsters!"

The guy doesn't even look concerned. He just stares at me blankly without saying a word. I swear I will never again use one of my father's men for a delicate job. He thinks he's living in a gangster movie.

"I promise this was not my intention. Jesus, I would have been scared too," I say more calmly.

She seems to relax a bit, but not enough to let go the scowl. "What do you want? I told you to take care of this problem. I don't have the kind of money you do to get rid of the paparazzi!"

"Did they bother you?" I ask. I didn't have time to check if there were other pictures online.

"Are you kidding me?" she asks incredulously. "I had to jump out the back window of the café where we met yesterday because they mobbed me as soon as I stepped foot outside."

"Shit," I curse under my breath and turn to Matthew who seems concerned but not panicking.

"Did they find out where you live, or work?" my campaign manager asks her, assessing the situation.

"No, not yet. But I don't know if they asked around. I didn't say much to the baristas that work there, but I'm not one hundred percent sure."

I can feel the concern in her voice, studying her more carefully. She seems guarded, but I can't figure out what's going on in her head.

Matthew intervenes with a reassuring smile and calm voice. "That's good. We can make sure they won't find out. They only know you get coffee there, so if you avoid it for a few days they'll give up and turn on Raphael. He's easier to spot, considering his public life."

What I like about Matthew is that around other people he never loses his cool. With me, it's a different story, but we've known each other since forever and I expect him to be less guarded.

"Good, can I go home now? I'm honestly tired. It was a long day," she pleads.

I watch her carefully. She seems tired, she's shivering a bit, and she looks almost small in her oversized hoodie and black leggings. She looks both helpless and strong, a combination that makes me want to protect her again. But she doesn't want my help, she made that loud and clear at the nightclub.

"Just a few more minutes, please. We need to figure out how to handle this situation and contain the damage, and I need you on board with it. I want to give clear directions to my staff as soon as possible so they can get on it first thing this morning. Can you do that for me?" My voice comes out soft and a small smile graces my lips.

I don't want her to freak out again and end this meeting in flames.

"I suppose," she murmurs, nodding.

She's still pissed at me, but at least she is obliging. There's hope she won't make a fuss.

"We need to find common ground to deal with this…inconvenience." I dare to wink and smile at her. She stares blankly at me. Okay, I've got a long way to go to gain her trust.

"Inconvenience is when you finish the toilet paper and you don't have another roll handy. This is a nightmare. At least for me," she blurts out, and I can't stifle a chuckle.

"Yes, maybe your definition is more accurate," I agree. "Matthew, do you have any suggestions about the direction we should take?" I turn to my best friend.

He smiles shyly and I have a bad feeling. He only does that when he wants to appear innocent, but I know him way better than that.

"You should get married." He drops the bomb.

"No way!" I spit at the same time Silver squeals, "What?"

I warn him in a stern voice. "Please, be serious. We don't have time for bullshit. It's almost six, we didn't sleep, and we're all tired." I know where this is going, and I want to give him the chance to backpedal.

"I *am* serious. This is going to be a huge scandal: you were caught on film with a massive erection and she's looking at you like you're her entire world," he starts but Silver interrupts him.

"I am not! And I don't want even to hear this ridiculous so-called solution!"

"Yes, you are. You can pretend you're not, but you totally are. Do you know how the press will spin this if we tell them it's nothing and you disappear? You'll be the slut that opens her legs for powerful men, and he's the asshole taking advantage of you." He states all of this sternly and I glare at him. I'm okay with hearing his solution, but I'm not okay with him insinuating she's a whore, even if it's clear he doesn't think she is.

"I don't give a shit about what people think about me. I'm not marrying him. This is insane!"

And I agree with her, this is insane. "Is there another solution? Like an ex-flame I bumped into or something?" I try to mediate.

"Yes, exactly." She sides with me.

Matthew shakes his head and lowers his gaze, a small smile on his lips. "Can I be totally honest?" He bores his eyes into mine, asking silent permission to share something strategic in front a perfect stranger, Silver, and my father's ears, Jordan. I silently nod.

"You need a wife. If you don't get married soon, your father will cut your funding. People who vote for you will demand you commit to someone. This scandal looks like you're having an affair. Your erection makes it look purely sexual, and you don't need a sexual scandal right now. You can absolutely not look like a disgusting pig taking advantage of a woman. No one gives a shit if that's what really happened. They don't want the truth; they want to sink you and they'll use this against you in the campaign. They'll dig up so much dirt on her, fabricate so much shady business you won't even see the midterms. Your career will end here. It will take you years to clean up your image." He lays out the raw truth and I am breathless.

I look at Silver and wish I could read what she's thinking. She seems surprised by the speech, completely incredulous at the proposal, and maybe a bit concerned about all of it. I can't blame her. The political world is wild. It takes years to figure out how to navigate it and understand the dynamics. You're always tiptoeing around situations that could bust or sink your career. It's unnerving even when you willingly jump into it. I can't even fathom how it feels to be dragged into it kicking and screaming.

"Shit," I whisper rubbing a hand over my face.

Matthew pushes, knowing I'm about to give up. "Listen, it's March. You have nine months until midterms. You can get married and Silver can slowly fade into the background until you get a quiet divorce, and that's it." Then he adds, looking at Silver, "We can pay you a lot."

Her mouth hangs open as she stares at us like we are complete freaks. "You are nuts! And how did you even know my name?"

I don't answer her question, but study her for a long moment. I try to imagine what it would be like to live with her and I'm surprised to find I may like it. She's gorgeous and seems smart. She is not intimidated by my presence, and she undoubtedly doesn't get shy when she has to call me out. Of all the women

I've met in the last couple of weeks, she is the most interesting. Maybe it's not the way I would have expected to solve this problem, but why spit on a solution that fell into our lap?

"He's not completely wrong. It's just nine months of a fake relationship, and in one year tops you're free to step aside. I'll pay you. I'll pay for everything while we're together, and we can arrange a payout when you walk away."

Saying it out loud, it doesn't sound like too crappy of a deal. It could work. I don't have to love her. I just need to get along with her. Feelings are out of the question; it will be a normal business transaction. Well, maybe 'normal' is a bit of a stretch, but who cares?

"You're insane," she whispers, taking a step back like we're the danger she has to run from. "I will never agree to something so crazy!" she says more firmly.

"Please. My staff can spin this thing to make it look good for both of us. I promise it will be worth it. I'll pay you whatever you want." I see Matthew snap his wide eyes on me. It's risky to give her free rein about the money, but she looks she's not convinced, and I have to do what it takes before she leaves this place.

"Absolutely not!" she shouts nervously.

Before I can even process what I'm doing, I kneel on the bare concrete floor. The cold seeps into my bones as the small pebbles dig into the expensive fabric of my suit. It's uncomfortable, to say the least, but I can see the surprise on her face. It's a different reaction from the absolute closure before.

"Do you want me to kneel to ask you to marry me? Here I am, asking you. Please," I plead.

There is a moment of absolute silence in which she seems caught off guard, but then the warm in her brown eyes becomes icy. And in that split second, I know I royally fucked up. The next thing I know, she's giving me a swift kick in the balls.

A grunt escapes my lips. I can't catch my breath, the searing pain between my legs bends me over until I'm resting my forehead on the concrete. I cup my crotch and grind my teeth trying not to cry. And just when I think the worst pain is behind me, it starts to expand from my lower belly to my sternum. I almost shit my pants, and I struggle to hold back tears.

When I can finally catch my breath, I grunt in pain again and say, "I fucking knew marriage would kill me."

CHAPTER 8
Silver

I grab as many clothes as I can fit in my duffel bag. I can't believe that prick asked me to marry him. Who does he think he is? Does he think he can play with other people's lives like that? For eight years I did everything to disappear. And he wakes up one day demanding I step into the spotlight. Is he crazy?

I let out a breath and plop down on my bed. I feel like a deflated balloon, scared and spinning out of control. No, he is not crazy. He doesn't know. I rub a hand over my face and sigh. This isn't happening. This is a nightmare that can't be happening.

I have to admit that for a split second I considered staying for the money. I could ask for what I'd need to live a comfortable life without worrying about how to survive, but the truth is it would be suicide. Being with him means being on the front pages of every paper, on every website. Everywhere. I can't afford that.

"Hey," Lola's sweet voice comes from my bedroom doorway.

I turn around. She's smiling at me, but I can see she's concerned. When I came back this early morning I found her in the kitchen, worried because I didn't come home last night. I had to confess where I was, without going into detail about the marriage proposal.

"Hey."

She walks into my room and sits down next to me, glancing at the bag with a sad expression. She grabs my hand and intertwines our fingers. She's the closest thing to a friend I've had in the last eight years, and I'll miss her.

"I talked to the guy I told you about. He said if you go there at noon, he can take your picture and have a fake ID ready in a couple of hours." She says this in a low voice, as if scared someone can hear our conversation. We're alone in this apartment, but I have the same fear.

"Thank you. You're saving my life." And she is, literally. With my face, and probably in a few hours my name, all over the web, I need a new identity and I need it soon.

She stares at me for a long moment with concern in her eyes. I know she wants to say something, but she's not sure if she can. Over the years, I've shut down every conversation about my past. Not in a mean way, but I made it clear that I don't want to talk about it, and she always accepted that. But I know this time she's worried, and she wants to know more about what's happening.

"You can ask me, you know?" I try to smile at her.

"I don't want to know." She smiles at me, and I frown, surprised by her answer. "I mean, I'm obviously curious, but if you haven't told me all these years there must be a reason. I don't know if you've done something or are running from someone, but I don't want to know what happened before you moved here. I don't want to be an accomplice if you've killed someone, and I don't want to unconsciously betray you if you're running. I love you. You're the best roommate and partner in crime I could have wished for, and I want the best for you. And if this means you'll disappear from my life, so be it. Because I'd rather know you're safe somewhere else than dead here in Los Angeles." She kisses my forehead and tightens the grip on our fingers.

I don't deserve her. I don't deserve the unconditional love she gives me. She's done everything for me, and I've lied to her face every single day since I met her. Sure, I did it because I had to, but a lie is a lie no matter the reason behind it. I'll miss the shift at the nightclub, our raids on Rodeo Drive, our late nights watching TV. I'll miss her, and I'm not surprised when she dries a tear running down my cheek.

"Thank you. I'll miss you," I whisper.

She nods and lets go of my hand. "Pack something and then go to bed. You look like shit, and you don't have to be down-town until noon. I'll wake you up," she promises before standing up and strolling out the door.

I walk to the dresser and start to empty the first drawer. Then the second. By the time I reach the third, I startle when someone clears his throat. I turn around toward my bedroom door and find Lola next to Raphael.

"Sorry, he was very insistent." She glares at him, but his eyes are focused on me, and the duffel bag I'm packing.

His face is unreadable, but the muscles on his jaw twitch slightly. I stare at him, anger simmering under my skin.

"You're so full of yourself that you dare to come into *my* house after what you pulled earlier?" I hiss and Lola frowns slightly. I'm sure she thinks there's a lot more than what I told her, and the truth is there *is*.

He's wearing a different suit than before. It's a navy blue three piece with matching tie and crisp white button-down shirt. It fits him so perfectly it looks painted on him. His posture is relaxed, with his hands conveniently tucked into his pockets, so I can't read his mood. I wonder how long he practiced this nonchalance to make it look this natural.

"Well, it appears it won't be your house for long." He gestures toward the clothes in my hands.

"You know, when some asshole messes with your life, you have to make some hard decisions sometimes." And I'm not referring just to the scene at the café. My life is dotted with painful decisions I've been forced to make because of men.

I notice Lola's smile and Raphael lips curving up in an amused grin he tries to hide.

He nods.

"What do you want?" I press him. If he tries to kneel in front of me a second time, I'm going to kick him in the balls. Again.

"We need to talk," he states firmly.

I clench my jaw and squint at him, trying to figure out if he's dumb or just arrogant. "Wasn't it enough that I told you no last night? My answer hasn't changed. So, turn around and move your ass away from me. Far, far away."

"Do you want me to call the cops?" Lola intervenes. I glance at her, then at Raphael who seems not to hear her. He's still staring at me, same relaxed posture as before.

I shake my head at my friend, silently communicating that I can handle another prick in my life, but she doesn't move from the door.

"We need to talk. Privately." He tilts his head slightly toward Lola, the only sign that he acknowledges her presence.

"No, we don't *need* to do anything," I stubbornly tell him, even if I am curious about how far he'll go to get what he wants. I'm guessing not many people tell him no.

He inhales deeply and tilts his head toward the ceiling. It's the first time since stepping in my bedroom that he loses his composure. It's not a major fit of anger, but enough to let me know he is losing his patience.

"Please. Just hear me out and give me a chance to hear *you* out. Explain to me the reasons why you can't accept my proposal and I swear that if I can't convince you, I will personally come back and help you pack. Half an hour in the *privacy* of my home. That's it. Not a minute more," he pleads. The way the word 'privacy' rolls off his lips makes me shiver and not in a pleasant way.

I don't know if he knows something about me, whether he did some research, dug up my past or whatever else, but the way his gaze pierces my soul makes me feel unsafe in the only place I've felt protected in the last eight years.

I consider his proposal. I have to be downtown in three hours anyway, and maybe he'll give up when I tell him no for the umpteenth time. I don't care about his reputation or the reasoning behind his insane request, but if this helps me to get rid of him, why not?

"Half an hour, I will hear what you have to say, tell you no, and then you will leave me alone." I scowl at him, and he seems relieved.

There is almost smug victory in his eyes. Just a flash of *Nobody can tell me no* that disappears as fast as it appears. Well, Mr. Wyden will learn a lesson today, and I'm glad to be the one to teach it to him.

"Please, turn around. I'm going to film you dragging her out along with that bodyguard of yours. If she doesn't come back or call me telling me she's safe, I will take this video to the police and to every single media outlet I can think of. Smile for the camera, Raphael Wyden," Lola says with a fake smile.

God, I adore how she looks out for me.

Raphael studies her with an expression I can only consider respect. He's not annoyed, angry, or anything. He seems impressed that she's making sure I don't get hurt and it throws me off balance. I expected a lot of things from him, most of them not good, but not showing respect for someone threatening him.

"It won't be necessary, I assure you." He nods solemnly and I almost smile.

I doubt he'll make me disappear, but I appreciate my roommate effort to keep me safe. "See you in a while. It won't take long," I whisper in her ear as I hug her.

Outside, I head straight for the SUV with tinted windows waiting in the shadows of the warehouse in front of our complex. I notice the car isn't visible from the streets and the plates are mostly hidden from the view. They sure know how to make a luxury car look inconspicuous in a not so stellar neighborhood.

The bodyguard who was with him last night accompanies us to the car, opens the door, and waits for Raphael to help me in before going to the driver side and pulling out into Los Angeles traffic.

It takes us an hour and a half to reach his house in Malibu, and I curse under my breath for it. I didn't consider the distance and the slow Los Angeles traffic when I accepted. I didn't even know where he lived until now. We're from such different backgrounds we might as well be from two different planets entirely.

We don't talk much during the drive, mostly because Raphael receives call after call about his campaign. There is always someone asking for his opinion, his decision, his time. It's tiring just being in the car while he deals with all this. I don't know how we can talk about anything if he keeps answering the phone.

We arrive at his house after a long climb up Canyon Road and a two-mile stretch along his private driveway behind high walls and a sturdy wooden gate dotted with iron bolts. The sun is high over our heads and the greenery surrounding us is surreal. The road snakes between tall and ancient looking olive trees and ends in front of a roundabout with tall trees surrounding a fountain tiled in blue and gold mosaic, like one of those Mediterranean villas you see on TV.

My mouth hangs open when we step out of the car. The house is covered in pale salmon stucco with terra cotta tiles that wrap around the entire perimeter of the terraced roof. Bougainvillas and vines cover the pergolas climbing a good chunk of the walls, offering shade to the massive reddish wooden door carved with an intricate design of a tree.

I'm startled when Raphael puts a hand on my lower back and invites me toward said door. A small smile graces his lips, maybe because he sees the effect this house has on me. It's like visiting another country entirely. I forgot my anger, annoyance, and everything that happened in the last few days. For a second I taste the sweet experience of being far away from my problems, like I've stepped off a plane and walked straight into a small town in Spain.

Unfortunately, when we reach his office, with its massive bookshelves covering two walls and window facing a vineyard, there's nothing to distract me from the conversation I'm about to have. Raphael turns off his phone and gives me all his attention.

He waves a hand toward an orange velvet sofa. "Please, sit down."

"No. This will be a fast conversation and you will bring me back to my place as soon I tell you no for the umpteenth time." I cross my arms over my chest and I notice how he leans against the carved wooden desk, gripping it with his hands and slumping his shoulders, almost defeated.

He closes his eyes, takes a deep breath, then reopens them and looks straight at me. There is concern in his face, but he is not angry. I wonder how important it is for him that I agree to his proposal. It's not like there aren't other women willing to jump into his life and his bed. He's handsome, successful, and seems smart too. Why me?

"Is it because you don't want to share your private life with the public? You're not on any social networks or anything available online. Why?" he asks.

He has done his homework.

"None of your business, but yes, I don't like to share anything about myself with strangers."

He seems to think about that. "We can agree to share only campaign and public appearance related information. You don't have to share anything personal. You don't even have to handle the social accounts; your publicist would do it for you," he explains and I sigh.

"I don't want my face online," I hiss between my teeth.

"Why? Is it a matter of money? We can pay you a lot for the inconvenience of having people recognize you."

I let out a humorless laugh. "You don't understand. I don't want to people to recognize me." I scoff.

"Why? Is it better to work half naked with people harassing you for a blowjob?" He's trying to fight back and I can see the disbelief in his eyes.

"Yes! It's way better than having my face all over internet. There's not enough money in the world to convince me to marry you!" I raise my voice and now I understand why he wanted to talk with me here. Nobody can hear me getting angry and shouting his indecent proposal through the paper-thin walls of my apartment.

"Why?" he repeats, raising his voice too. "Give me just one reason and I'll leave you alone!"

"Because I'm in the witness protection program. That's why!" I shout.

The silence that follows is absolute. My heart hammers in my chest after the confession I've told nobody about. For eight years, this secret has gnawed at my heart and made my life lonely and miserable. As soon as the words leave my mouth, I feel the weight leaving my chest.

"Fuck," he whispers without moving, his eyes never leaving my face.

"Yes, fuck. Now do you understand why I can't show my face to the public?" I ask angrily.

He shakes his head, like he just realized what this information means and what the consequences are. "Can you tell me what happened? If you're comfortable. Nothing you say will leave this office." His voice softens and I feel my legs tremble from the rush of the confession leaving my body.

I sit down on the couch and Raphael takes a spot next to me.

"Have you ever heard of The Hangman of New Jersey?" I ask, looking him straight in his green irises.

He frowns. "The head of the criminal organization?"

I nod. "I was the one who filmed him as he shot the fifteen-year-old in cold blood. I testified at the trial and was responsible for putting him in jail for the rest of his life. Afterwards, the government helped me to change my identity. Gave me a whole new life."

He rubs a hand over his face, probably trying to process how messed up my life is. "Do you have a family? Did they make them disappear too?" There's a slight pain in his voice I can't place. It's not like it's his family that's in danger.

"Yes, my parents and little sister are in the program too. I asked to be separated from them to keep them from danger in case I get caught. I know nothing about their identities or where they live. It's been eight years since I last saw them." My voice breaks from the emotions clogging my throat.

"I'm sorry." His voice is quiet and somehow, I know he means it.

"Now do you understand why I can't do what you're asking me?"

"No." A half-smile curves his lips.

"Are you dumb or high?" I ask, making him chuckle. "Did you not hear what I just told you?"

He turns his body toward me, giving me his full attention. He exudes power, confidence, and I find myself wanting to hear what he has to say.

"Your face is already out there. Your name will be soon. I got your name, number, and address from the prick you work for. How do you plan to disappear?"

I swear I want to kill Ice. I knew he was a bastard, but I hoped at least he could keep his mouth shut about my personal information.

"I'm getting a fake ID made. I already have a fake name. My parents weren't crazy enough to name me Silver Argent."

He smiles and nods. "Okay. How do you plan to find a job, withdraw your money from a bank, or just rent a house or a car with a fake ID? Do you have enough cash to pay without a credit card or something? What about background checks for basically anything? Are you ready to live like an outlaw? Because that's exactly how you'll have to live."

I don't know what to say because I didn't plan that far ahead, but he's right. I lower my head and lock my gaze on my hands in my lap.

"I thought so," he adds.

"I don't know, okay? I'll cross that bridge when I get to it," I snap, bringing my eyes to his.

He's determined and I can almost see his brain running a thousand miles an hour. Like he already has the solution in his back pocket. "Or you can accept my offer and let me deal with the rest. I can protect you and your family," he states, and my heart sinks into my stomach.

I spent years praying that somehow I could find a way out of this life, but I lost hope after every attempt to make it right. I've come to accept that there is no happily ever after for me.

"It's not fair," I whisper.

He frowns, not knowing what I'm referring to.

"You can't feed my hope. You can't tell me you'll change my life for the better. When they asked me to testify, they promised that after a while my life would get back to normal. Well, guess what? It's not true. My life never went back to normal, there is no normal for me. There is no husband, no kids, no future. There's nothing for me. And you can't just waltz into my life giving me false hope. It's not fair." I feel my throat constrict in a vise and tears pricking my eyes, threatening to fall.

Raphael reaches out and grabs my hand, smiling kindly. "I can't give you your old life back, but I can keep you safe in this one. I can keep your family safe too. I have connections, I have money and I have men that can make this happen. You will be safer with me than out there alone. And the most important thing is, I know your secret. You don't need to lie with me, you don't need to pretend, you don't need to be guarded around me. You can be yourself."

I forgot a long time ago how it feels to be myself. Even my real name sounds foreign on my tongue. What he's offering is so much more than money that I feel my resolution slip between my fingers.

"Give me one year to show you I can keep you safe, then you can go wherever you want. I'll give you enough money to last a lifetime and a new identity. I promise. I'll make you disappear again." His tone is calm, reassuring, warming.

I should trust no one, run out of this place and catch the first bus out of town, but the hope he planted in my chest is already blooming. He's promising a shoulder to lean on, help with carrying the weight of this secret, and the temptation is so inviting I find myself nodding at his marriage proposal.

CHAPTER 9
Raphael

"Are you nervous?" I study Silver, wrapped in a green silk dress that graces her curves without being too sexy. It's elegant, paired with her light makeup and a new, more natural shade of red hair.

It's been a week since our enlightening conversation in my office where she agreed to pretend to be my fiancé, and now we're waiting in the back of a conference room at the Hilton to announce the engagement and answer some questions from journalists. I would have done something more discreet with a press release, but Matthew pointed out that the paparazzi are going wild, and they won't stop until they get pictures of us together. Doing this joint press conference means their shots will be worth nothing because we're publicly confirming our relationship and they won't have the coveted *inside scoop* about our romance.

"A bit, but I promise not to throw up." She smiles and I chuckle.

I put my hands on her shoulders and squeeze lightly. "Remember what we talked about, the fake interview we practiced, and you'll be fine," I reassure her.

"And if you don't feel up to answering, let Raphael handle it," Matthew intervenes, smiling. "He's used to these kinds of situations, and nobody's expecting you to jump in and answer every question during your first public appearance."

She moves her eyes from my face to my best friend's and frowns. "You mean the only thing I'm required to do is be the pretty fiancé clinging to his arm?"

I like the way she challenges him. I witnessed a couple of banters between them yesterday when Matthew suggested more politically correct ways to answer the sexist questions. She can hold her own just fine.

Matthew shakes his head and smiles. "I can't win with you."

I chuckle, and she smiles a bit. I get closer to her and whisper in her ear, "You're safe out there. Never forget that."

She nods and I'm reassured by the sincerity I can read on her face. This week we've gone through all the security procedures of my team at least ten times, until she was convinced she'll be fine if she sticks with me. I understand her worries, and I have to admit that when I told Matthew and the head of my security about her story, they were concerned too. We had to adjust and improvise some to make this work.

"It's time," Cindy says as she approaches us and guides us toward a door. When she opens it for us, the flashes of the photographers go wild. I grab Silver's hand and guide her to the podium in front of the chairs where the journalists are waiting for us.

I stand tall in front of the microphone, reluctantly letting go of Silver's hand. Maintaining contact with her helps me know how she's feeling. I notice her tensing when we enter the room, almost tugging me back, but then she trusts me again and follows me in front of everyone.

This is a massive leap of faith on her part. She is literally trusting me with her life and the lives of her family members, and I feel the weight of the responsibility on my shoulders. It's a big burden I'm willing to carry for her.

"Wow. You really like gossip, don't you?" I say, assessing the thirty plus journalists seated in front of us and the twenty more photographers standing in the back.

The room comes alive with chuckles. I wait until the murmurs die down again before speaking.

"You all know why we announced this press conference, right? The woman next to me, the one you haven't stopped harassing for days, is my fiancé, Silver. We wanted to keep our relationship private, but you clearly had something else in mind, didn't you?" I scold jokingly, but I'm damn serious.

The way they unleashed the manhunt against us was disgusting. I had to double the security at my home because they tried to jump over the eight-foot wall to take pictures of me and Silver, not knowing that she doesn't live there. Miraculously, Matthew worked his magic and they haven't discovered where she lives yet, but we have a couple of men at her apartment to be sure there's no trouble.

Cindy steps beside me and points to a journalist, a woman I often see around because she writes a political column for a local newspaper. She stands up, paper and pen in hand.

"Mr. Wyden, isn't it convenient that we're just now finding out about not a girlfriend but a fiancé when there are rumors surfacing about you being gay?"

We went over these kinds of questions a lot because we know how they can backfire. Silver knows it too, but I can sense her tensing besides me. She was infuriated when we told her someone would ask these kinds of questions. She can't understand why people feel entitled to ask such private questions.

"You're the ones who spread those rumors. I've always had a girlfriend first, then a fiancé by my side. I just respected her wish to stay out of the public eye." I glance at Silver and smile, partly to reassure her, partly to play the role of a person in love. She smiles back shyly and I'm not sure she's pretending being uncomfortable.

Cindy points to Greg, an old school journalist who is a pain in the ass. "Are you going to marry before your potential election or are we going to see her disappear a few months after the midterms? You know, a convenient breakup?"

I want to punch him in the face, but I smile instead. "Sorry, Greg, you're not invited to the wedding, which is why you don't have the date noted in your calendar. Trust me, our closest friends know exactly when we're getting married and they're excited. But we'll shoot out a press release to let the public know."

Someone chuckles, someone murmurs, the flashes go off from time to time, but we're not here to satisfy their perverse desire to know everything about my private life. It's to put out the word that I'm going to have a wife soon, so I suddenly become reliable and trustworthy. This press conference is a farce, and they know it too.

A younger journalist stands up. I don't know his name, haven't seen him much before. He clears his throat then looks down at his notepad. "Mr. Wyden, some are saying that your relationship with the woman is purely sexual and that you were looking elsewhere to find a wife. Is that true?"

The room goes quiet, everyone waiting for my reply. They probably got tipped off by my dating history in the last few weeks, and the list my father gave me.

I'm about to call it quits when Silver grabs my arm and gently demands my attention. I turn and study her carefully for a moment.

"Can I answer this question?" she asks loud enough for everyone in the room to hear.

She's not shy, or even intimidated. The fire in her eyes reveals an angry woman and I can't wait to hear what she has to say. Anything is better than me launching into a lie that could be found out if some of the women I dated talk.

"Of course!" I step aside to give her space at the podium.

"Sorry, I didn't get *your name*. Can you repeat it, please?" she asks the journalist, and he's a bit confused. I take it she didn't much like him referring to her as *the woman*, like she's not a person in this room.

"Jared."

"Tell me, *Jared*, do you have a wife?" she asks in a polite but firm tone.

"Yes," he answers a bit amused by the situation and I'm enjoying where this conversation is going.

"How many times a week do you have sex with your wife and which is your favorite position?" she asks with a smile, and I almost choke trying not to laugh.

The flashes start bombarding her and a murmur rises from the crowd, but she seems completely unaware of it, staring down the poor guy with a smile on her face. The guy blushes a bit and rubs a hand on the back of his neck.

"That's kind of private. Don't you think?" he counters in a condescending tone, not getting where she's going with her questioning.

Silver gasps and puts a hand over her chest. "I'm so sorry. I thought your line of questioning was about *our* private sexual life. I didn't get that it's inappropriate to ask a person if a relationship is purely sexual. I'm new here and I don't know the etiquette. My bad," she counters back innocently, making everyone laugh and the flashes go wild.

The guy sits down, embarrassed, and the roars of questions for Silver are deafening.

"Did you choose your dress yet?" a woman asks, completely ignoring me.

Silver is the center of the attention, and she announced her presence in this room with the power of a bomb detonating. She's no longer just a figure at my side, she is front and center, and I hope I can keep the promise I made to protect her.

I glance at Matthew standing next to the door. He smiles and winks at me. He's looking at her with admiration, and more relaxed than before. He's obviously impressed by Silver and I'm happy to have him in my corner.

"Not yet. I've tried on a few but I didn't find *The One*," she answers, smiling, and I stand beside her watching her juggle questions about the wedding. She looks like a woman excited about her big day, and I have to wonder how many times she's thought about it and put the idea aside because of what happened to her.

The press conference flies by, and when we finally leave the main room, we meet Matthew's grinning face.

"We streamed the interview on your website and Silver's official Twitter account is exploding," he announces, and I frown.

"In a bad or a good way?" I imagine it's good, considering he's smiling like a maniac, but you never know.

"You were fantastic," he tells Silver, and I can see she's proud of herself. "Women adore the way you put that prick in his place. They are absolutely ecstatic that you didn't get intimidated, and you defended yourself without Raphael sweeping in like a knight in a shining armor."

I sigh in relief. It was a risky answer, but she pulled it off. We're probably going to have to defend her from the bigot who got offended by her blatant honesty, but that's something we can easily handle. She set a very important precedent this morning about what kind of wife she's going to be. She could have chosen to be quiet and submissive and let me handle everything, or be a strong independent woman at my side who handles her own battles. She chose the second and I admire her for it.

***

I hit the white ball and send it flying toward the orange one that rolls into the hole. Aaron curses under his breath because this is the third time I've kicked his ass at pool this afternoon. After the press conference, Silver went with the movers to pack up her things at her old apartment to move in with me, and I needed some time off to relax and process the fact that my life from now on will radically change. So, I took refuge at the Hunting Club and Aaron joined me.

"Are you going to tell me the news or are we playing until our arms fall off?" he asks as soon as two other members of the club leave the room, giving us some privacy.

I smile and hit another ball sending it into the right corner. I expected this line of conversation. He's always seen me with random women that last less than a month. Now I'm announcing my engagement with a person I've never even dated. He's one of my closest friends, he knows something is up. I expected nothing less from him.

"What? Did you start reading gossip magazines?" I wink at him, and he shakes his head.

"Someone once told me I can learn a lot from reading between the lines. But I can't figure out what's going on." He is studying me carefully.

I can feel his gaze on me, his frowning eyebrows tip me off that he's puzzled over my behavior. And I get it. I would be puzzled too if a friend of mine who has never had a serious relationship suddenly announces his engagement to the world.

"He's a wise dude." I chuckle. "But there's nothing to say. I will get married, and you will be invited." I stand, waiting for him to play after my ball bounces without falling into the hole.

He grips his stick and stares at me. "She's a bartender in a nightclub."

"Was, but yes, that's correct," I point out, never diverting my eyes from his.

I can see he's trying to figure out what my intentions are but can't get a picture. This situation is so out of character for me that even my friends can't figure out where I'm going with this.

"Is it a campaign stunt we don't know about?" he asks tentatively.

I breathe in deeply and close my eyes for a second. I shouldn't tell him much. The less people know the better. "Sort of," I blurt out finally.

He puts down the stick and crosses his arms over his chest. "Okay. I get that you can't tell me the details, God only knows how complicated your life is, but if I have to lie for you, I need to know more than a 'sort of.' I can't blow your cover because I have no idea what is going on."

One thing I love about Aaron is his honesty. He's had some bad shit go down in his life in the past, and he knows exactly how these things works, how you can't trust anyone. He's offering me his friendship and his help. I shouldn't be so guarded, and I definitely need someone other than my entourage to have my back in this charade.

"You know about the pictures of Silver and me at the café? Long story short, instead of trying to avoid a sexual scandal, we just went with the flow and told everyone that we're getting married. They're breathing down my neck because they want to vote for someone reliable with a family, so we're giving them a wife."

He nods like this is the most normal thing in the world. He knows what it means to sacrifice for the sake of your career. He's been there, got burned badly because of it, and learned his lesson. He understands what I'm doing.

"She is...*was* a bartender at a shady nightclub. Are you ready to explain that? Your opponents have eyes in there, they can use it against you," he points out with a practicality that amuses me. He's the one who owns an empire, so he knows exactly what people are willing to do to take you down. His own father stabbed him in the back.

"If they say anything, they'll have to explain to their wives and voters why they pay girls younger than their daughters to have sex with them."

He's silent for a moment. I can see his brain working to put the pieces together, then he nods. That's it. It's enough for him to know I will be fine. He doesn't question my decisions, the way I handle my campaign, and I appreciate that. It's a breath of fresh air to have someone who doesn't judge you for every decision you make.

***

When I step into the living room not even a couple of hours later, I find absolute chaos. I've never seen my house with so many people around, boxes scattered everywhere, and Silver on the verge of a breakdown. When she turns around her eyes widen and a smile lights up her face.

"You're here! Thank God. I have no idea where to put all these things." She waves toward the chaos.

"How is it even possible you fit all of this inside your tiny apartment?" I ask, laughing because the amount of the boxes is bigger than her entire bedroom.

"I don't know!" She shakes her head incredulously like she doesn't know where it all came from.

I chuckle and rub my face. I have to direct the people staring at me, but I can't think about it right now. This is exactly what I warned Matthew about when he told me my life would be basically the same. It's not. I've never lived with a woman and I've never shared my space. There is a whole other life in this living room right now that doesn't fit with mine.

"Okay, guys, go home! I need time to figure out where to have you put everything," I shout, and the movers can't escape fast enough from this nightmare.

I turn to Silver, who is studying me carefully. "Can we talk?" she asks, nodding toward my office, and I guide her there.

When the doors closes behind us, she frowns. "It was your idea to have me here," she points out and I lean against the desk nodding.

"Yes. It's better for both of us. I can keep you safe here," I assure her.

"So, why don't you want me here? You disappeared and left me alone, and now you don't give a shit whether or not my things get put somewhere. I'm changing my entire life for you. The least you can do is give me some attention while I try to fit into yours."

I feel like an asshole. I should have been here helping her feel at home instead of going to the club. I didn't even think about it.

"You're right. Can you find what you need for now? Tomorrow, I'll call the movers back and stay here with you and go through your things. I honestly didn't think I was needed here," I confess.

Her features soften a bit. "I packed a duffel bag for tonight. I wasn't sure I'd be able to find everything in the middle of this chaos."

I nod. "Good. Now that we're here, can we go through some rules about this whole roommate-slash-fiancé situation?"

"Yes, sure. I figured there would be some."

"We need to look like we're in love." I say, trying to gauge what she thinks about it.

"Yes, of course." She frowns.

"I mean, in the house too," I explain. "I have a lot of staff coming and going. We're never entirely alone. They've all signed non-disclosure agreements to work here, but people talk anyway. If they sense something is off, they'll blow this whole charade."

"Oh," is her only answer.

"Are you okay with that?" I didn't expect enthusiasm, but words would be nice.

"You mean we have to act like a couple in this house too?"

I nod.

"Like being affectionate? Hugging…?" she guesses.

"Kissing too, if you're okay with it," I add.

She nods. "Yes, sure. I can kiss you. I mean, you're not that ugly, so I won't be too disgusted." She giggles and I chuckle.

"Well, thank you. You're not so bad either." I wink at her.

She blushes a little. "Do we have to…you know…do more?"

I frown. "Like what? Sex? God no! I would never ask you to do something like that!" I rush to explain.

She chuckles and lets out a sigh. "Sorry, I had to ask. You never know."

I study her, amused. "Besides, I wouldn't have sex in front of my staff even if this were a real relationship. Are you into public sex and exhibitionism?" I tease her.

She rolls her eyes and gives me the middle finger. She's relaxing, I see.

"I have a rule too," she says firmly.

"Shoot."

"No funny business. I'm not the kind of woman who's okay with a man making a fool of her by cheating or publicly humiliating her. I will give you my complete loyalty, and I demand the same. You fuck up, I'm gone." Her resolution burns in her eyes.

"Absolutely. You have my word on that."

"Good. That means escorts too."

She knows about Jenny. She probably saw me at the nightclub with her. I can't tell her what is happening, not without messing everything up. "Okay," is the only thing I can say.

"Good." She assesses me for a long moment, then turns around and walks out of the office.

I follow her into the mess of the living room.

"I can't deal with this right now." She sighs looking at the boxes.

I approach her from behind and hug her shoulders. She stiffens a bit when I lower my chin and whisper in her ear. I inhale deeply and take in the strawberry and mango scent that is so her.

"The movers are still out back, packing their things. They're looking through the window," I explain before she freaks out.

She turns around, putting her hands on my shoulders and smiling at me adoringly. If I didn't know this is all pretend, I'd believe she has feelings for me. Damn, she's good. I envelope her waist and hold her against my chest. Her soft curves mold perfectly in my arms.

"Should we practice that kissing?" she asks, surprising me.

"We should," I whisper when she tiptoes and brushes her nose with mine.

She pecks my lips, once, twice, tentatively. Then she presses her lips firmly on mine and I open for her. Her tongue strokes mine in a sensual way. We may be pretending for the sake of the movers, but it's no less pleasant than a real kiss. I like it. I like the rhythm we have, her sweet taste, her fingers trailing up until she buries them into my hair.

It surprises me. Damn, this is a good kiss.

A fantastic one.

Damn.

Damn.

CHAPTER 10
Silver

That kiss was—wow! It's been half an hour since our lips parted and mine are still tingling. And the way he hugged my waist—like I'm his and nobody better take me from him?— that was some serious touch-her-and-you-die energy. If this is Raphael pretending, I envy the woman who has a real relationship with him.

"And this is our bedroom," he says, opening the door to what looks like a master bedroom.

Like the rest of the house, this room is colorful, with salmon walls, reddish wood furniture and a king-size bed against the wall on the right.

"What do you mean, *our*?" I ask.

"We'll share the master bedroom," he explains like it's the most obvious thing ever.

"No way! You said no sex!" I hiss.

He turns around and closes the door behind us smiling. "And I meant it, but we have to share this room."

"Why? You have a gazillion bedrooms in this mansion!" It's already strange living with a man who's not my husband. But sharing the bed too?

He sits down on the bed and folds his hand on his lap. He's so calm about it all it freaks me out.

"I have staff that clean my bedroom and make the bed every morning. They'd notice if you slept in a guest room. Think about it, wouldn't be weird if two people in love don't spend the night together?"

I can't argue with his logic. But still. "Well, maybe you snore and I'm a light sleeper," I mumble, but it's not convincing.

He raises his eyebrow in a challenge. He has this way of making you do what he wants, and making you feel like you're the one suggesting it. A politician at his finest.

"Listen, the bed is a California king. It's huge. We can share it and not even notice the other person on the other side."

"Why do you need a bed so big if you sleep alone? For you and your huge ego?" I ask, because compared to this, my old queen size looks like a cot.

He barks out a laugh. "Maybe. You'll find out soon enough," he teases and I smirk in response.

I accepted this agreement because he has the power and the connections to keep me safe. Nobody can walk into this manor without being invited or shot trying to gain access illegally. But I didn't think about all the implications, like the PDA in front of his staff or sharing a bed. I mean, he's hot, he kisses like a champ, and I'm not complaining. It's just awkward sharing a couple's life with a stranger.

He stands up and reaches out a hand for me to grab. "Come with me, I think this will convince you it's not all bad."

He drags me into the adjoining bathroom and my mouth hangs open. The floor and walls are covered entirely in an intricate mosaic of red, blue, and yellow tiles. There is an enormous shower on the left and a double sink on the right, but what gets my full attention is an antique clawfoot tub in the middle of the room in front a huge window that faces the vineyard and the hills surrounding this place.

"Are you serious? I could live in this room alone and never come out!"

He laughs and strolls next to the tub. He turns on the hot water and beckons me. "What do you think? Want to relax in here while I make a couple of phone calls?" he suggests with a grin.

"Do you even have to ask? Of course, I will spoil myself with a hot bath."

He smiles like he feels satisfied making me happy. It's obviously not the case, considering we barely know each other, but it's nice having someone taking care of me for once instead of doing it alone.

"I'll bring your bag. The towels and bathrobes are in the linen closet next to the sink and the window has one-way glass installed. You can see out but they can't see in, just in case you see one of my men doing a round of the garden," he explains before leaving the room.

When I slip into the hot water fifteen minutes later, I feel like I've hit the jackpot. I close my eyes and enjoy this turn my life has taken recently. I still can't process if it's a good turn or a bad one, but I've learned to take life one day at time. Today I'm soaking in a tub surrounded by luxury. It's a good turn today, and I'm not wasting this opportunity thinking about what shitstorm will hit next. I'll deal with it when the time comes.

"Are you still alive in there?" Raphael's voice comes from behind the door.

"Yes, why?"

"Because it's been more than two hours and I thought maybe you'd drowned." He chuckles.

"Really?" I didn't realize how much time had passed, but now I notice the water is lukewarm.

"Really!" He laughs.

"I'm coming," I shout as I stand and grab the fluffy bathrobe I found. God, I could get used to this life.

As soon as this thought crosses my mind, I feel a pang in my chest. This isn't my life. This is an existence I'm borrowing while I decide what to do with my future. I can't get used to it because as soon as I get comfortable in it, someone will pull the rug out from under my feet, and I'll be back to my miserable existence.

I walk out of the bathroom, not even bothering to change out of the bathrobe. "I've decided to spend the rest of my life in this fluffy cloud," I tell Raphael when I reach him in the kitchen.

He looks up and grins. He's changed into gray sweatpants and a white t-shirt. I've never seen him out of a three-piece suit, and I have to admit he's even more handsome. He looks almost younger than his thirty-five years. I googled him after I agreed to this arrangement, and learned the basics about his public life. Nobody, however, mentioned how that t-shirt stretches over his defined pecs and drool-worthy biceps.

"Are you cooking?" I ask, smelling something delicious coming from the pan in front of him.

"Reheating what the chef prepared for us."

"Oh, you have a chef." I don't know why I didn't think of that. Money is clearly not a problem for him like it is for me. Hiring someone to cook for me is so far from my reality I could be on another planet.

He glances at me for a second before turning around and grabbing two plates from the cabinet.

"I can cook but I don't have time, so I have a person come in and cook for me when I eat at home. Now that you're here too,

I can ask him to come daily." He puts a plate on the counter for me and the other one in front of the stool next to mine where he sits down.

"There's no need for that, I can cook. I'll have to go back to work anyway, so there won't be many chances to eat at home, especially in the evening." As soon as I say it, he stiffens.

"You're not going back to that place." He pins me to the stool with a stern look.

I stare back, not intimidated by his order. I'm used to far worse creeps than him to be scared by that pretty face. "I *am* going back to work," I insist.

"No, you are not. You are my future wife, and you're not going to work in a nightclub." He is so adamant I'm not sure I can win this argument.

I cross my arms over my chest and raise an eyebrow. I can understand where he's coming from. Running for senator when your wife works in a public place wearing lingerie doesn't scream family and mother of your future kids, but it's the principle of him telling me not to work that irks me.

"I'm not the kind of woman who stays home all day while her husband goes to work. I'm not swiping your card on Rodeo Drive while I wait for you to show up after your meetings or whatever you do during the day. I'm used to working, contributing to the expenses and supporting my family since I was a teenager. My parents didn't raise me to be just a pretty face with a husband who provides for me." My rant dies on my lips when I see the smug smile on his face.

"Trust me, I've known you for not even a couple of weeks and I get that you're not a trophy wife. And to be honest, it's what I like most about you. You don't depend on anyone; you have your own life," he says after swallowing a bite of this amazing broccoli and cheddar soup. Who knew broccoli could taste so good?

"You do?" I didn't realize he'd studied me so intently and picked up on those things. Men usually label me as "difficult" when they're being nice, and a "bitch" when they're being honest.

"Yes. And the problem is not you having a job, it's the nightclub. Ice is not a—how can I put it—reliable person, and it would be difficult to set up security in there," he explains.

"So, it's not that being a bartender there is a not a respectable job for a senator's wife?" I raise my eyebrow, challenging him to contradict me.

He nods. "That too, but that's not *my* problem, it's the bigots' issue and I'm not one of them," he states firmly.

I study him for a long moment. He is an enigma. He seems so progressive with all this feminist propaganda, but then he pays women to have sex. It doesn't fit with his personality.

"Okay, so what am I going to do?" I ask, curious about what he thinks is right for me.

He shrugs his shoulders and shakes his head. "I don't know, what *you* like to do, I suppose. But I asked Matthew to prepare a list of jobs suitable for your role and maybe you can start there." He stands up and walks to the sink, then rinses his plate and puts it in the dishwasher.

I lower my gaze and fidget with the spoon. The problem is I don't know what I want. I knew up until eight years ago but none of it is achievable now. When I look up, he's studying me intently and I feel naked in front of him.

"So, what do you normally do after dinner?" I ask to change the subject that's making me uncomfortable.

He frowns. "What do you mean?"

"What do you do for fun, to relax?" I explain but his expression doesn't change.

"I don't know," he replies tentatively.

"What do you mean you don't know? Don't you have a hobby? Some passion?"

"No, I mean, I have, but it's usually…work." He is totally awkward right now.

"You work for fun?" This is a first.

He shrugs. "I usually have a lot to do, so after dinner I do the things I enjoy working on." He says it like it's something everyone does.

My mouth hangs open. "Jesus. That is sad."

He snorts to hide a laugh. "It's not sad. I'm just a busy person."

"No, you're not busy. You're a workaholic, and you don't know how to enjoy your time off work. I bet when you were a kid, they called you lazy when you spent time doing nothing or just relaxing in front of the TV." From the way his mouth opens and closes silently a couple of times, I'm sure I hit too close to home.

I stand up, put my plate in the dishwasher, and start to open the cabinets.

"What are you doing?" he asks, puzzled but a bit amused.

"Teaching you how to enjoy the small things," I answer, grabbing a bag of popcorn.

Fifteen minutes later, we're comfortably seated on the plush cushions of one of his couches watching the opening credits of an action movie.

"I can't believe you have a theater room, and you never use it," I murmur as I grab a handful of popcorn and stuff my mouth with it. I glance at him and notice he's picking in the bowl and putting kernels in his mouth one at time, sitting up straight. I wonder how many times he was scolded for slouching on the couch and now he can't fully enjoy it.

"I bought this house for its style and the vineyard that comes with it, but I wasn't particularly interested in the amenities."

"You really never thought to sit here and watch a movie?" I'm genuinely curious about his disinterest in everything fun-related.

"Alone? What's appealing about that?"

"I don't know. Taking some time for yourself, I guess."

He seems to think about it but doesn't say anything.

Two hours, countless shootings, a gazillion explosions, and a destroyed city later, he's finally slouching on the couch with popcorn peppering his t-shirt.

"So? It wasn't that bad, was it?" I say, grabbing the remote and shutting the massive screen off.

He chuckles. "No. It wasn't bad."

"Look at your phone," I suggest.

At the beginning of the movie, he kept checking his cell-phone, but after a while he completely forgot about it. He grabs it from the sofa and his eyebrows shoot up in surprise.

"See? Nobody called or texted you. The world kept turning without you pushing it," I tease.

"Smartass." He smirks at me, standing up and offering a hand to help me stand too.

"So, what next?" he asks.

"It's almost midnight. We're going to bed. I think?" I notice him stiffen as I say it.

He played it cool before, when he was convincing me to sleep in his bed, but he's uncomfortable too. It's an awkward situation: we're two grown adults perfectly aware that we can share a bed without being intimate, but it's still unsettling, even if the reasoning behind it is right.

I head to the master bathroom first, and when I walk out to the bedroom, I find him wearing dark gray boxer briefs and a black t-shirt. My mouth dries and my eyes pop as I watch his perfect body bend to peel down the duvet just enough for him to slip under it. I can't do it. How can I sleep next to a gorgeous, half-naked man and not have wet dreams about him? This is pure torture.

"Are you wearing that?" he asks, puzzled.

I look down at my hoodie and leggings and sigh. "When I packed, I thought I was going to sleep alone in another room, and I didn't pack anything appropriate." I feel my cheeks blushing.

"Please, put on what you normally wear. Don't change just because I'm in the same room. It looks uncomfortable to sleep in that," he pleads.

"Trust me, this is uncomfortable but way better," I insist.

"Listen. We're going to spend a lot of time together. We're going to see very intimate aspects of each other's life, and I'm not even talking about sex. Can we just rip off the band-aid and get it over with? It's already weird choosing one side of the bed when I usually sleep in the middle, I can't wake up and find you strangled by your hoodie. Unless you sleep naked, I can handle it!"

I huff. "I don't sleep naked, but remember that *you* wanted this when I walk out of that door." I point a finger at him.

He stifles a laugh and shakes his head, clearly not fazed. When I walk out five minutes later in a silk gray camisole and matching culottes—without underwear—his eyes widen and his mouth drops open.

"Fuck," he blurts out under his breath.

I stroll to my side of the bed with a smug smile. I warned him my hoodie and leggings were better, but he didn't listen to me.

"Fuck," he whispers again after turning off the light.

Yeah. This will be one hell of a year, living with an attractive stranger, surrounded by luxury, pretending to be his fiancé. A hell of a year for sure. Hell, I suppose, seems to be the operative word for my entire life.

CHAPTER 11
Raphael

I lightly kiss the spot under her ear. She catches her breath. I smile because I knew it. It's been a month since Silver moved in with me and we've had the chance to make out a lot. I've learned that she whimpers in pleasure if I grab the hair on her neck, she molds herself completely to my chest when I kiss her, she likes to snuggle in my arms when she sits on my lap like she's doing this morning. Her skin smells like mango, like her bodywash, and her hair has the strawberry scent of her shampoo.

I've learned a lot about her in this month and it's addictive. I've never spent enough time with the same woman to learn the little things about her. I've forgotten how it feels. How familiar and comfortable it can be. There's something so attractive about sharing small, intimate moments with the same person and not feeling the need to go out and have sex with someone new. Don't get me wrong, I'm always horny when I'm around her because she's sexy and smart, but sex is not the only thing that crosses my mind when I'm with her.

I nip at her neck, and she squeals. "Raphael, seriously. There's a limit to what I can take without jumping you. My nipples are poking out of my bra. Stop it!" she whisper-shouts.

I chuckle. "Well, you'll give a hell of a show to the pool guy." I glance at the dark-haired dude staring at us. "He's been cleaning the same spot in front of our window since we started breakfast."

She stiffens. "Is he still there? We've been here half an hour!" I know she wants to turn and look, but she can't without getting caught.

I nod. "Yes. That spot is thoroughly clean by now. But he's not watching us, he's ogling your ass. These leggings will be the death of the pool guy."

And mine too. The way the fabric wraps her round ass and hugs her trim waist is right out of a magazine. She's perfect.

"So, that's why your erection is poking my ass?" she smirks, holding my gaze as she pops a blueberry in her mouth.

I shift a bit, adjusting her in my lap to avoid the crotch area. "Sorry about that. I didn't notice it was pressed there." It's useless to deny my evident attraction.

She shrugs. "It's okay. I just said I'm so horny my nipples are like rocks. We're human. We make out all the time, it's not like I'm disgusted by it."

God, this situation is so messed up I don't even know where to start. On paper it looks so easy. Like making a movie: you play a part, you kiss, hug, pretend to be in love. No big deal, right? Wrong! I can control my actions, but I can't control my body. And I'm attracted to her. A lot. I don't know how not to look like a horny teenager in front of everyone. I mean, it's perfect for the role I'm playing, but it's creepy when she can feel the effect she has on me in the form of my hard shaft pressed against her ass.

I kiss her cheek and when she turns toward me, I peck her full lips. "Sorry honey, but I have to go or Matthew will bust my balls this time." I help her slip onto her chair as I stand up.

One thing I've discovered living with this woman is that I stay at home a lot. Before, I had no one to come home to and would walk out the front door as soon as I got dressed in the morning. Now, I take my time, enjoying conversations with Silver and looking forward to coming home earlier at night. It's a pleasant surprise, one I didn't anticipate.

"Please, don't piss him off. I have a meeting with him later this morning along with the stylist to upgrade my wardrobe. Apparently, we have a lot of official events coming up and I can't wear the same dress twice," she complains.

"I know, it's a waste, but think about it, you'll have more dresses to auction off on your website and donate to the Los Angeles women's shelter." I kiss her on the lips again. This one wasn't forced, since the pool guy finally moved out of view, but why not? I like kissing her.

"At least there's that," she mumbles.

She was outraged when the stylist, with Matthew backing him up, told her she couldn't reuse a three-thousand-dollar dress she wore only once. She went on a rant that involved the stylist, Cindy, Matthew and me, all having to listen to why this is so wrong. She's right, but we had to compromise. She buys a new dress, wears it and ends up in the newspaper, and then auctions it on her official charity website, donating the money to a cause she chooses. I'm proud of her for coming up with this idea.

I leave her to her day but first slip into the bathroom before heading out to start my day. I look at my reflection in the mirror and there is no chance my erection will disappear. So, I do what I do most mornings: take out my stiff shaft, pump it imagining Silver's lips wrapped around it, then come all over the sink and feel guilty about it. Because there is no good way to put it: I'm a perv masturbating at the thought of her.

***

"How's it going?" Matthew asks me for the umpteenth time this morning.

We're going through the plan for next month's campaign. We're still too far from the midterms to focus our attention on the communities that are still undecided about me. So many people don't want to vote at all, considering it a waste of time and effort, and those are the ones we have to convince.

"You tell me. You're the one running my campaign," I pretend, for the umpteenth time, to misunderstand his real question.

Since having Silver move in with me, my best friend's been keeping a close eye on our interactions and he's become a bit worried. He's monitoring my every reaction, probably because he realizes that fake it or not, I *am* living with a woman. I am kissing her, having important conversation with her, sharing a bed with her. He was there during the worst time of my life, when my heart got broken into thousands of pieces, and I swore I would never give it to another woman again.

I'm still planning on not falling in love with anyone, Silver included, but there is undeniable chemistry between the two of us that I haven't had with anyone else since I was twenty-one. And this is probably throwing Matthew off balance because he was the one who forced us together; he suggested this solution without fully understanding that I would have an intimate life with this woman. He underestimated that what we're sharing goes beyond sex and he probably doesn't know how I'll react.

"I mean with Silver," he points out and I lift my eyes from my computer to watch him on the other side of the desk.

"I know you mean Silver, but isn't it too late to worry about it?" I snap.

Guilt crosses his gaze before he nods.

"Listen, I'm sorry. But I don't know what you want me to say."

"I want to know if you're okay." This is my friend talking, not my campaign manager. Sometimes his two roles are so blurred I don't know it it's the friend or political expert talking. Right now, the worry on his face leaves no room for question.

"I'm okay. It's a bit weird because Silver is sort of the perfect politician's wife, but I'm dealing with it," I admit.

He studies me with a couple of fingers over his mouth. He always does this when assessing a potentially dangerous situation. "Are you attracted to her?"

"Mentally, yes. Physically, hell yes! Emotionally? No. I'm not attracted to her in that way." I'm honest with him.

He nods, a bit of worry leaving his face.

"I promise I'll tell you if I'm spiraling again, okay? I promise you, I'm fine right now." And it's true. I'm really fine. I feel the urge to protect Silver because this is what I always do, but I'm not going to give her my heart.

This seems to reassure him because he goes back to business, and I sigh in relief.

***

"Look at who's finally showing his face!" Harrison laughs when I walk into the private cigar room at the Hunting Club.

Aaron and Leonard seated next to him chuckle while sipping from their glasses. The air is dense with cigar smoke, and I curse myself because this suit is new and it will be a nightmare to get rid of the smell. I like the smell of cigars, but not on my clothes. I should have gone home to change, but I would have seen Silver and then never left the house to see these three idiots.

"Now that he has pussy at home, he never leaves Malibu!"

Leonard laughs and I glare at him.

"Don't even go there. First, it's sexist, and second, we don't have sex," I counter and he rolls his eyes.

"I know, I know. It was a joke. A bad one, but still a joke. Damn, you're a pain in the ass these days."

They chuckle and I fill a glass of whiskey. I sip it and sit in the comfortable leather armchair.

"How is it going?" Aaron asks. He was the one with the most doubts about this arrangement, but with that grin on his face he doesn't look so worried anymore.

"It's weird," I say honestly. "I'm living and literally sleeping with one of the sexiest women I've ever met, and I never have sex with her."

"Not once? Not even a blowjob? A hand job? Nothing?" Aaron clearly doesn't believe me. According to him there's no chance a man and a woman can live together without fooling around and fucking like rabbits.

"God, no. Nothing. It's not part of the agreement."

"This is bullshit. How can you make out like a teenager and not get horny?" he insists and they all look at me like I'm an alien who just dropped his disguise. Their faces are a mixture of skepticism and amusement, and I can't blame them. It's difficult for me too to understand this situation.

"You have no idea. I'm horny all the time and it's driving me crazy," I confess, rubbing a hand over my face.

They laugh. I'm here baring my soul and they laugh.

"Are you at least getting off?" Harrison chuckles.

"Alone in the bathroom like a teenager."

Another heartfelt laugh erupts and this time I laugh too. It's refreshing to tell someone what I'm going through.

"How do you do it?" I ask Harrison. "How do you shoot all those sexy scenes and not sport a hard-on for the rest of the day?"

He shrugs and swallows a sip of his liquor. "When you film those scenes, you have so many people around you don't really get aroused. You have to shoot the scene over and over again from every angle, and at the end of the day it doesn't even get up."

"Not even once?" My heart sinks. I hoped he had some magic trick actors use to avoid embarrassing situations.

"Oh, yeah, sometimes, but then we usually end up fucking in the trailer and it solves the problem." He says it like it's normal to get rid of an erection by fucking your co-star.

Aaron turns to me and smirks. "You do know that at some point you'll fuck your brains out and end up married for real with kids, right? You can try to resist all you want, but you live together, you'll give in at some point."

I smile but my heart sinks. I will not end up like him. I will not fall in love.

"He's been there, done that. Trust him," Leonard adds as I down the entire contents of my glass.

Silver is hot and smart and the perfect wife, but I will not fall for her. I can't. I don't have a heart anymore to give love a second chance.

***

I walk into my living room at midnight, expecting to find the lights turned off and nobody in sight, surprised when Silver's head pops up from her computer. She's sitting on the couch surrounded by papers scattered all over the cushions and the coffee table.

"What are you doing still up?" I ask.

She looks at me with sleepy eyes and a messy bun on her head. Like she just rolled out of bed, and gorgeous still. "Sorry.

I didn't realize it was so late." She grabs the papers to make me some space.

"No worries. What are you doing?" I'm curious. I've never seen her so focused on something she didn't notice the time.

I sit next to her, and she wrinkles her nose. "God. You smell like an ashtray. You stink!" She laughs.

"Sorry. I met some friends in a cigar room and now I think I have to burn this new suit." I chuckle. "What is all this?" I gesture toward the papers.

"I was catching up on some homework."

I frown and she sees my puzzled expression and clarifies. "I never got a chance to finish college. I was a senior at NYU when I testified and got put in the protection program. I couldn't stay enrolled there and couldn't transfer because with the new identity I had no records from a previous school. But I had this one professor who's been helping me study for my courses, as though I'm still a student there. I think he suspects who I am, but we have this silent agreement where he doesn't ask, I don't tell. I'm studying for my MBA, but without the pressure of tests and finals. Isn't that cool?"

She's trying to be positive about it, but I can tell it's forced. That testimony fucked up her life and my heart aches for her. I wish I could help, but even with all my money and connections, I can't change her situation.

"I'm sorry to hear that. What were you studying?"

"Criminal Justice. I was going after a career in criminal law. I wanted to catch the bad guys, but apparently the bad guy got to me first and ruined that for me." Her smile never reaches her eyes.

A pain stabs at my chest. God only knows how much I wish I could go back and save her from this life. If only I could carry this burden for her, give her a chance at the life she dreamed of.

We're so alike in our aspirations it's almost ridiculous. The only difference is that I can and I'm working for it, and she got her wings clipped before she even learned to fly.

I lean closer to her, weave my fingers into her hair and crush my lips on hers. At first she's surprised, but when my tongue slips between her lips, she melts in my arms. I drag her to my chest; her hands trail up my shoulders and get buried in my hair. A moan escapes her lips and I'm ready to catch it with mine. I need to feel her closer, kiss away her sadness, make her feel better. She doesn't deserve the life she got. She doesn't deserve to be punished for doing the right thing. She deserves to be happy, and I'll do anything in my power to make it happen. She chose to help me because she wanted to do the right thing. Again. And I don't want to be her punishment.

Someone once told me I have a hero complex because I want to save everyone who's in need, even when they don't ask for my help. I don't want to be a hero. I just want to be the one that erases her sadness.

CHAPTER 12

Silver

I've been hiding for years. Ever since the trial, I've been trying to be less noticeable than possible. I'm used to blending with the crowd, becoming part of the wallpaper, avoiding situations where other people notice me. I've never hidden from a kiss.

I'm still in bed when Raphael wakes up and goes to the bathroom. I'm wide awake but pretending to be asleep. That kiss last night was incredible. It took my breath away and for a long moment, I forgot we were pretending.

It was easy to forget because no one was around, we didn't have to put on a show. He just kissed me out of the blue and now I don't know how to act around him.

I can hear Raphael walking around the room, getting ready for his day. He steps lightly to the door of the bedroom and stops for a long moment. I don't know if he knows I'm awake, avoiding a confrontation with him, but he seems to hesitate before walking out the door and closing it softly.

Half an hour later, I'm heading to the kitchen and there is no trace of Raphael. I sigh in relief and immediately feel guilty for it. It's immature to avoid facing him, but I need to wrap my mind around that kiss before I speak with him.

On the counter I see a plate under a plastic cover with a post-it on it. Raphael's horrible handwriting makes me smile. He's perfect in many ways, but handwriting is not his strong suit.

Eat breakfast, then try this.

There's a key under the note. I frown, not sure what does it means. Putting post-it and key aside, I remove the plastic lid and smile when I see toast, jam, yogurt, and fruit. He knows this is my favorite breakfast and I appreciate that he remembers it. A pang of guilt hits my chest because avoiding him sounds awful after he took the time to prepare this. Maybe that kiss was nothing to him and this is just another normal day. I'm the one overthinking it, and the guilt turns to disappointment.

I shouldn't be disappointed. I should be indifferent, and this realization scares me.

I sit down and eat my breakfast, picking up the key from time to time. I wonder what it is. As soon as I finish eating, I walk around the house looking for a door to open. Excitement bubbles in my chest. I feel like a kid trying to spy what her parents got for her birthday: a bit eager, a bit scared to be discovered, very naughty for doing it. It's silly, but it's been a while since anyone thought about me enough to surprise me with anything.

It doesn't take me long to find the door. It's to one of the many guest rooms in this mansion, and the only locked room besides Raphael's home office.

When I open it, my jaw drops. The room is completely stripped bare, the bed and dresser gone. The only things left are a desk and a chair in the middle of the space. I walk into the room and see my laptop and notes neatly laid out on the desk. A post-it similar to the one in the kitchen is attached to my computer.

It will take a lot of work to make it feel like home, but this is a start. This is your office, where you can study, work, or spend personal time. You deserve a place where you can be yourself.
Raphael

I feel tears threatening to fall down my cheeks. He gave me an office. He gave me an office to be myself. I'm so used to being someone else that I don't even know who I am. He understood that and gave me a space where I can find out.

I have no idea how he pulled this off without me noticing, but this is the best present anyone has ever given me. And the weight of that kiss becomes even heavier.

***

"I thought he'd locked you up in his bedroom and thrown away the key." Lola greets me with a scowl.

I cringe inside. My life has been so hectic in the last month that I forgot about her. It's like I stepped into another dimension and my previous life was completely erased. Sort of what happened eight years ago, but without the trauma of a murder.

"Sorry about that. My life is upside down right now." I cringe at the bland explanation.

She rolls her eyes but smiles while we sit in the sand on a Malibu beach. I chose this place because it's less crowded than Venice Beach or Santa Monica, so less people will notice the huge bodyguard dressed in a black suit a few feet behind me.

Lola glances at him and her eyes sparkle with amusement. "Does Death follow you around everywhere?"

I turn toward Sven in time to see him struggle to hide a smile but pretending to look around.

I nod. "Yeah. Every time I walk out of the house. He's stuck with me."

She takes another good look at him and from the way she bites her lip, I think she'd like a ride on Sven's carousel. I smile.

"How's life in the political spotlight?" she smirks.

It's my turn to roll my eyes. "Weird."

"Oh, come on! I want details!" she pouts.

"There are no details. I live in a mansion and my life is turned upside down. I can't do my job, but I make a lot of official appearances. No details, just massive twists and turns in my life," I complain.

She chuckles and shakes her head. She sweeps her gaze around then lowers her voice to a murmur only I can hear. "Can we skip the part where I ask you if this engagement is real and you come up with a bunch of lies? You walked out the door one day fighting with a complete stranger and you walked in a few hours later engaged to him. I'm not a fool, Silver. I know you didn't know him two days before your engagement."

I feel a weight lift from my shoulders. "God, yes, please. I'm glad you brought it up."

She nods and smiles at me. "I won't tell anyone."

I know that. I trust her. She never pushed me for details about my previous life and she always kept quiet when our colleagues asked about me. She's loyal and I like her for that.

"Thank you. Are they asking about me at work?" I'm eager to know. I'm probably *the* gossip going around right now.

"They're all wondering how you got your hands on the most handsome bachelor in town. They're asking me if I knew you had a relationship with him and things like that."

"Are they giving you a hard time about it?" My voice is small. I'm sorry for causing her all this trouble.

She turns around and raises her challenging eyebrow. "Do I look like someone who's easily intimidated?"

I chuckle. "No."

"So, don't worry about me. I can handle a bit of questioning. Not a big deal."

"Thank you."

"How are you doing? Seriously, how is living with Mr. Handsome?" I can feel the curiosity in her voice.

"Weird. I'm not joking. It's strange because we act like a couple, but we barely know each other." I've been able to get to know him better this month, but I'm not even close to knowing the real him.

She giggles, bumping her shoulder against mine. "How is he in bed?"

"What? No! We're not having sex," I whisper-shout.

She studies me for a long moment, then her eyes widen when she realizes I'm serious. "Are you kidding me? You haven't had sex with him? Is he gay or something?"

"No, he's not gay, trust me. But we keep it professional." Nothing is professional about what we're doing.

"Professional? There are pictures of you making out, how is that professional?"

She has a point.

"We're pretending, okay? We don't cross the line and sleep together. We don't mix the job with pleasure." But my job *is* pleasure, sometimes.

"And how is that going so far? Keeping it separate, I mean," she challenges me.

"I don't know." I let out a breath.

She hugs her legs against her chest and rests her head on her knee. She looks at me, waiting for something more.

"There was a kiss last night that I don't know how to read," I confess.

She nods and I continue. "We're usually affectionate when are people around, to make the relationship believable, but last night there was no one around, we didn't have to convince anybody, but it was the most intense kiss I've ever experienced. It was earth-shattering."

"Who made the first move?" she asks without judgment.

"Him."

She nods. "Have you told him how you felt about the kiss?"

I shake my head. "That's the problem. I pretended to be asleep this morning to avoid the conversation. Because the truth is, I don't know how to feel about it."

She falls silent for a long moment then she moves her gaze toward the ocean in front of us. "This is messed up. A relationship that's not a relationship, I mean. It fucks with your head, and I'm worried it will fuck with your heart too," she finally says.

I'm worried, too, because nothing has changed on my end. I can never have a family, and falling for the guy I'm pretending to love, is not on my to-do list. But the lines between fake affection and real intimacy are blurring, because if there's anything Raphael and I have in abundance, it's chemistry.

***

When I get home after an entire day out, I'm surprised to find Raphael already changed into sweatpants and a hoodie, lighting up the grill on the patio next to the swimming pool.

"What are you doing home so early?" I'm curious because it's just six in the evening.

He shrugs. "I was craving some grilled steak and decided to cook dinner tonight."

"You went to buy steaks?" My eyes bulge out of their sockets.

He laughs. "Yes. I did"

"Wow. Dave must have had a heart attack when you asked him to drive you to the market." I chuckle.

"He didn't believe me at first," he admits.

"I can imagine. Can I help?"

He shakes his head. "I'm all set; just sit and eat when it's ready. But if you want to keep me company, tell me how your day was and where you went, I'm happy to listen."

A warm feeling expands in my chest. He already knows where I've been because his bodyguards tell him every detail for safety reasons, but I appreciate that he asks. I'm not used to it anymore and it's a pleasant return to the past.

"I went to see Lola." I sit down on the stool next to the built-in grill.

"How is she doing?"

I study him for a second. He is genuinely invested in this conversation.

"She's okay. She wants to find another roommate, but she's not in a hurry."

"Sorry about that."

"Don't be. She doesn't need one, and I'm pretty sure she won't rent my room anytime soon," I explain and he nods.

"Listen, thank you for the office. I really appreciate it." I finally have the guts to say it.

He stops cleaning the grill and turns around to face me completely. He smiles as he grabs my hand and comes closer.

"Do you like it? There's a lot of work yet to do, but I can call an interior designer to help you set it up like you want," he rushes to explain.

"I love it. It's the most amazing gift anyone has ever given me."

He seems to think about my answer and moves closer, nestling between my legs. He brushes a strand of hair behind my ear, and I have to tilt my head up to look into his deep green eyes.

"It's nothing, really. It's just a room." He says it so quietly it's almost a whisper.

"No, it's not. It's so much more for me."

I straighten up and brush my lips on his. He tenses a bit, but when I kiss him a second time, he gives in and grabs my hair, making me moan softly. I put my arms around his neck and enjoy his embrace. I enjoy his tongue exploring my mouth, his possessive grip around my waist, his erection pressed between my legs.

After a very long time, I feel like I belong somewhere. Even if this life is just a pretense, it feels more real than the last eight years of barely surviving on autopilot.

The thought is scary enough to make me want to run far away before my heart shatters.

CHAPTER 13
Silver

I peel my eyes open and the first thing that comes to my mind is the searing kiss Raphael and I shared last night. Just one kiss, like the night before, but it's more confusing than anything. If we were having sex it would be easier. It would be just that: sex. You can have fun with someone attractive without having feelings for him, right? But just kissing—something between platonic and fucking each other's brains out—that feels more intimate.

I turn toward Raphael and sigh. He's still asleep. He is on his back, one hand over his chest, the other bent under the pillow. His hair is messy, giving him an innocent look. A ray of sunlight filters from the window and illuminates his face. His long lashes caress his high cheekbones, the tanned skin making his straight nose stand out, and his full lips are so kissable they're hard to resist. He is gorgeous and he is not mine. I have to remember that.

He stirs slightly and opens one eye. I'm still staring at him when he smiles.

"Good morning." His voice is rough and does funny things to my lower belly.

"Good morning," I whisper back, hoping he doesn't notice I was ogling him.

He rubs his eyes with the heel of his hand and turns toward me. Far enough to not touch me, but close enough to make me quiver.

"What time is it?" He frowns.

"It's almost nine thirty. We slept in."

"We're late." He smiles but doesn't move.

"Late for what? It's Saturday." I try to remember if we have some appointment I forgot about.

He smiles. "Remember when I told you I was craving a steak yesterday? I may have gone a bit overboard at the market, and I invited a few friends over today for a small gathering."

His lips are still curved upward, but I read expectation in his eyes, like he's not sure if I'll agree to this or not. This is his home. I would never tell him to not invite friends over.

"Oh, okay. I'll find something to do. I can shop for some furniture for my office." I'm not sure it's the right thing to say because his smile fades.

"What? No! You're invited too. I'm not kicking you out."

"Okay…" My answer comes out sounding insecure.

"And for the record, if you want to invite someone over, you can. You know that, right?" he rushes to add.

"Now I do, thank you." This time my voice is firmer. "What time are they coming?"

"I told them to get their asses here by ten to help me set up." His guilty smile makes me quiver, but his words make me sit up with a start.

"Ten in the morning? Like in twenty-five minutes?" I scramble out of bed.

"Yeah. Sorry about that." He chuckles as I run into the bathroom.

Ten minutes later, I'm showered and dressed in a tank top and shorts, popping grapes into my mouth while I watch Raphael sort out the steaks he bought yesterday.

"Oh, honey, that is not craving a steak, that is full-blown shopping spree. At least, the male version of it." I giggle when he realizes he bought way too much.

He laughs. "Shit. This is why Dave was looking at me like I'd gone crazy."

"Probably."

The doorbell rings and I stroll to the front door. I swing it open and almost choke on the grape in my mouth. In front of me stands Harrison Bates, multi-award-winning actor, Dakota Anderson, Hollywood up-and-coming movie star, and a face I recognize from the press as Aaron Steel, producer and business genius. Basically, Hollywood royalty at its finest standing here looking at me awkwardly.

"Can we come in?" Harrison asks hesitantly.

I'm staring. Thus, their embarrassed expressions.

"Yes, of course! Sorry, I was freaking out on the inside but frozen on the outside," I say nervously and they laugh.

"Raphael didn't tell you who was coming, did he?" Dakota asks as she walks in with the other two.

"Even worse. I found out we had guests coming literally twenty minutes ago. I was still in bed." She gasps, horrified.

"Are you serious?"

"Yep." I nod.

"Raphael, we need to kick your ass!" she shouts as we reach him in the living area.

"Why would you do that?" He feigns offense.

"You didn't tell her we were coming? A woman needs time to get ready!" She explains like he's a child who doesn't understand adult stuff.

He frowns and waves at me. "Have you seen her? She doesn't need to get ready; she rolls out of bed looking gorgeous like that."

Complete silence follows. My cheeks go up in flames, both at the compliment Raphael just gave me, and at their faces, all grinning in my direction.

"So, you're Silver, right? I'm Dakota, this is Aaron, and the other pain in the ass is Harrison." She reaches out her hand and I shake it.

"Nice to meet you!" I blurt out in a rush.

I look at Raphael, who winks at me then turns to his two friends and starts giving them orders about what to do. Still, their curious gazes linger on me, and I'm saved from more embarrassment when the doorbell rings again. I bolt toward the front door like the house is on fire.

When I open the door, I'm greeted by the smiling faces of Matthew and Cindy and the brooding one of a guy I've seen a lot on the cover of *Forbes*. He always has that expression, and I thought it was his mysterious way of striking a pose for the camera. Apparently, he has a severe case of resting bitch face.

"We found this one taking a selfie in front of the flowers," Matthew says, stepping aside and showing me Lola's grinning face.

"What are you doing here?" I ask her as they file in and she hugs me tightly.

"Raphael told me there was a party and you know I can't miss one!" She kisses me before walking into the room and turning around looking at the faces. "So, where is Sven?" she asks Raphael and I can't stifle a chuckle.

"What? You have *la créme de la créme* of Hollywood in this room and you're looking for Sven?" Harrison asks outraged.

Lola walks over to him, puts a hand on his chest and purrs. "Sweetheart, I don't date guys who wear more makeup than me at work. I like a man who can fuck me with the same hands he uses to kill someone who looks at me the wrong way." She winks at him and walks away.

Harrison gasps, putting a hand to his chest like she just ripped his heart out, and the room explodes with loud laughter.

"I'll pass along the message," I tell her when she walks by me.

"Thanks, honey." She winks at me.

I join Raphael as he's seasoning the steaks and put a hand on his bicep. "Thank you for inviting Lola," I whisper.

"I thought you'd be more comfortable having someone you know here." He smiles sweetly at me.

"I appreciate that." I tiptoe to kiss him on the lips.

I turn around to see all eyes are on us. Someone is smirking, someone is frowning. There are various reactions on their faces, but they're all focused on us. I feel my gut clinch nervously.

"So, anyone want something to drink? I'm a bartender, you know. It's the only thing I know how to do at a party." I smile and everyone seems to snap out of their thoughts and walk toward the kitchen counter.

"Is it true that you know what a customer drinks just by looking at his face and how he's dressed?" Harrison asks me.

"Why don't we try?" I wink at him, and they all seem entertained by the idea. Even broody resting bitch face.

I gather as much as possible from the liquor cabinet, grab a bucket of ice from the freezer, and start to do what I know best. Fortunately, Raphael seems to own a bar; he not only has the best liquor, but almost everything I need to make cocktails. He even has passion fruit in his fridge. Who buys passion fruit?

"Shirley Temple for Dakota." I put the glass in front of her.

"Thank you!"

"Why a Shirley Temple?" Harrison asks.

I look at him, curiosity written all over his face. "Because she is refreshing, genuine, and has a smile only a child-like person can pull off."

He nods and Dakota blushes.

"Cosmo for Lola. I cheated with this one. I know her favorite."

Lola sips from her glass and moans.

"For Cindy, a vodka tonic, sparkling like her personality." I put the glass in front of her and she nods.

"My favorite!" she confirms.

"Aaron, Scotch. Neat. A glass of water on the side." I give him his glasses.

He smirks at me and Harrisons gasps. "How did you know that?"

"He's wearing a polo, khakis, and sneakers. He wants something easy, not fancy, colorful or pretentious," I explain.

"Why not a beer?" Harrison challenges me.

"He's wearing a sixty-thousand-dollar watch. He has too refined taste for a cheap beer."

Dakota gasps and looks at Aaron's watch, then at the smirk he's giving me. He didn't expect I would actually get it right.

"What about Leonard?" He points to resting bitch face. So, he has a name.

"Old-fashioned for him." I put a glass in front of him and he almost smiles. Almost. "He showed up in black trousers, elegant shoes, and a perfectly ironed white shirt. He probably ditched the tie and jacket before getting out of the car, after he saw what you all were wearing. He likes expensive things, like Aaron, but he wants you to put an effort into making his drink."

This time he actually grins.

Harrison's mouth hangs open.

"For you, my dear, a Pornstar martini. It's refreshing, frivolous, and over the top with a bit of exotic that you love so much," I say, putting half of the passion fruit into the glass and handing him the cocktail and the shot of champagne that goes with it.

Everyone laughs and Harrison grins and sips it, winking at me.

"Matthew, I just saw you down an antacid. I'm guessing you're not doing alcohol today, right?" I smile and he waves at me.

"I'm sticking with water. Thank you."

"What about Raphael?" Leonard asks, speaking for the first time, and everyone seems to hold their breath.

"He's a shot of tequila, salt and lime." I give him his shot, but he doesn't touch it.

His arms are crossed over his chest, an amused smile dances on his face. "Why am I tequila?" There is a challenge in his tone.

"Because you're good at making people do the unthinkable, even the most stupid things. But, if you have too much of it, you end up hungover in some Vegas hotel, married to a guy you barely know and with no memory of how you got there in the first place," I explain and his amused smile morphs into a full belly laugh.

He grabs my hand and drags me to him. A mischievous glint burns in his green eyes. My breath catches in my throat when he lowers his lips in the crook of my neck and licks it. An audible moan almost escapes my lips as my heart hammers in my chest. What the hell is he doing in front of everyone? He grabs a pinch of salt, puts it on my damp skin then licks it again. He downs his shot of tequila and then suck at the lime without his burning gaze ever leaving mine.

My lower belly tingles with desire and my nipples stand at attention. If he touches me between my legs, I will come faster than a shooting star.

"Damn! That was hot." Harrison's voice startles me and I turn around to find everyone staring at us.

"Now I know why you chose her," Leonard tells Raphael, but his eyes never leave mine. A naughty grin is plastered across his face.

And just like that, with Leonard's approval, I feel like I've been introduced and accepted into this new group of people. His people, not mine, and I'm not sure how I feel about it.

***

I stare out the window with a smile. Raphael is laughing at something Harrison said and everyone is relaxing around the table like an old group of friends. Today couldn't have been more perfect. We chatted, laughed, and had fun. I haven't smiled so much in a long time and a sense of happiness warms my chest.

For the first time in a long while, I glimpsed what my life could have been if I had chosen differently eight years ago, if I hadn't done the right thing. Hope has been trying to bloom in my chest all day, and even if I did try to snuff it, it hasn't gone away. If I look carefully, it's still there, feeding false hopes I can't afford to trust and let grow.

"He'll never love you." Matthew voice startles me.

"What?" His words hurt more than I expected.

He is staring out the window at the same view I am. "I've never seen him fall in love with anyone else. He never got over her."

I have no idea who he's talking about, but I imagine it's someone they both knew. "I wasn't thinking about that," I lie. Hope is still there, the kind that imagines a different future for me. I could learn how to love someone like Raphael.

Matthew smiles sadly and a lump forms in my throat, making it hard to breath. "I see how you look at him. Don't go there. I'm telling you because I don't want to see you get hurt."

I force a smile. "Don't worry. I'm not planning on sticking around for long. I know this isn't my life. After he gets what he wants, I'll disappear."

He studies me for a long moment with an unreadable face, then he nods and walks out to sit around the table. The same table I will not be part of in the future.

As if sensing me stare at him, Raphael turns around smiling and something in his eyes seems to burn with an intensity that makes my legs weak. I put my hands on the counter to keep from crumpling to the ground. He winks at me and motions for me to come out. I nod, swallowing once, twice, three times to push down the lump constricting my throat.

I put on a smile on my face as I reach him and his friends. They are loud and happy, and I suddenly don't fit in anymore at this table.

Raphael grabs my hand and makes me sit on his lap, dragging me closer to his chest.

"What happened?" he whispers in my ear. Concern clouds his eyes.

"Nothing, just a bit tired," I lie.

He doesn't seem convinced, but Harrison demands his attention. "Can I just say that you are a shitty friend? You got engaged and didn't invite us to the party." He's teasing. Everybody here knows the situation between the two of us.

"Who says I didn't?" Raphael challenges him and everybody goes quiet. I turn around to watch him and he winks at me. "What?"

I don't understand, but when he pulls out a blue velvet box from his pocket, my mouth goes dry. Dakota gasps and Lola squeals. I, on the other hand, am frozen in place.

"I'm not a shitty friend, but I'm a shitty fiancé. I announced to the world we were engaged, and I didn't get you a ring first."

He opens the box and shows me a simple rectangular diamond on a ring that I suspect is platinum.

I don't know what to say. I look at the diamond shining under the California sun, then at Raphael's smiling face, then at the ring again.

"So, what do you think?" he asks.

"Yes?" What am I supposed to say? It's still fake, I didn't need the diamond.

Raphael laughs, putting the ring on my finger.

Harrison sighs loudly. "Thank God. For a moment I thought she'd say no."

Everybody laughs and cheers but when my eyes lands on Matthew, I see he's frowning. He didn't know about this. The fact that Raphael kept this from his campaign manager and best friend makes my head spins. This is fake, this has nothing to do with my future, but the ring feels heavy on my finger.

"Okay, we have a ring, but what about the date?" Leonard asks.

"September sixth," Raphael replies without missing a beat, and I'm so stunned I can't even speak.

I didn't know I was actually getting married before the mid-terms.

CHAPTER 14
Raphael

"You need to go on a date with Silver," Matthew says out of the blue.

I lift my gaze from my computer to look at him. "What?" I ask, puzzled by his proposal

"Silver. You need to be seen out on a date with her," he repeats.

"Yes, I heard you the first time, but I don't understand why," I explain, and he sighs.

"Because you're not gaining voters like we thought, and you have to push it. People adore Silver, especially women, but she's out of touch," Matthew pushes, and I clench my jaw.

We've gone over this many times. He knows Silver's situation, and I don't think she wants to push her luck.

"We started this relationship playing on the idea that we could hide for a long time because we value our privacy, and now you're saying we have to go out on a date? Are you planning to call the paparazzi and stage something?" I arch my eyebrow in a challenge. He knows I don't like to use gossip to get people talking about me.

"No, of course not. But people will take pictures of you, they'll talk online. Real people, not gossip magazines. She feels distant. They adore her because of her public appearances, but they can't relate to her. There's not one picture showing her doing something normal like having breakfast or going for a run. Only official pictures in glamorous dresses. Normal people can't relate to that," he points out.

"You know why she doesn't do it. It's a risk, and you're willing to put her in danger for my sake." There is accusation in my voice and Matthew's face clouds with disappointment. I know he is doing everything to win this election, but there are some things I won't do, like exploit the woman who agreed to help me.

"She knew what she was signing up for when she decided to help you. She likes the money you're throwing at her, so don't pretend she's doing it out of the goodness of her heart." He raises his voice and anger starts boiling inside me.

"She never asked for my money!" I shout. "I put a figure on the table and she accepted it without even glancing at it. She's helping me because I screwed up her cover and I'm the safest option for her, and you know it."

Now anger crosses his heated gaze. "Literally ten days ago you gave her a freaking diamond she can keep after this is over. A million-dollar diamond and you're telling me she doesn't want your money?" he shouts back.

Here we go again. Matthew is furious I gave her that ring, and I don't know why. "Is this about that fucking diamond or the money or what? What's the difference if I gave her cash or a diamond? Please tell me why you are so pissed about that ring. We're engaged, everyone is expecting a rock on her finger!"

"Because she's falling for you!" he shouts, and this time I'm speechless.

"What?"

"Have you seen the way she looks at you? Are you sleeping with her? Because if you are, stop it. Snuff it out now because you are going to hurt her. You're giving her a taste of a life she can't have and when you dump her, she will be crushed," he spits out in anger.

What the hell is he talking about? She's not like that. She knows the deal, doesn't she? We both know that there will never be a real relationship between us, and she's on board with that.

"You don't know what you're talking about." I rub a hand over my face.

Matthew studies me for a long moment and I can see the anger leave his face, a mixture of resignation and fear replacing it. "I hope so. I really hope so," he mumbles before standing up and going for the door. He stops before grabbing the handle and walking out. "Go on a date. I'm telling you as your campaign manager, not your friend, this is the right thing to do."

"I'll talk to her, but I can't guarantee she'll agree," I say firmly, and I can see his shoulders slump a bit. He seems defeated.

"Remember that you chose her because of your campaign, not to play hero and save her. Do what's right for you, not her," he adds, never looking back at me, then walks out the door, leaving me here with my chest tightening and an uncomfortable dread seeping into it.

***

I walk through the front door almost hoping Silver wouldn't be here, even though I know she is because Sven keeps me posted about her every move. The conversation with Matthew churned in my mind all morning, and when I couldn't keep my head in work anymore, I just gave up and came home.

I take a deep breath and walk into the living room where Silver is sitting at the table in front of the windows, a gazillion pamphlets and magazines in front of her.

She looks up from what she's reading and frowns. "I didn't expect you home so early," she says and I smile.

"If you want, I can walk out and come back later." It comes out like a joke, but I'm not sure it's so far from reality.

"Come on in!" She laughs, waving me closer.

When I reach the table, my heart drops. Wedding pamphlets are scattered everywhere. She's smiling as if excited about it and I wonder if she is taking my proposal more seriously than intended.

"What are you doing?" I hope she can't hear the panic in my voice.

"Cindy came by and dropped these off. She said I have to start planning the wedding," she explains as she giggles, and I can't tell if her excitement is for the big day or something else I can't pinpoint.

"Listen, I know I didn't tell you about the ring and the wedding date, and it sounded more romantic than it actually is, but nothing's changed about the plan to split after the election. You know that, right?" I blurt out in a very messy way. It's ridiculous how nervous I get when I talk to her about something that could upset her.

She frowns and nods. "Are you worried about it?"

"No, it's just that I came home and found you planning a wedding and I don't know what to think," I answer honestly.

She bites her lip trying to hide a smile, but she's doing a really bad job of it. "You should see your face right now," she giggles.

"What about my face?"

"You're panicking." Her giggle becomes a full-on grin, lighting up her face.

"I am not!" I scoff.

"Yes, you are." She nods. "Listen, don't worry about it. I get your concern, but I'm not thinking about spending the rest of my life with you. I know nothing has changed and I'm aware that I need to plan a wedding that is as fake as this relationship." There is a seriousness in her tone that puts my heart at ease, but there is also a bit of longing in her gaze that does nothing to erase Matthew's words from my mind.

She is smart, she knows the deal, and she's never pushed for more. But that doesn't mean she can turn her feelings on and off like a robot. And I get what Matthew said, at least in part. She will do the right thing, but that doesn't mean her heart won't break.

"So, did you find anything interesting?" I point to the pile of material laying on the table.

She laughs, handing me a hideous pamphlet with a goat carrying the rings. I mean, the goat is cute, but the whole idea is hideous.

"What the…"

"I know, ridiculous, right?"

"Yes. Is there really someone who can get a goat to do that?" Sometimes I think those things are just publicity stunts to click on the website. A cute goat can be terrific click bait. Not for a wedding, though.

"Any preferences for the big day?" she asks, dropping the question with a smile on her face but a seriousness in her voice.

"About the animals I want at the wedding?" I joke but I know what she means.

She rolls her eyes and bumps her shoulder against my hip. "No, about what you like. It's your fake wedding as much as it's mine, so it should be a choice we make together."

I wish I could be one of those men who leaves the wedding planning to their fiancé, but I think doing something like this together is a good way to determine how your marriage will go. It shows how you both cope under pressure when you'll have to make difficult decisions as a couple in the future. The problem is, I don't want to know something that intimate about my relationship with Silver.

"I've never thought about getting married, so I don't have any particular preferences."

She frowns and studies me for a long moment, seemingly on the verge of asking me something but then doesn't do it. It's the same puzzled expression everyone has when I say I don't want to find a woman and settle down.

"I got my chance once but it didn't go as planned. I'm not interested in repeating the experience," I add, hopping this explanation is enough to satisfy her curiosity. I don't want to dig up my past in front of catalogues of wedding dresses.

She assesses me for a while then she nods. "Let's start with something simple. Venue or church for the ceremony?" she asks, putting in front of me two different pamphlets.

"Are we even the same religion?" I can't hide a smile at the absurdity of this situation.

"Catholic, but I don't go to church. You?" She grins.

"Me too. Good, at least we can settle on the basics." I chuckle and she laughs too. "Listen, before planning a wedding, shouldn't we go on a date at least? You know, to get know each other a bit outside this house? I know what you wear to bed, but I don't know what your favorite ice cream flavor is."

The smile dies on her face. "You know I'm not comfortable with leaving this house. I'm aware that up until now we haven't had any threats, but official events are one thing, being surrounded by people on a date is another."

"What is it that scares you the most? You know we have security, so we're not going to be completely alone. It's like when you go out shopping or meet with Lola." I try to figure out how I can make her feel more comfortable.

"It's not the same. During official events, we know exactly who will be there. I trust your staff to check people that come and go during those events. And when I'm alone it's easy to hide, I'm not as recognizable as you are. Do you have any idea how many people know your face? You're like a rock star, and everyone wants to shake your hand, take a picture with you. You're the reason I'm in this mess in the first place. It's easier to get to me when I'm with you."

Her explanation opens a pit of guilt in my chest I don't even know how to fill it. I'm so ashamed by my request that I don't even have the guts to look her in the eye. She's right. If I were a John Doe, she wouldn't have gone viral or had her life turned upside down.

"Give me a chance to prove that we're safe even when we go on a date, please. If you're not comfortable, I promise we'll come back, and I'll never ask you to do it again." I hold her gaze as she bites her lip and seems to think about it.

"They asked you to do it, didn't they? That's why you're home so early," she states, and I'm not surprised she saw right through me.

She's not stupid, far from it, and despite what Matthew says she has a good heart. I'm almost resigned to drop the argument and tell my campaign manager to fuck off when she nods.

"If for any reason I feel unsafe, we're coming back. Promise?" she demands.

"Promise," I agree, and feel bad about it.

She does anything I ask of her because she understands my position and wants to help me. And what am I doing for her? Nothing but making sure some crazy mobster doesn't kill her, and as she pointed out earlier, there isn't even a small threat of that happening.

***

"You were serious when you said you wanted to learn what my favorite ice cream is." She smiles when we enter the ice cream parlor.

"Of course, I was serious! This way I know how to make up to you when I screw up. Because it's not a matter of if, but when." I chuckle and she leans closer, snuggling to my side.

My heart picks up speed and I'm so overwhelmed by the urge to protect her that I wrap an arm around her and pull her even closer. She stiffens a bit, but then relaxes and presses her back against my chest as I wrap my other arm around her.

I lower a bit to reach her ear and whisper my question so no one can hear. "Are you uncomfortable? Because we can walk out of here whenever you want, just say the word and we ditch the date."

I feel her shiver under my touch and my cock stirs in my trousers. This embrace is so intimate that I forget for a minute we're pretending and kiss her neck lightly. The scent of mango and strawberry does strange things to my body, like giving me an overwhelming urge to sink my erection between her thighs and bury myself inside her until she comes, screaming my name. It's a thought so vivid in my mind that I realize I'm pressing my hips against her round, perfect ass.

She turns her head to look at me straight in the eye. "I'm okay, I promise. But if you keep dry humping my ass, I'll ride you here in front of everyone. I told you, there's a limit to how much a woman can endure when she's dating such a hot, power-ful man," she whispers back before lightly kissing my lips.

I almost choke, stiffing a laugh and coughing at the same time. "Noted." I nod grinning.

"What can I get you?" The smiling teenager behind the counter brings me back to reality.

I notice at least ten people in here watching us intently, and from the smiles on their faces, they recognize us, or at least me. I dropped my defenses, the guarded, calculated behavior I keep when I'm in public, and the feeling is so unsettling I almost want to bolt out of here. I smile down at Silver and see how she's trying to gauge what I'm thinking. She probably sensed the shift in my behavior and now she seems almost worried.

She puts a hand on my cheek and smiles at me. "What do you want, honey?" Her voice is sweet and calming and she grounds me.

"You first," I say, regaining my composure.

It occurs to me that she settles me, makes my world right again. She sensed my discomfort and knew exactly how to calm me. It's a warm feeling, knowing someone in this world knows you so well they know how to make your worries disappear with the right word, the right voice. At the same time, it's unsettling because she's someone I've known for barely two months. Yes, I know she's smart, and she can figure out a person on the fly—she made that clear the day she made cocktails for everyone without missing a beat. But it's the way I eased into this life with her that makes my stomach clench.

"Two scoops of vanilla, whipped cream, and a cherry on top, please," she says without hesitation, like it's what she gets every time.

"And for you, sir?" the teenager asks me, handing Silver her ice cream.

"Two scoops of chocolate, please."

I look around, assessing the people nearby. There's a woman filming us, and while I want to rip her phone from her hands to protect Silver going viral again, I know this is the exact reason why we came out in the first place, so I just smile and nod at the camera. She blushes a bit and bites her lip.

"I'm going to vote for you," she says, confirming that she recognizes me.

"Thank you! I appreciate your support." I grab my cone and step back, ready to pay and walk out of this place.

"Do you want to take a picture with him?" Silver surprises me, asking the woman.

I look at her and she is sporting a genuine smile on her face.

"Do you mind?" the woman asks, and I shake my head and stand next to her.

Silver grabs her phones and takes a couple of pictures of us, but when she hands the phone back, the woman surprises her.

"Can I take a picture with you too? Both of you. You're such a cute couple!" she almost squeals.

I glance at Silver, trying to pick up her discomfort, but she seems at ease, maybe because we're not being mobbed and the crowd is small.

"Sure!" She steps on the other side of the woman.

"I loved how you handled that journalist. They think they can stick their noses everywhere." The lady seems more confident after another few pictures.

Silver puts a hand over her heart and smiles. "I know, right? How can they even think to ask someone about their sexual life?"

The woman shakes her head and sighs. "Sometimes they have no limits, and no morals either."

I'm enchanted by how Silver is handling her conversation with a complete stranger for my sake, for my career. She would be a perfect first lady, and the thought makes my gut clench in discomfort. If she sticks with me that long, the marriage wouldn't feel so fake even for us, not just the public. That's a thought I don't want to indulge in.

***

We return home at almost ten in the evening. After our ice cream, we spent the day strolling around the beach and going to dinner at one of the restaurants on the oceanfront. We both enjoyed it and Silver relaxed. Matthew sent me a text congratulating me for approaching the woman at the ice cream parlor and I didn't bother to correct him. For the first time since I've know him, I'm annoyed by his insistent presence.

"Do you want to relax on the patio?" I ask her.

"Sure." She grabs a blanket and strolls outside as I fill two glasses with red wine. It's still the end of April and the temperature is a bit chilly at night.

We settle down on the double sunbed and I put an arm around her shoulder as we lean close together and she snuggles up to my side.

After a long moment of silence, Silver breaks the ice. "Can I ask you something? Feel free to not answer if you think it's too personal. I understand." She looks me in the eyes.

Her phrasing makes my blood chill, speculating about the topic of this conversation, but she stuck with me all day doing what was best for me. The least I can do is to listen to her question. I nod and she goes on.

"Why do you want to fake a marriage? I mean, when I first met you and you asked me to do this, I thought you were a freak who couldn't get a woman to stay with him. But now that I know you, I don't understand why you don't want to find someone. You're smart, funny, caring. There is no doubt you're rich, and that's a perk, plus you are insanely attractive. You're the complete package. I can't figure out why a woman would ever say no to you."

There is honest curiosity in her voice, no judgement.

I inhale deeply, and for the first time in a long time, I feel the need to tell someone else about Kelsey. I don't talk about it often, and only with people who already know the story, never a stranger. But Silver is not a stranger, and her presence grounds me. She showed me today that she can be by my side in a real way, even if our relationship is fake.

"I had a fiancé when I was young, and she died when we were both twenty-one," I explain and then wait for her reaction.

She gasps and puts a hand on my chest, where my heart is hammering. She feels it, but I don't feel any urgency to take her hand away. Somehow, it's comforting that she can sense what's going on in my chest.

"I am so sorry, Raphael. I didn't mean to pry into such a hurtful memory," she whispers.

I shake my head and pull her closer.

"It's okay. It was a long time ago. Kelsey, Alba, my little sister, and I were very close. We grew up together and we spent a lot of time hanging out. Kelsey and Alba used to go for a run every day, they loved running." I smile at the memory. "One day, they were crossing a street a few blocks from home and a drunk driver hit and killed them both." I take a deep breath and I can feel Silver tense besides me.

"Oh my God. Your sister too? I didn't know you had a sister." I can hear the pain in her voice and my heart beats harder.

"It turns out that the driver was the son of a rich mogul and got away with it. There wasn't a trial or anything. Just a slap on the wrist and he went on with his life."

"Are you serious? Nothing? Not even court-ordered community service?" she asks, dumbfounded.

I shake my head. "I was devastated. I lost the love of my life, my little sister, and a few months later, my mom. She couldn't endure the pain, so she just packed her bags one day and left my father and me to deal with it. But all of that is what made me decide what I wanted to do in life. Becoming a lawyer or a judge wasn't enough—I wanted to change the world. I wanted to make laws that punish people for the pain they cause. It was also the day I decided never to get into another relationship. I'm not strong enough to endure another loss like that." I sip my wine and avoid eye contact with Silver.

She snuggles against me without saying a word and I appreciate that. A lot of people tried to console me when it happened, but nobody understood that there are no words anyone can say that could heal a shattered heart.

We stay there in silence for a long time, hugging as though we could glue the pieces of our broken lives together. I don't know if we can ever heal from what's happened to us, but the fact that my heart isn't exploding in my chest when I hold her tight makes me want to never let her go. My world is spinning less since she walked into it, and that thought is terrifying.

CHAPTER 15
Raphael

I study Silver as she asks Cindy questions about the people we're going to meet in a few minutes. Her eyebrows knit together when my assistant explains something, her mouth pouting in an adorable expression. She looks beautiful wrapped in a silky blue dress that falls elegantly at her knees.

"Are you done drooling over her?" Matthew's voice brings me back to reality.

"I'm not drooling," I say defensively, like a teenager caught lusting over a girl.

"Yes, you are, and I can't blame you. She's gorgeous. But right now, you have to focus on the veterans waiting for you in the other room." He doesn't even bother to glance at me as he attaches an American flag pin to my suit.

"I was just making sure she's comfortable. She's asking a lot of questions."

Matthew sighs and finally turns his stern look on my face. "That's just Silver. She asks a lot of questions because she wants to be prepared about what will happen in a few minutes. She's asking about their names, their backgrounds, everything. When you picked her, you didn't choose a trophy wife who just smiles at your side. You got me a fucking pain in the ass to handle." He scowls at me, and I can't stop a smile curving my lips.

"You're welcome." I grin at him, and he flips me off.

I walk toward Silver and when she notices me, she smiles, making my heart skip a beat or two.

"Are you ready?" I put a hand on the small of her back and guide her toward the doors.

She nods. "Yes! It's a lot of names, but I think I can handle it."

"You know that you're not expected to know every single detail about them, right? Nobody will blame you if you don't remember their names." I try to reassure her, but she pins me with her stern look.

"I'll be disappointment in myself if I don't remember their names. They served our country, and they deserve my respect. Learning their names is the least I can do." Her words are so heartfelt that the only thing I can do to express my pride in her is cradle her face between my hands and softly kiss her lips.

When I let her go, I find her stunned expression staring back at me.

"What was that for?"

I lean in close to her ear and whisper, "For being the perfect future fake wife. You are gorgeous in this dress, but your brain and your heart are what make you the most incredible woman I have ever met." And I mean every single word.

Strangely, I don't feel like I'm betraying Kelsey in saying this. She was my sweet fiancé; we were high school sweethearts and I loved her. But we were young and hadn't yet experienced life as adults. We both needed to grow up, a lot. Silver is a woman any man would be proud to have at his side, not just as a wife but as an incredible human being.

She blushes at my words and looks down at her feet before looking up again and smiling. I glance at Matthew waiting for us at the door, and his expression is a mask of worry and doubt. I stare him down to determine what is going on in his head, but his face relaxes, and a sad smile appears on his lips. I don't know which of his moods is more unsettling, but I don't have time to ask because he opens the door for us and we walk into a room full of veterans and journalists waiting for us.

All eyes are on Silver and me. There are a lot of uniforms in here but also a few journalists. I sense her hesitate for a heartbeat, take a deep breath, and then exhale slowly and relax next to me. She is ready and I feel more confident when we walk forward and start to shake hands.

Many of the people in uniform have been on a battlefield, and their bodies show signs of it. But some of them have no idea about what war is, and they're the ones who approach me first. They flash their perfect smiles, trying to convince me they're the ones I should be talking to.

Indeed, they're the ones who pull the strings of everyone in this room, so I need to engage as they boast of their accomplishments, nodding and smiling to appease them. What they don't know and underestimate is that I've asked Silver to do my job and greet those who need this encounter the most.

I keep an eye on her as she moves around the room, then pauses to talk with a small group of guys including one in a wheelchair, one with a prosthetic leg, and another with a brutal scar across his face. The four are engaged in a conversation, and they seem enchanted by her as she asks questions, listens, nods, or offers a sympathetic smile. She has them charmed not even twenty minutes into our visit, and I'm completely amazed by her ability to make other people feel at ease. You can see them relax after a few words, something Silver does even with me. She has a calming, grounding presence about her.

"What are your plans for the future? After becoming senator, are you aiming at something more?" The colonel in front of me is not one for subtle, political banter. You can tell he's used to handling situations that require a clear vision of your surroundings to survive and, in his case, keep your men from being slaughtered. The black glove disguising his two missing fingers and the scar on his neck tell me he's not someone who climbed the military ladder sitting behind a desk.

"Isn't everyone aiming for more?" I reply with a hint of amusement, and his lips curl up in a grin.

"You're ambitious." He seems to press further in order to determine for certain whether I'm aiming for Washington DC.

"I know what I want and I'm not afraid to get it. What about you? What are your plans for your future?" I ask while keeping an eye on Silver. She's surrounded by more people now, but she seems not to mind it one bit. On the contrary, she appears almost happy to be here.

The colonel chuckles and I divert my attention back to him. "I will enjoy my retirement with my wife. I already gave a lot to this country," he says, waving his gloved hand in front of me.

I doubt he'll retire soon, or he wouldn't be here, talking with a politician about his future. There is a reason he wants to know, the same one every powerful person in this room has: what I'll do for them if I get elected.

I decide not to play his game and take this chance to excuse myself. "Well, in order to enjoy my retirement with my wife in the future too, I should go and rescue her." I motion to where Silver is surrounded by a dozen veterans.

He chuckles. "Are you sure she wants to be rescued?" he teases.

"That's the point. They're handsome, in uniform, and they can fight. I don't stand a chance against them!" I wink at him, and he laughs heartily.

I reach Silver and she turns toward me with a smile when she feels my hand on the small of her back. "Here you are! We were just talking about you."

"Good things, I hope." I smile back at her.

"Capitan Grant was telling me how not every veteran has accessible Medicare," she explains.

I turn toward the guy she's referring to, the one in a wheelchair, in his mid-forties with a hard look on his face.

"That's a problem we're aware of," I say, looking him straight in the eye. "But I can't promise you it will magically disappear. It will take time."

I'm honest with him, even though it may not be in my best interest since someone else could sell it like a done deal. I'm not that kind of person. I don't want to insult his intelligence.

He doesn't miss a beat. "I'm aware of that, but there's a lot of talk that doesn't include the actual people who are affected by the problem."

"I think Silver has something in mind for that, yes?" I look at her with a smile. I can see the determination in her eyes and her brain working overtime for a solution.

What I like about Silver is that she sees these encounters as a chance to solve real problems, to dig into what people need and what would make their lives better. She's not jaded by politics, power games, or corruption. She still believes that things can change, and she's someone who can do it, with her determination, her passion, her kindness.

"Why don't we meet, and you can explain what the problem is? I think your experience is an invaluable resource of information for people who are working for a solution," she suggests and the guys around her seem to light up. Even Capitan Grant smiles. Not a grin like the others, but his lips are curved upward.

"We can do that," Grant agrees.

"Listen, compile a list of ten to fifteen people who are experiencing this problem," she adds. "I'll send Cindy to get your contact information and tell her to set up a meeting. Don't focus just on the physical injuries. I'm sure you have friends who need psychological support as well but couldn't get it. Mental health is important too."

I see the admiration forming on these men's faces. She gets it. She knows what it means to struggle every day to survive and she understands them. Her ordeal was different than theirs, but she's a survivor too, and she has the empathy to prove it.

"Is it true you were a prostitute?"

My blood freezes in my veins. We all turn toward the middle-aged journalist who joined our conversation. As soon as my eyes lands on his smirk, the ice inside me turns to simmering hot rage. I'm about to kick his ass when Silver smiles at him. Everybody around us seems to want to punch the guy in the face, but we're all waiting to see what she'll do.

"I don't know who gave you this information, but it's a complete lie. I've never had sex with anyone in exchange for money or presents. Write that down very carefully, because if I read some other version of this conversation, I have fourteen witnesses that will testify against you in court." She's calm and still smiling, but there is a firmness in her tone that makes me want to kiss her and kneel in front of her. She is a queen.

The journalist shrinks a little but doesn't back down. "So, you're telling me you never worked in an exclusive nightclub where baristas are also escorts?" The smug smile on his face makes me almost snap, but it's Capitan Grant who turns on him.

"Listen, dude, I don't know what your problem is, but she answered your question very clearly. She's not a prostitute, so stop digging into something that isn't there and get a life," he snaps, and I silently thank him. My rage is boiling so hot it's difficult to keep my temper under control.

Silver is tense next to me, and when I see one of the security guys come closer and gently grab the journalist's elbow, I relax a bit. I look around and see Matthew controlling the situation without making a fuss. People nearby notice the tense atmosphere but I don't think they followed our conversation.

The security guy bends to whisper something in the journalist's ear and the man walks out escorted without making a scene. I'm glad he's out of here, but I'm not happy about this situation. I keep a smile on my face, pretending to be unaffected by it all, but inside a storm is brewing. Someone better explain how the hell this happened. Everyone in this room should have been thoroughly checked, background and all. How did he get on the list?

"Capitan Grant, come with me. I want to make sure I have all your contact information before we sit down for lunch." Silver smiles at the man, managing to diffuse the tension and awkward silence that follows the outburst.

"Thank you," I whisper in her ear, kissing her temple.

She doesn't say anything, she just smiles at me and puts a hand on my chest, calming me down. I search for Matthew in the crowd, and when I lay eyes on him, he knows he has a lot to explain.

***

"How the fuck did that shit happen?" I shout.

Silver flinches and Matthew lowers his gaze to the floor. We're locked in my home office after the event and all the anger I suppressed in public is exploding like I've never experienced before.

"Why was that prick in there? I pay you to take care of these things and check every single person that steps foot within a mile radius from us. Why was he in there?" I shout again at my best friend.

He snaps his head up and I see anger, disappointment, and maybe shame in his eyes. I don't care. That man humiliated Silver in front of everyone, tried to smear my campaign, but what scared me most is that he wanted to hurt Silver and me. What if someone else, the one Silver's running from, got this close to her? In that moment I realized I'm not sure I can keep her safe. I promised her, but I'm not certain I can do it.

"He was screened like everyone else. He's never been a problem before," he says firmly, raising his voice a bit.

"Bullshit!" I get in his face. I know it's not fair, but I can't stop blaming him.

"Maybe the guy that harassed me at the bar tried to sell the story," Silver chimes in, and I turn to her.

She seems unsure as to whether she can speak or not, and I'm ashamed at my outburst. I say nothing because maybe she's right. I don't know. I can't know.

She continues a bit more confidently. "You humiliated him in front of everyone, he probably wants some kind of revenge because of that or because I didn't sleep with him. Hell, if something like that came out, he'd sink us both with the same story."

I turn to Matthew, furious. "How is this possible? You told me you took care of the story about her past and where she's worked all these years. Why is this coming out now?" Anger drips from my words.

Matthew straightens his spine and briefly glances at Silver, like he's annoyed at her theory. "I took care of it," he hisses, "personally. Without delegating to keep questions about her identity hidden like you asked."

"Cleary, you did a sloppy job." I know this is a low blow, but I can't stem my fury.

It's like I slapped him in the face. Surprise and anger make his jaw clench. He stares at me, challenging me, wanting to hit me square in the face. I can see it clear as day.

"Matthew, can you leave us alone for a moment, please?" Silver's voice is calm but firm.

He turns to her, staring her down and gritting his teeth like he wants to tell her to fuck off. I'm sure he's restraining himself because he knows if he says something to her, I'll punch him in the face.

"Leave," I order, and after a moment of hesitation he walks out of the room without looking at either of us.

Silver comes closer to the desk I'm leaning on. She puts her hands on my chest and looks at me straight in the eye. A sweet smile graces her lips and the fury simmering in my chest dies down a little bit.

"Matthew can't control everything, you know that, right?"

"He should. I pay him to prevent these things," I mumble, ashamed because she's right. You can't foresee everything.

"But he can't. It could be anyone. The guy that harassed me, Ice, or anyone who works or goes to that club. It's probably someone who knows I worked there. I met literally thousands of people during the eight years I worked there. We were prepared for this eventuality and did the damage control," she murmurs, coming closer.

She's standing so close I reach out and grab her waist to press her perfect body against mine. I like the way she feels in my arms, the way she relaxes and surrenders when she's close. It's like she's waiting to let her walls down and only does it when the heat of my body envelopes her. It's strange what we have, the intimacy forced on us that seems more natural than faked.

I lower my forehead on hers and close my eyes. I inhale her sweet scent deeply and let my hand travel to the back of her head, grabbing her hair and enjoying the shiver that run down her spine. She whimpers softly when my lips brush hers, and when she opens her mouth for me, I sink into her sweet taste and bask in the pleasure of this moment.

She grips her arms around my neck, sinking her fingers into my hair, pressing her body firmly against mine. I need more, I crave this closeness like my life depends on it. And maybe my life will crumble into pieces if I let her go. I don't know, but I don't want to find out yet. There will be a moment in the future when she'll have to walk away, but right now all I need is here and I don't want to think about the future.

I turn around, pulling her with me, then push her against the desk and help her hop up on it. The kiss becomes frantic, and when I slip between her legs, pressing my erection against her core, she lets out a soft moan. That's it. I'm done for. Every restraint I had, every excuse I fabricated to not sleep with her, goes up in flames. I slip my hand under her dress and enjoy the silkiness of her inner thigh. I reach the apex of her thighs and brush lightly against her soaked lace panties. She whimpers, pushing her hips against my hand, wanting more, craving that contact we've denied ourselves for months.

A loud knock and the door opening abruptly startles us both. "What the hell?"

I turn around and find my father's furious face. My blood freezes. I can sense Silver jumping down from my desk and discretely hiding behind me.

"Leave!" he booms, looking at Silver.

She hesitates for a moment, then she steps in front of me and looks at me a bit scared and a bit perplexed, silently asking me what to do. God, she's beautiful, with her hair a mess from my fingers and her lips swollen from my kiss. I nod slightly and she reluctantly turns around. She assesses my father for a long moment, straightening her spine and raising her chin. She is not intimidated by him and I admire her for that. Not everyone has the guts to stare down my father like that.

She stalks out of my office with confidence, and when she closes the door behind her the air is sucked out of the room. I pull my eyes back to my father.

"We need to talk."

"About what?" I ask with more confidence than I feel.

"About the fact that your wife is a whore!" he booms.

And just like that, my nightmare begins.

CHAPTER 16

Silver

I grab the handle of Raphael's door, not sure what to do. There is such a storm in my chest I can't even think logically. The way he touched me, lighting up every part of my body, is something I've never experienced with a man. It was like he was trying to brand my lips, my skin, my blood, my heart. Raphael is intense, he exudes power, but the way he demands access to my body is another level of passion.

Then his father's booming voice echoes through the door, saying I'm a whore, and here I am, stopping in my tracks to go back in there and tell him *No, I'm not*. But his icy words are like a cold shower that extinguish the fire in me. He's scary, and I need that fire to go face to face with him.

"No, she is not!" I hear Raphael shout and the spark reignites in me.

I should be in there defending myself. Not Raphael, not Matthew, not anyone but me. Anger starts to rise in my chest and it's enough to make me open this door again and barge in on their conversation.

Raphael's eyes widen when he sees me and when his father turns toward me, his fury so scorching it terrifies me. But I swallow and stare at him.

"Silver, please, let me handle this." Raphael's voice is slightly more than a whisper, his plea almost desperate, like he doesn't trust his father. It sends an icy shiver down my spine.

"No, I'm not going to leave it to you. This is my life, my mess, and I will take care of it," I tell him without taking my eyes off his father.

"Silver..." His voice fades when I don't leave this office.

"I'm not a whore. Never have been and never will be," I tell the man in front of me.

His features morph from fury to scorn and my anger steps up another level. "Oh, really? Then tell me why I had to take care of a story that was going to hit every website by tonight. It was very explicit, lots of detail about the lingerie you wear in that fucking club." He barks out the words and it takes all my strength not to flinch.

He's an imposing man, exuding power like his son. They have the same green eyes, same brown hair, but while Raphael makes you feel safe, this man gives the impression he could kill you in cold blood and then turn around and forget about your dead body on the bare concrete. There is authority in both men, but behind one there is a big heart, behind the other a cold one.

"*You* took care of it?" Raphael's voice makes me turn toward him. He seems unsettled by this news, and it's the first time I've seen him without his usual confidence.

"You didn't do your job so I had to do something." He's not apologizing for overstepping, he's scolding him, and I don't understand how this is even possible. I thought no human was able to overpower the man I've lived with these last months.

"What do you mean?" I ask and both turn to me.

"You don't want to know," Raphael says so firmly a chill runs down my spine. There is such determination in his eyes and voice that I don't dare ask for an explanation. Who the hell is this man?

"When you told me you did your job choosing her, I didn't dig into her past, but clearly you fucked up." He says this like I'm not even in the room, annoying me greatly.

"I did, and I know what I got myself into and she knows what she signed up for," Raphael answers.

"So, why the hell did you pick her knowing where she worked?" his father shouts, anger simmering in his eyes.

"Because I fucked up and the paparazzi were all over her!" he shouts back.

"So what? Since when do you care about paparazzi?"

"Since she's in the witness protection program, and I blew her cover!" The anger radiating from Raphael is so intense it almost knocks me to my knees.

His father turns his wide eyes toward me in surprise, realization and anger spreading on his face.

The silence that follows is almost deafening. Nobody even moves when the realization of what Raphael just confessed hits all of us.

"Fuck!" his father shouts. "Fuck! Fuck! Fuck!" He kicks the couch in front of him with such force it moves back an inch. He turns to me. "That's why there's nothing online about your childhood."

I nod. "I didn't exist before eight years ago." My voice is a lot less firm than before.

"Is someone looking for her?" he asks Raphael.

I know what he means: is The Hangman after me. The thought that *he* knows where I live now is something that has tortured me in the last two months.

"Not that we know. My security picked up nothing about this, but it's safer if she stays with me, considering everyone now knows her face and new name." His explanation is firm, but I can see his hands in his pockets clenching in a fist.

"So, you'll just willingly marry him and have kids? You agreed to that?" he asks me suspiciously.

I know he thinks I'm doing it for money, and in part it's true, but that doesn't mean I'm a bad person.

"Until he become senator, then he helps me disappear." I nod and I know it's the wrong answer when I see him turn around toward his son and Raphael pales a bit.

What the hell is going on? I want him out of this house. The urge is so intense I clench my hands into fists to keep from pushing him out of here.

"Are you fucking kidding me? You want to step foot in the White House with a divorce on your shoulders and no kids? Are you insane?" He steps toward Raphael and by instinct, I grab his arm.

Raphael's eyes snap to me as his father turns, angry and surprised. "You are ruining his life, you know that?" he shouts at me, and Raphael jumps in front of me, pushing his father away with both hands.

The gesture comforts me—I've always wanted someone who takes care of me—but the murderous gaze on his father's face makes my stomach churn.

"Enough!" Raphael shouts and everyone stands still.

There's so much tension in the room it's almost impossible to breath. His father seems to want to argue, but just one furious glance from his son shuts him up. It's so surprising that I'm almost stunned. Since entering the room, he's been the more powerful force, but after shouting in my face the balance has shifted. Raphael is willing to go against his own father if he thinks he's a threat to me, and the feeling is so foreign to me that my knees almost give out. Nobody has ever stood up for me like this, and the warmth that invades my chest makes my heart speed up and slow down, then pick up speed again. Not even my heart knows how to react.

"We are dealing with *this* election right now. She's doing great and they adore her. So, shut the fuck up and get out of my house. I appreciate your help, but you are not allowed to say one more word about how I handle my campaign," Raphael says, and I'm shocked by the anger that simmers in his father's eyes.

If I thought he was menacing before, I was a fool. This is not your average argument between father and son. He is a dangerous man, a deadly person who won't stop at anything to get what he wants, not even his son. I recognize that look, I saw it in a courtroom, it's the one I'm running from. For the first time since I stepped foot inside this office, I fear for Raphael.

The man stands there for several excruciating moments then storms out without a word. We stand still until we hear the front door slam shut. Only then does Raphael dare to let out a slow sigh and sit down on the couch with his elbows on his knees, hands in his hair. I sit next to him and put an arm over his shoulder. He immediately tenses, but then he crumbles under the weight of this conversation and snuggles his head in the crook of my shoulder.

I hold him tight, not sure what to do. I've never seen him so defeated and vulnerable. Gone is the confident man who charmed me, who swore to protect me, who persuaded me into a marriage I never saw coming. He seems almost defenseless, like a child dumped alone in the middle of the street.

I hold him tight. "Please let me help. We can get through this together, I promise," I whisper, lightly kissing his hair. He wraps his arms around my waist in a strong grip but says nothing. He trembles in my arms, and I can't tell if he's angry, or just exhausted after a long, challenging day.

I don't know how to help him. I have no idea how to drag myself out of this mess, let alone the two of us, but the feeling that creeps into my chest is strange and unexpected. Would it be so crazy if the idea of sticking around a bit longer helping his career crosses my mind? It's so foreign I've never given it a second thought. But his father's words keep pestering my mind with questions and the one that stands out the most is: *What happens to Raphael when I disappear from his life?* I always thought he'd be fine; he'd thrive like he always does. But I'm not so sure anymore, and this realization hurts more than I expected.

I watch Silver sitting in a deck chair going through some notes Cindy dropped off yesterday for an upcoming public appearance. We've decided to base our campaign on people. We're trying to stay in contact with voters and she's a key element in this strategy.

When I was looking for a wife, I thought I'd find someone who would accompany me to galas or parties. Someone who had her own life and wanted only the glamorous parts of being a politician's wife. With Silver, it's the total opposite. She took this job to heart, and she wants to help me. I ripped her away from the life she knew, and she's looking for a new purpose in life.

And she likes it. She likes being involved in helping people on a level she would have never reached as a barista. She was studying law before having her life torn in pieces, and I can see why she wanted a career that helped people—she's a natural at it.

I can see a future alongside someone like her. Someone who shares the same goals in life, the same desire to help people. I can be the cynical one, used to dealing with politics, knowing how to compromise between idealism and reality, but she can be the heart, the passion, the purpose of this career. We could be a damn good team if she decides to stay longer.

It's been seven days since our discussion with my father. Seven days since she came into that office like a tiger and fought him. I've never seen anyone go after him like that. Even if she was scared, she didn't back down and I admire her for that. I'm not nearly brave enough to stand up to him like that.

But my father is right. Divorcing after I get elected is potential suicide for my career. And I don't know how to tell her that. After what Matthew insinuated, her falling for me, I don't have the heart to ask her to stick with me longer. The point is, I don't have a choice.

I walk out onto the patio and bask in the mid-May warmth I enjoy most about living here. Summer is way too hot, but I love spring.

"Do you have any questions about that?" I ask, sitting on the deck chair next to her.

She lingers a few seconds on the page, then looks up at me. Yes. She has questions. Her knitted eyebrows and pouty lips tell me she's a bit disappointed about what she's reading and I have to fight to keep a smile from forming on my face. I really need to pay Matthew more since she came into our lives and started giving him hell.

"A lot, but I'd rather address them when Matthew's here. I don't want to have to repeat them," she affirms, and I don't say a word.

When she's like this, she means business and I know not to challenge her.

"Listen, I've thought a lot about what my father said." I focus on her face to gauge her reaction.

We didn't talk about what happened in that office, and I don't know if that's good or bad. It was a very intense moment, and I showed some vulnerability I haven't revealed to anyone except Harrison and Matthew, my best friends.

Her face is unreadable, so I go for it. "I think my father is right. In the midst of all the hurtful words that came out of his mouth that day, he got one thing right. We should stay together longer."

She's quiet for a while, her face clouded by a sadness so deep it hurts to see it. Then a small smile slightly curves her lips, though a trace of sadness still remains. Tupac Shakur once said, "Behind every sweet smile, there's a bitter sadness that no one can see and feel." But what if I can see that sadness, what if I can feel it because I have it too? What if I can't erase it from her heart?

"I can't. I thought a lot about what he said too. I've tried to imagine my life in the White House, and I can't," she whispers. Her voice trembles with emotion and the knot forming in my throat is difficult to swallow.

"Why not? You've come so far, why not a little more? I can pay you for every year you decide to stay with me." I can hear the desperation in my voice.

She shakes her head and a tear runs down her cheek. "Because this isn't real, Raphael. It's an illusion I'm living, and at some point, the bubble will burst. I have no past, and I have to hide the fact that I worked in a nightclub for years—wearing only my lingerie. You can divert public attention from that now because you're just one of many senators, but what happens when you become the president of the United States? How do you think you can hide something like that?"

"We can figure something out. I have a team that handles exactly these kinds of things." I try to convince her, but I know it's a losing battle.

"And then what? Will you ask me to pop out a couple of kids too? Because at some point they'll ask you for that. And if I do it? My past will always be looming over us. It won't just disappear. You're giving me the illusion of a normal life here, Raphael, and it's not fair. It's not fair because I can't have a lovely husband and laughing kids. I came to terms with that a long time ago, and it's not fair to ask me to believe in something else. All you're doing is instilling hope in my heart, and at some point, it will break, and I can't deal with that. Not again."

She takes a shaky breath, and continues. "I already lost an entire family. I have a father, a mother, and a sister out there somewhere, and I don't even know if they're okay, if they're still alive or not. You can't ask me to surround myself with another family and then risk giving it up again. I will die, Raphael. This time you will kill me." Her voice finally breaks with emotion, and the tears streaming down her cheeks are so raw my heart breaks for her.

How could I ask that of her? How could I destroy someone as amazing as Silver and live with myself?

I reach out and pull her toward my chest, squeezing her tightly. I have no words to make her feel better. Maybe I can protect her from threats, but I can't give her happiness. I can't give her the life she deserves, the stability she craves. And my heart breaks again for her.

***

"Why did you choose all rich schools?" Silver asks Matthew.

We're in my office and the air is tense after the discussion we had seven days ago, and the moment Silver and I shared this morning when she broke down in tears. I would smile at her question, but I don't have the strength or the heart. I'm wiped out and it shows.

"Because we're focused on reaching communities that can change the outcome of the vote." Matthew's voice is strained.

I can't tell if he's just tired or if he thinks Silver isn't a good choice anymore. We've been discussing all week what happened, and he seems to almost regret pushing me to marry her. What everybody seems to forget is that I fucked up her life. I have no other choice but to make it right.

"So, rich people vote for a billionaire? That's your strategy?" she challenges him.

Matthew takes a deep breath and closes his eyes for a moment. I know he's struggling here, but I can't find the strength to help him out.

"They're all public schools. It's not like we picked private schools where parents pay thousands of dollars to send their kids." He's doing his best to convince her, but I can see the stubbornness in her eyes. I should have warned Matthew that I pissed her off this morning.

"They're all in rich neighborhoods," she points out.

"Where there are higher rates of registered voters," Matthew shoots back.

Silver grips the papers in her hands so tightly they crumple. She's gone from annoyed, to stubbornly defending her position, to angry. And this time, a small smile crosses my lips.

"So, you're avoiding poor neighborhoods because there're mostly illegal immigrants? They're the people who need him the most!" she spits angrily.

"They can't vote, so we'd be wasting our resources!" he shouts back.

"They can't vote but they have friends who can. And you know what? They can't vote now, but they may in the future. He wants to run for president, in what? Four years? Eight? The kids that you're ignoring now they may be the ones voting for him then. Are you even thinking that far ahead or am I the only one doing that?" she shouts back.

Matthew turns toward me with wide eyes and a desperate expression.

"She has a point," I say and he scoffs indignantly.

"Are you fucking serious right now?" he asks in disbelief.

"Just see if you can add in some of the schools on her list," I tell him. "We may not visit every one of them. In some neighborhoods there's real concern about safety," I add, nodding toward her.

She nods but Matthew is not having it. "Is she calling the shots now? Do you want me to resign as your campaign manager?"

I look at him in surprise. I've never seen him act like some kind of jealous boyfriend threatening to leave me if I listen to someone else's suggestions. I make a mental note to dig deeper in this new development in our professional relationship. It could be nothing, but it could also be something that turns ugly if we don't vent our frustrations now.

Silver responds angrily, "I'm not calling the shots, but you added this leg of the campaign because you saw an opportunity to exploit my presence to bump up his ratings. I'm putting my face out there and I have an opinion. I'm not your puppet. You can't tell me what to do and expect me not to speak up when I disagree!" She slams the list of schools on my desk then turns around and storms out of the office.

There is a long silence where I study Matthew and try to figure him out. I can't tell how deep his frustration runs, or if it's something bordering on resentment. It's always been the two of us dreaming up how to change the world, no one else understood what we wanted to do. Even Harrison started to call us crazy at some point. And now that Silver has entered the equation, wanting to help, he seems to have a hard time accepting it.

"Are you regretting letting Silver onboard?" I flat out ask him.

He doesn't say a word, just lowers his gaze to the floor. That's all the answer I need.

"She's helping me, Matthew. She put herself in this for me. I'm sorry if you expected someone more malleable who wants to please you, but that's not who she is."

"Why is she doing it?" he finally asks. "She could just take the money at the end of your agreement and disappear. I don't get why she's putting all this effort into something that will end."

"She has nothing to lose. She wanted to change the world in her own way by studying law, but her world imploded eight years ago. She has a second chance, why not take it?"

He looks at me for a long time. "Are you in love with her?"

I expected this question at some point. I smile and shake my head. "No. You know I'll never love anyone like I loved Kelsey, but she's an amazing person and I'll do anything to put a smile on her face, even if this relationship isn't real."

He sits on the couch and rubs a hand over his face. I see the tense shoulders, the dark circles under his eyes, the muscles in his jaw clenching as he grinds his teeth. What we're trying to do is massive. I don't come from a family with a political history, my father has a not-so-crystal-clear reputation, and I'm running without the support of a party. I'm a lost cause on paper, but we're not just surviving, we think we can win this election. It's fucking exhausting.

"Do you think you can stay with her for the long run? For the White House?" There's hope in his voice.

"She's the only person I would consider living with for that many years. She's smart, caring, she has a big fucking heart," I admit without hesitation.

"Sounds a lot like a real marriage to me. A loving one too." He frowns.

I look down at my desk, not sure I can look at him in the eye. "But it's true, right?"

"Do you think she'd agree to do it?" There is a timid, hopeful smile on his lips, and I hate to be the one to wipe it from his face.

"No. She won't be here for the long run," I murmur, and feel an uncomfortable grip squeezing my heart.

CHAPTER 18
Silver

I look out the tinted window of the luxurious car and feel pain spreading through my chest. The houses are a bit run-down and the front yards are so far from the manicured lawns of the richer part of the city this could be another planet entirely.

A woman with a toddler in her arms looks out the window at our car driving past her house. I raise my hand to wave but then I remember we have tinted windows and she can't see me. I wish I could smile at her, stop and ask how her day is going, ask what we can do to help her fix the broken steps leading up to her house. But I can't. We're stuck in this car, with security and blacked-out windows, so far removed from the real world that it feels like I can't reach it.

"This is why we didn't choose these schools. The neighbor-hoods are not as good as the ones you're used to." Matthew chooses this moment to speak to me for the first time since leaving home this morning.

I turn toward him. Raphael insisted I take him with me today. He said it's because Matthew can help answer questions about my past that I can't navigate, but we both know he wants to be sure I'm safe, and he trusts his best friend with his life and mine.

His attentiveness makes me smile. I like when someone is invested enough in my life that they pay attention to those kinds of things. On the other hand, I don't know what Matthew has against me, but I don't feel comfortable in his presence. He pushed Raphael to marry me, and now he seems to regret his decision. There's no open hostility between us, but we're not best friends either. I get that he wants to protect Raphael, but I'm not the enemy here.

"I'm not worried about the neighborhood." My answer is a bit more clipped than I intended.

"Your face suggests otherwise." He raises an eyebrow, challenging me to contradict him.

"I'm annoyed by the fact that people can't see inside the car. I wanted to wave at that woman, but I can't. We're so out of touch in here, we could be aliens for all they know." I don't make an effort to hide my annoyance.

He stays silent for a while then adds sternly, "So you're saying you removed your engagement ring *not* because you're worried they might steal it?"

I frown and study him. I can't tell if he really thinks I'm someone who would do that, or even be worried about something like that. It's so far from my reality and my actual concerns that I don't think he's made one ounce of effort to get to know me.

"I removed it because it would be insulting to have a gazillion-dollar ring on my finger when these people don't even have money to buy school supplies for their kids. Yes, I'm worried about these visits, but not because of the neighborhoods. You shove the cameras in my face and put my image out there without caring that you're putting my life in danger. I agreed to help Raphael and I knew what I was signing up for, but don't insult my intelligence by assuming things about me that are not there," I spit back at him.

He seems taken aback; he opens his mouth to say something but hesitates. When we pull up in front of the school and Sven opens the door for me, I'm glad our conversation is over.

I step out of the car, and cameras start to photograph me, kids cheer, and I'm pulled into a new reality, almost forgetting the discussion I just had with Matthew. It's in the corner of my mind, but I'm so overwhelmed by the welcome I receive that it's not nagging at me.

The principal, a woman in her fifties with black wavy hair and a smile that could brighten up a stormy night, comes to greet me. "Welcome to our school! We're glad you chose this neighborhood to visit. The kids are so excited." She shakes my hand.

I smile at her and can't contain a bit of nervousness creeping into my stomach. These kids are welcoming me with colorful signs, smiles on their faces, and hope in their eyes. I feel like I'm betraying them; I won't be here to keep my promises a year from now. I hope Raphael will do it for me, will do something for them. I know he has the heart, but I won't be here to help him.

I focus my attention on the kids, to a girl around six or seven years old, with two brown braids cascading over her shoulder and a gap where her two front teeth are missing. She's wearing a bright pink dress with a pair of beaten-up white sneakers. She's so happy her eyes are shining. My chest caves in a little bit more. What promise can I make to this girl if I can't be here to keep them?

I return my focus on the woman in front of me. "I'm happy to be here with you today. I hope I'm not disrupting your routine too much."

She waves a hand and smiles, dismissing my concerns. "Trust me, they're thrilled to not be in class today. And to be honest, the teachers are excited to have you here too. It's not every day that someone acknowledges our school." She winks at me.

"I'm here to make sure that you're not forgotten in the future," I tell her and her smile broadens. I hope this is not a big fat lie.

"Please, come meet the kids." She puts a hand on the small of my back and guides me to the giggling bunch of elementary school students.

We spend the morning walking from class to class, assisting with some of the lessons. The teacher explains the challenges they are facing, from kids not coming to school because their parents work three jobs and can't get them here during school hours to the lack of money for basic things like paint for art class or pencils and paper for math.

The more I walk through these halls, the more I feel like an impostor. I'm here, faking my fantastic life in Malibu, promising these people I can change things, and I don't even know where I'll be next year. The thought of sucking it up and sticking around Raphael for the long run crosses my mind a lot this morning. I'll never have a normal life anyway, so why not stay here? Every time I think about it, I'm overwhelmed by emotions I have difficulty controlling.

I look at Matthew, who's observing me with an unreadable face, quietly present to solve any problems that may arise while I'm here, but he's Raphael's campaign manager. He solves my problems because they are also *Raphael's* problems. If something that concerns me doesn't affect Raphael, I don't know if Matthew would step in. I feel alone in this life, and I don't know if I can think about having a family if it's just me against everyone. Raphael doesn't even have real relationships. He has sex with prostitutes. I saw him walking out of the club with one of them with my own eyes. I'm his fake fiancé and he doesn't even touch me if it's not for a show, for Pete's sake! How can I think of starting a family like this?

"Are you enjoying your visit?" Andrea, the principal, asks me.

"I love the energy in this school. The kids seem happy to be here."

"They are. For some of them, this is their only chance to live a normal life. Most of these families are living in poverty with four or five children, and sometimes sending them to school is the only way to give them a decent meal every day," she explains as we walk toward another class.

I peek through a small window at four rows of kids who are enraptured by something their teacher is explaining. They're looking at him like he can change the world and, somehow, he's doing exactly that. One kid at time.

"Do you offer free meals at this school?"

She shakes her head. "No. But families decided to share the costs among everyone, so those who can pay a bit more make it possible to offer a hot meal to everyone in the school. No one is excluded," she explains with a pride in her eyes I didn't notice before.

I turn toward those kids and wonder which are the ones starving at home. They're all the same, smiling and raising their hands to give an answer. But some won't have a decent meal when they go home. Is it the girl with blond hair and pigtails or the boy with jet-black hair and a hoodie two sizes too big?

"What are you thinking about?" she asks politely.

I glance at Matthew, talking with the assistant principal and a couple of janitors, probably asking them to do something to accommodate me. I feel guilty for disrupting their day, just by being here and parading around the school like I'm someone important.

"There is no way to say it without coming off like a total bitch." I smile at her, and she chuckles. If Matthew knew I was cursing in front of the principal, he'd scold me like a child.

"You can speak freely. Nobody will judge you here." She invites me to continue and I'm a bit hesitant.

This could be her way of framing me into saying something compromising to sell to the press, but she seems genuinely interested in what I have to say.

"Why have kids if you know you can't feed them? I'd never have the guts to do that," I finally say and she studies me for a long moment.

She nods and then looks through the glass window. "I understand what you're saying. How many people can you count on?" She glances at me.

I don't answer. There aren't many I trust. Once I would have said my family, but now? Raphael maybe, but I'm not sure about Lola. Not with a kid, at least.

"The extraordinary thing that happens when you live in a community where people don't have much is that everyone helps his neighbor. Maybe there's not enough money for daycare or for new clothes, but there's usually someone willing to watch your child during the day if you keep an eye on theirs during the evening. There's always an older kid who grows out of clothes you can pass down to your neighbor. What I mean is, sometimes when you're poor, life doesn't seem so scary because you have people around you that can help you."

I nod in understanding. How many times did a neighbor kid have dinner with us because her mother worked long hours and my mom worked in the morning? The school bus dropped her in front of our door and my mom let her stay until her mom came to pick her up. I'm so used to being alone, to counting only on myself, that I forgot what it means to have a normal life, relationships, friendships. I've spent so much time lying to people that I don't even trust myself, let alone trust someone else.

The rest of the day is a blur, eating with the kids in the cafeteria, reading stories during one of the classes, taking pictures and doing interviews for the press. All the time, feeling my chest splitting in two, divided between what my heart wants—what those kids have, the happiness in their eyes—and what my brain is reasoning against.

When it's time to walk out of the school with the kids, I'm exhausted and watching them run toward their parents makes me smile. They wave goodbye to me like I'm one of them, and their parents give me curious glances. They knew I was coming today, and they're probably just wondering how it went. But the crowd is lingering, taking pictures, and the wall of faces, smiles, and voices is a little overwhelming.

I start to panic slightly, scanning the crowd for someone I wouldn't even recognize. How could I spot someone who wants to hurt me? I know the face of the person I sent to prison for the rest of his life, but I don't know the people working for him. What if they decided this is the best time to kill me? In the middle of a crowd of kids, nobody is looking for a man with a gun.

I glimpse a guy on the other side of the street, a bit isolated from the others. He's wearing a baseball cap, but I can see his eyes staring at me with an unreadable expression. A shiver runs down my spine. The feeling of cold ice expanding in my stomach is so sudden and unexpected that it takes my breath away. I'm so terrified I can't take my eyes away from him. I want to call Sven and Matthew, but I'm petrified.

Just then, one of the kids crosses the street and the guy grabs his hand, smiles and says something, and walks away with one last glance toward me. The relief is so overwhelming I'm not sure I can keep standing. I let out a shaky breath and look around to find Matthew watching me from not too far away.

"Are you okay?" he asks as he comes closer.

"Yeah, sure." I fake a smile and let him guide me to where the car is waiting for us.

Realization hits me hard in the chest. I was scared out of my mind for a few seconds out there. I put myself in the public eye, leaving the comfort of my anonymity, and I thought that guy came to kill me. And the worst part was that no one was there to reassure me that I would be fine, that nobody would have hurt me. Not that I expected someone to save me, I've always made it just fine on my own, but I realized that nobody has my back. When Raphael is not here, I'm totally alone. Everyone is here for him, not for me.

I sit down next to Matthew, and after closing the door, I relax a bit.

"Are you still reluctant to have kids one day?" he asks after a while.

I don't know if Raphael told him something or if he just has a feeling about what I think about my future, but it irks me that he's implying I'm some sort of monster that doesn't want to become a mother.

"My reluctance to have a family has nothing to do with not wanting kids," I spit a bit too harshly.

His lips curve in a contemptuous smile. "Why? Isn't Raphael paying you enough? What would it take for you to help him out? More money? Name your price."

The anger rising in my stomach is almost painful. "I don't know what your problem is with me and I don't care. Do you think everything is about money? Because I've got news for you, honey. Not everyone is greedily going after your best friend."

"So, what do you want? For him to love you back?" He mocks me with an irritating smile.

I overlook the fact that he thinks I have feelings for his friend. I don't even want to go *there* with my thoughts. "I know he'll never fall for anyone. Do you think I don't know about Kelsey?" He seems surprised, probably not expecting Raphael to tell me. "Yes, he told me, and I'm not dumb enough to think that he'll forget her and fall madly in love with me. And honestly, I don't care. I would settle for a loveless marriage if that was a possibility."

He grinds his teeth, clearly uncomfortable with where this conversation is going. "So, what do you want?" he barks.

"Do you have my back, Matthew?" I ask with a smile, studying his every expression.

He frowns, genuinely thinking about my question. "I'm in a car with you instead of at the office running a campaign—what do you think?" he asks angrily.

"I didn't ask if you were here because Raphael asked you to be. I asked if you have *my* back. Do you realize I panicked in front of that school because I thought someone was following me? Are you prepared to keep me safe? If I agree to give my life to Raphael and stay until he steps foot in the White House, are you willing to protect me? Because I'll have a massive target on my back, not only from the people I sent to prison, but from everyone who digs up my past and wants an explanation. Are you willing to protect me from that? My kids, because at some point they'll demand kids, will become a reason to blackmail me. And are you ready to protect them? Do you have *my* back Matthew?"

He clenches his jaw and looks down before shifting his gaze out the window.

"Because if I have to be honest with you, Matthew, I feel completely alone. The only one who gives a shit about me is Raphael. Everyone else sees me as a pawn in their own game."

CHAPTER 19
Raphael

As soon as Silver comes home from her first visit to a school, I know something is wrong. She smiles at me, but she looks like she's holding back tears.

"What happened?" I ask, my heart hammering in my chest.

Matthew would have called if something alarming had happened during the visit, but he wouldn't bother if she's just upset for something not life-threatening.

"It was a good day. I loved being around those kids," she answers meekly.

I study her. She's not lying but she's not telling me everything either. "It doesn't seem like it. What's bothering you?" I insist and hope she opens up with me.

There's something haunting in her eyes that wasn't there this morning and it breaks my heart.

"It's just… Nothing, it doesn't matter," she mumbles, looking defeated.

I stand up, come around the desk, and grab her hand to pull her to me. I hug her tightly, hoping to convey all the warm she needs to chase away the clouds in her eyes.

"It matters to me," I whisper and she pushes back a bit to look me in the eye.

She strips me naked of my walls, baring my soul. For the first time in my life, I'm not scared to show to a woman how vulnerable I feel. Maybe it's the intimacy of my office, or maybe I've just become comfortable with her during these three months together, but I don't feel the need to hide from her.

"Today I went there looking for problems to solve, but I found nothing. Or at least, nothing that more funds can't solve. They're happy, they help each other out, and they don't need us to do anything but open our wallet and give them the money they deserve," she explains, but I'm more confused than before.

She senses my puzzlement and continues. "It's the kind of community where every kid is taken care of. Maybe they're not rich, but they have each other's backs. I don't have that. I can't afford to think about having a family because I am utterly alone. Nobody has my back. Nobody will take care of my kids if something happens to me. And the chances of something ugly happening to me are pretty high."

I hear the tremble in her voice and read the pain in her eyes. She feels hopeless, and I don't know how to fix it. It breaks my heart seeing her like this because part of this unhappiness is my fault. I dragged her into this mess, showing off what she could have and asking for more, without giving her the certainty of a future. Of course, I can give her money, a comfortable life, but she never wanted those things. She needs them, but she never sought them out greedily. What she desperately craves is a family to belong to, and all I have to give her is a fake one.

"I have your back. You can count on me. Maybe I don't love you in a romantic way, but I care about you. You're smart, funny, beautiful, and you have a big heart. If I have to imagine spending a life with someone, the only person I could think is you. I can take care of you. I can take care of your kids if something happens to you and you can't take care of them. I can be that man for you," I end almost in a whisper.

Tears well up in her eyes and a mixture of hope and fear cross her face. "I knew you would say that, and I really appreciate it. But you're the only one. Nobody else will stick around for me. Nobody in their right mind should *want* to stay by my side. The people around me now, they want to protect *you*, not me. They are loyal to *you*, not me. I'll always be the outsider." Her voice cracks with emotion.

The desperation in her eyes tells me she thinks she can't be loved. She's trying to push everyone away in an effort to save them. Like she did with her family.

"You're always the one trying to protect everybody, but you don't let anyone protect you. You don't let anyone in because you're scared you'll lose them. I get that. Trust me, I understand that feeling. I'm asking you to let me help you get what you want," I whisper, cradling her face between my hands. I dry a tear escaping the corner of her eyes.

"I had a family, and I don't even know if they're alive or not. I don't know if I can handle losing another one. I won't survive it," she whispers back.

"They're alive and well," I tell her, gauging her reaction to the news.

She frowns. "What?"

"I got a phone call yesterday; I was waiting for more info before telling you. I called in some favors, and I asked about your family. They couldn't tell me anything about their location or their new names, for security reasons, but I know they're alive, and they're doing fine. Your mom, dad, and sister are living their lives because you chose to sacrifice your happiness for theirs. You kept them safe, Silver. Now it's your turn to be happy," I say, and I see all her walls crumbling.

"They're alive? You checked on them? You did that for me?" she whispers, her eyes glowing with gratitude.

She puts her hands around my neck and kisses me with the fierceness of someone who wants to show how grateful they are. "Thank you. I don't know how you did it, but this is the best gift anyone ever gave me," she whispers against my lips.

"I can't tell you what will happen in ten or twenty years, but I can promise to make you happy now." I peck her lips.

She tightens her grip around my neck and molds her body with mine. I wrap my arms around her waist and press myself against her. She is so perfect in my arms I can't stop my erection from growing in my pants. I've always found her gorgeous, but the more I know her, the more difficult it is to hide my attraction to her. The physical reaction has been there since day one, and I don't know how not to make her feel like I'm sexually pressuring her for more.

I should probably stop kissing her. But she's kissing me back and biting my lower lip like she wants a piece of me. A groan escapes my lips, and she seems invigorated by it. She slips her fingers in my hair and fists them fiercely. A sting of pain and pleasure runs down my spine as I moan.

"Silver," I whisper not sure what to ask. To continue this torture? To stop because she's driving me crazy and I can't fuck her?

She puts me out of my misery by deciding for the both of us. She pulls away from my chest and lowers down to her knees in front of me with determination in her eyes. A mixture of shock and anticipation runs through me, and I have to lean against my desk because I'm not sure my legs will hold me.

"Silver, you don't have to…" My voice trails off when she starts to unbuckle my belt.

She looks me straight in the eye and smiles. "I know. I *want* to."

Her long fingers unzip my trousers, and I can't keep my eyes off her as she lowers them with my boxers. My erection springs free and the surprised gasp from her lips makes me almost smile. She looks up at me and a grin curves her lips. I have to admit, my ego swells at her pleased reaction.

When she grabs my shaft with a firm hand, I close my eyes for a brief moment, enjoying the pressure around my sensitive skin. I force myself to open them again when I feel the tip of her tongue licking from the base to the tip. Her eyes never leave mine as she sucks the leaking precum and then wraps her lips around my engorged head.

She seals her perfect mouth around the shaft and slides down, taking a good part of it down her throat. Her eyes water a bit, and the view is so mesmerizing I have to grip the desk I'm leaning on to keep from kneeling on the floor. I groan her name and she takes me in deeper.

She sucks me, bobbing her head up and down, and I realize there's nothing I wouldn't do for her. She's on her knees but I'm the one who would bend to her will. Maybe I can't give her the love she deserves, but I can give her the family she wants, and anything else that will make her happy.

CHAPTER 20
Silver

I watch Raphael taking off his jacket and put it on one of the armchairs in the bedroom. We didn't last long in his office. Once we opened the pent-up dam of physical attraction between us, we can't stop. We need more and we need the privacy of our bedroom to get what we want.

He unbuttons the cuffs of his white crisp shirt. He never takes his gaze from mine as he unties his tie and puts it over the jacket. It's a slow deliberate gesture that makes me want to crawl to him and take his cock in my mouth like I did not even half an hour ago. The salty taste of his manhood still lingers on my tongue. I've never been a fan of oral sex, but there's a satisfying feeling filling my chest at having such a powerful man at my mercy.

He slowly unbuttons his shirt and drops it on the floor. He strolls barefoot over to the bed where I am seated and stares at me. The bedroom is dimly lit, but I can see the defined muscles of his chest and abs. He is gorgeous in the most drool-worthy way. Everything about him is breathtaking, from his beautiful face and tanned skin to his sculpted body. Everything makes me want to nip, lick, and suck until he comes again. He's still in his trousers and boxer briefs, unfastened and lowered on his hips. He is drop-dead sexy.

"Are you not undressing?" he asks me with a smirk.

"I was enjoying the view." I coyly smile back.

He rests his hand on my jaw and grazes my lower lip with his thumb. I dart out my tongue, lick it and suck it in my mouth. I love seeing his eyes widen and his jaw clench. I whimper a bit when he moves his fingers from my face to lower them around my neck. He squeezes, just a bit, making my heart flutter in my chest. He feels it. He feels the blood pumping in my veins faster than before. He stares at the spot on my neck where my heartbeat is stronger, then he raises his eyes on mine and smiles mischievously.

He kneels in front of me and start to undress me slowly, from my shirt to my panties, taking his time to remove my clothes and enjoy the view. He reaches out one hand and presses a finger between my folds. I'm so wet he slips inside me without resistance, and I moan when he bends his knuckle just a bit to tease me.

"You really are enjoying the show," he whispers, pressing his mouth against my bare breast and sucking on a nipple.

"Yes," my answer comes out like a whine.

He sucks again and I moan. He bites and I groan. He fucks me lazily with his fingers, slowly building my orgasm but never bringing me to the peak. I move my hips, seeking the contact I'm craving to get this pleasure going but he draws back his hand.

I open my eyes and frown at him. He chuckles, standing up and lowering his trousers and boxers, discarding them on the floor. He grabs my wrist and drags me toward him. I stand up and follow him to the other side of the room: I don't know what he wants to do, but when he puts one of the armchairs in front of the full-length mirror, I get an idea.

"I want a show too," he whispers in my ear before sitting down on the chair he just moved, facing the mirror. I look at his reflection, his erection resting on his stomach, his legs sprawled and his gaze on my naked body. It's the most erotic thing I have ever seen and I don't want to miss a second of it.

I sit on his lap, my back resting against his chest, my legs outside his. His chin rests on my shoulder and when I look in the mirror, I'm on full display. My wet, glistening pussy begs his attention.

"You are gorgeous," he whispers in my ear, looking me in the eye through the mirror. "You're so perfect I can't keep my hands off you." He slips his fingers between my folds, playing with my clit.

My breath catches in my throat, and a moan escapes my lips when he starts stroking slowly between my legs and pinching my nipple with the other. I push my hips against his hand, seeking pleasure, and rubbing my butt against his thick shaft. He pushes a couple of fingers inside me and picks up speed while looking at me.

"I want you inside me," I moan, and his eyes heat up with lust.

He pushes me away enough to raise my ass and position his hard cock against my entrance. We both look entranced while his thick erection sinks slowly but steadily into my wet pussy. I groan at the fullness of my inner core, at the pleasure of his cock hitting the right spot inside me.

I push on his thighs to raise up a bit and then lower myself on his shaft in a steady rhythm. The image of my breasts bouncing, his hand rubbing my clit, and the other one tightening around my neck, makes my orgasm build at lightspeed. When I'm on the verge of exploding, Raphael applies more pressure on the sides of my neck, reducing the oxygen flowing to my brain. His eyes never leave my face, looking for any sign that I don't like him playing this dangerous game. But I don't stop him. I trusted him with my life when I agreed to be at his side, I know he won't hurt me.

I completely abandon myself to his mercy and go off like a firecracker. The orgasm is so intense my pussy clenches around his thick cock ramming inside me. He slams his hips against my ass, chasing his own orgasm, and when he comes with a groan, he releases my neck and bites my shoulder.

My legs quiver from the effort, my lungs expand trying to catch enough breath, my heart hammers in my chest as it pumps blood in my ears. I'm exhausted and shivering but I've never felt so much pleasure in my life.

Raphael grabs my chin and makes me turn toward him. I look him in the eyes for the first time since he pulled me in front of the mirror and the softness in his expression is so sweet, I smile. He sticks his fingers in my hair and drag my lips to his for a long intense kiss that tastes of promises.

I rest the back of my head on his shoulder and turn to watch us in the mirror. I'm still on display for him, his softening cock slipping out of my wet pussy. My wetness combined with his release slips down the crack of my butt, making the sight dirty and erotic, but also raw and real. This is us, far from perfect, but honest to the bones.

Raphael squeezes his arms around my waist and kisses my shoulder, then helps me stand up and walk to the bed where we crawl under the blankets and I fall asleep wrapped in his arms.

***

When I wake up in the morning, I feel Raphael's grip around my waist. We're still naked from last night and the erection pressing on my backside tells me he likes us lying together like this. His breathing is still slow and steady and I'm enjoying the sensation of a warm body pressed against my back.

It's been a long time since I've slept with someone. Not sexually, but really sleeping with a guy after making love. In the last eight years, I've dated and had some one-night stands, but never woke up the morning after wrapped against the man I slept with. It's a foreign feeling I don't fully understand, but it's nice and I'm not complaining.

"Good morning," Raphael's raspy, sexy voice graces my ears.

"Good morning," I whisper back.

His grip around my waist tightens and he snuggles against my back, kissing my neck just below my ear. I shiver in pleasure, and I can feel him smile against my shoulder.

"Good to know." He chuckles and kisses my naked skin again.

I turn around to face him and get lost in his intense green eyes. I study his face, trying to gauge any signs of regret, but there are none. His face is relaxed, a smile slightly curving his lips. His hair is sticking out every which way, and I've never seen someone so sexy in the morning.

"What are you thinking?" he asks, caressing the side of my face. I enjoy his touch and briefly close my eyes, indulging in the pleasant feeling warming my chest.

"I was trying to figure out if you regretted this." I open my eyes to see his reaction to my words.

His forehead crinkles a bit to match his puzzled expression. "No, why should I?"

"I don't know. It was an emotional night and I don't know if you're feeling the same today, without all the confessions and the tears."

It's easy to be honest with him. He's so straightforward with the people around him that he trusts, I feel like I can talk to him without having to interpret his reactions. He is completely different from his public persona. When he becomes senator—because there's no doubt he'll be elected—he could say he murdered ten people with a straight face and somehow it would have a positive spin. He's a natural politician and it's a good thing he's got a kind heart and honorable intentions, or we'd all be screwed. If he was the villain in this story, we'd all fall for him.

"I don't regret it. Nothing that happened was something I didn't want. Are you regretting it?" There's a confidence in his question that I envy. He's not second guessing his actions or even wondering if I liked it or want to back out. He asks it like no woman in her right mind would refuse a second round with him.

And that's probably what happens on a regular basis when someone jumps in his bed. The way he tightened his hand around my neck without hurting me but intensifying my orgasm requires a lot of confidence and knowledge. It shows both a desire to pleasure the woman and a craving for control. It perfectly sums up Raphael—his drive to be the best at helping other people.

"No. I'm not the kind of person who jumps into something without thinking about the consequences. I wanted it and I'm sure about that." The firmness in my voice is convincing enough to make his smile widen.

"I believe that. I don't know if it's what happened to you or if your parents raised you this way, but sometimes you're so level-headed I wonder if you're even human," he chuckles.

"I've always been that girl who does the right thing, but what happened to me intensified my need to overthink things. Sometimes I feel overwhelmed."

His expression sobers up and his face becomes almost solemn. "You were brave to testify against him. Not a lot of people would risk doing something like that, knowing their life would be so disrupted. It takes a lot of courage and selflessness to decide to put aside your own needs and do the right thing." The pride in his words makes me want to hide my face in the pillow so he can't see me blushing.

"I don't feel so brave. I'm always looking back second guessing my decisions. Like yesterday, for example. I thought someone was staring at me outside the school, but it turned to be just a father picking up his son."

He frowns. "Someone staring at you? Did you feel threatened?" There is caution in his tone.

"At first, yes. I freaked out a bit, but I couldn't let on that I was having a panic attack. Then he picked up one of the kids and I relaxed. It was just a weird feeling, that's it. It's happened in the past, and the fear probably returned because I'm in the spotlight now. You said your men haven't seen anything weird these last few months, right?"

He nods. "They reported nothing unusual, and they're being extra cautious, but I'll check with them. Did you tell anyone?"

I think back to the conversation, or argument, I had with Matthew and I cringe inside. I don't know what he'll tell Raphael about it. "Matthew knows, but he didn't see the guy."

He nods before kissing me on the lips and hugging me tight. I wrap my arms around his warm body and even though we're naked, there's an intimacy between us that goes beyond sex. It's exhilarating and terrifying at the same time.

***

If I thought we'd reached a turning point in our relationship with the sex, I was greatly mistaken. Raphael comes home from work and strolls into my office where I'm working at some paper the professor assigned.

He leans against the desk. "What do you think about a movie night here at home?" The smirk on his face tells me that he already planned something, and I was right.

In the theater room, there's a banquet spread out over the low coffee table in front of us. Popcorns, chips, cookies and candy are just some of the things I recognize.

"You bought me vanilla ice cream?" I ask in disbelief. I didn't know he remembered that.

"With whipped cream and cherry." He points to two different cups next to the ice cream.

"You definitely know the way to a woman's heart!" I joke, grabbing his hand and dragging him onto the sofa.

He's changed into a comfy pair of sweatpants and a t-shirt, and he puts a blanket over our legs before grabbing the remote and turning on Netflix. He wraps an arm around my shoulder and drags me next to him. I snuggle to his side and when he speaks, I can feel the rumble of his voice through his chest.

"I talked to my staff today and asked them to look into the incident at school. They assured me there's no chance of someone following you. There's no one directly connected with your past in that school," he says without taking his eyes off the list of movies in front of him, but I know he's detecting my every move.

I don't know how he gets that degree of intel and I suspect his father is somehow involved, but I don't want to know the details.

"Thank you. I really appreciate that. It wasn't nagging at me, but I feel relieved just the same."

He says nothing but his grip on my side intensifies, and he kisses my head. It's such a mundane thing we're doing, watching a movie snuggled together like a normal couple, that my chest expands with a feeling that I'm terrified to recognize: happiness.

I don't know where this is going. I have no idea whether in one, five, ten years from now we'll be sitting on this same couch watching a movie like we love each other for real, but I decide not to overthink it. Raphael promised to keep me safe, and for the first time in my life I feel like I can trust someone.

CHAPTER 21
Raphael

I walk through the back door of the nightclub and immediately regret my decision to come here. The main dance floor is packed with bodies swaying to the beat of the music, and when I try to gain access to the VIP section, I have to shoulder my way up the stairs.

The usual bouncer recognizes me and lets me in. I left Dave at the back entrance. He's so huge he attracts way too much attention and I want to be as inconspicuous as possible. This is the first time since meeting Silver that I've set foot in here and it feels like I'm betraying her. It's been fifteen days since we slept together, and our relationship feels more real than any other I've been in since Kelsey.

I navigate through the crowded VIP section. Most of the people I encounter are too engrossed in their conversations to recognize me, but I try to not make eye contact with anyone to avoid having to explain my presence here.

I glance toward the bar hoping Lola isn't here tonight but I'm not that lucky. She's working her ass off preparing four drinks at the same time. She glances at the faces in front of her as she serves them, but fortunately she doesn't have time to look around too much.

I reach the other side of the bar where another girl is serving her customers, and I scope out the crowd looking to spot the familiar mane of red hair. It takes fifteen minutes before she makes an appearance and by the time she reaches me, I'm fuming.

"You're late," I point out when she greets me with a kiss on the cheek.

She rolls her eyes and dismisses me with a wave of a hand. I hate when she does that, but then I look at her in the heavy makeup and skimpy clothes and feel the urge to hug her and keep her safe.

"Buy me a drink!" she shouts in my ear.

"We need to go out of here," I answer without giving her the chance to get the bartender's attention.

She crosses her arms over her way-too-visible breast and pouts. "Okay, you pay me by the hour, but Jesus, can you cut me some slack and buy me a drink?" she complains.

I glance toward Lola, and notice she's moved closer to where I'm seated. I don't know if she notices me, but I start to feel uncomfortable. Lying to Silver about where I am tonight makes me feel a bit jumpy.

"We need to go now!" I repeat sternly and get her attention.

She looks at me like I'm a piece of smelly, disgusting shit that got stuck under her shoes. "What? Now that you have the perfect fiancé you're too good to be seen with an escort?"

The remark hits too close to home to not feel the sting of guilt. She hit the nail on the head. I can't risk being discovered with a prostitute, especially in a place where everyone knows that escorts have free reign to scour the place in search of clients.

When I don't answer, she scoffs. "You're an asshole."

"It's complicated," I try to explain, but she turns around without saying a word. I have to speed up to keep up with her. I guide her toward the car and the short drive to the diner is silent and tense. She's always been difficult to deal with but tonight she seems in a particularly foul mood.

We enter the diner and take the most secluded booth. Dave goes to the counter to order our drinks, and fries for Jenny, asking the waitress not to bother us. It's always like this with her. She won't talk if someone may be eavesdropping on our conversation, but she wants to be in a public place and not alone with me. She's probably scared I'll bring her back to her parents and wants to have an out. I've told her I wouldn't do that, but she doesn't trust me. She doesn't trust anyone.

"You wanted to talk, go ahead," I tell her when she doesn't speak for a long while.

She looks at me and shivers a bit. It's June, but she seems cold, and her gold sparkling dress is not covering nearly enough. I take a good look at her under the bright lights of this place and my heart sinks a bit. She looks skinnier than the last time I saw her, and the heavy makeup does little to cover the dark circles under her eyes. If I wasn't familiar with the brothel where she works, where they test regularly for STDs and drugs, I'd be worried she's become a junkie. I take off my jacket and offer it to her, but she shakes her head, refusing to wear it.

"There's a new girl," she practically whispers.

I nod and take in this news. Usually, when she calls it's to tell me something bad happened, and I don't know why this time I hoped it would be different.

"Okay, do you know anything more about that?" I ask, not really wanting to know the details. Every time she brings me news, I feel sick.

"She has a tattoo like the other one. On her foot."

I nod and wait for Dave to put our orders on the table and walk away.

"She doesn't speak English. She's from South America, but I don't know where exactly. We both speak a little Spanish and sometimes it's hard to understand each other," she explains.

"She came straight from another country?" This is new. Usually, they deal with girls that are in the United States long enough to be able to speak enough basic English to understand their clients' requests.

"She told me they put her on a boat back in her country, and when she arrived, she had to walk all night through a swamp infested by mosquitoes and alligators," she adds and knows this is important. She's been feeding me this information for years, and I taught her what to ask the girls and what's important to know. She's good at it, but tonight something is bothering her.

"Is there something more?" My stomach twists in a hurtful grip because I know I won't like it. I can see the fear in her eyes.

Years ago, when I agreed to do this, I thought it would be an easy job to hand over this information to people who could snuff out this nightmare. But I wasn't prepared for the stories I would hear while doing it. Sometimes I want to throw up at the thought of what these girls endure.

"She said other girls were with her, but only a few survived. They died on the boat. For days, she had to endure the trip alongside those dead girls. They also beat and raped her," she whispers and I reach out my hand to squeeze hers.

"We're going to find the people that did this to her. I promise." My voice shakes, because every time I think about what she's told me over the years I want to curl up in a corner and erase the information from my brain. I think I'm reaching the limit of what I can handle.

***

After dropping Jenny back at the club, I go straight to the warehouse I brought Silver to months ago. So much has changed since last time I was here it feels like a lifetime ago. The only memory branded in my brain is the excruciating pain when she kicked me in the balls. *That* is something I will never forget.

Dave knocks a couple of times on the tinted window of the SUV and I know I have to get out of the car. As soon as my feet hit the bare concrete, I can see the outline of the FBI agent walking toward me. I've known him for years and never saw him arrive in a car. It's like he just materializes a hundred yards from where my car is parked, like I summoned a ghost. And maybe he is a ghost, considering what a nightmare his job is.

"I thought you forgot about me." He smirks as he approaches, dressed in loose jeans, a black hoodie, and a black baseball cap. He looks like one of the hundreds of homeless people walking around Los Angeles, just a bit cleaner and showered. Even his beard is out of control. I guess this look helps to not attract attention.

"I haven't see her for a while."

He nods, becoming more serious.

"Maybe after the last bust they laid low?" I try to figure out if Jenny is missing something.

"We hit them hard last time. They need time to regroup," he confirms.

Something stirs in my chest: hope. Maybe we are doing something good here. Maybe we have been saving lives. Trying to stop human trafficking sometimes feel hopeless. You stop one criminal organization somewhere and another ten pop up overnight to take their place. Sometimes it feels a lost cause, but then I think of the ones who got free and a bit of hope blooms again in my chest. It's a continuous rollercoaster I never get used to.

"Well, I think they're active again, but with something different." I get his full attention. "There's a new girl, same tattoo as the other, but she didn't come on a truck like the others, she came in a boat, dumped off in a swamp. She had to walk through mosquitos and alligators."

He seems to think a lot about it. "They must have someone local helping them navigate the swamps. Otherwise, they would have ended up dead," he murmurs and I can hear the defeat in his voice. It's barely there, an underlying feeling that escaped his chest.

"I thought so. There were more girls with her, but just a few survived. The others died during the trip from South America."

I can relate to the grimace on his face. "Did she say how many? Where did they bring her after she walked out of the swamp?" he asks, almost expecting I'll have all the answers. I know his frustration.

I shake my head. "She barely speaks a few words of Spanish. It was difficult to communicate."

He snaps his head toward me. "Brazilian?" There's hope in his voice. Knowing where she comes from means he can track where the boat dumped her. Satellites give you very little privacy these days.

"I thought so, but I'm not sure. She didn't recognize the language. They had beaten and raped her," I spit out at the end.

"I had no doubt about that," he sighs, rubbing a hand over his face. "Do you have anything else?" he asks hopefully.

I shake my head. "No, but she promised to ask her more. She can't press too much because the girl is traumatized."

"Of course," he says, and before he turns to walk away, I stop him. He looks at me curiously.

"What do you know about the witness protection program?"

He frowns. "Not much, but I know not to mess with them. Why?"

"I may have messed with them." I study him and his eyes widen in surprise.

"Well, un-mess it."

"I can't."

"Why?"

"I'm marrying someone in the program in three months."

"Fuck! Are you serious right now?"

"Do I look like I'm joking? I know I messed up, but now I need to protect her. I can't just kick her out and hope they won't find her." I feel the shame spreading across my face.

He looks at me like I'm walking into a burning building. "I can see that. How can I help?"

"Can you look into her case and see if there's been any movement on his side? He's still in prison, life sentence without parole, but I don't know how much power he still has to get to someone outside and do the job."

He nods. "Who?"

"The Hangman of New Jersey."

The color drains from his face. "Are you shitting me? Fuck!"

His reaction is all I need to confirm how badly I've messed up with Silver, and a lump the size of a baseball forms in my throat.

"I'll see what I can do," he promises, and it's enough for now. I'm going to fix this. I have to.

***

When I walk into our bedroom it's almost dawn. Silver is sleeping peacefully, sprawled across the bed as if searching for me in her sleep. I walk over and watch her beautiful face. She's relaxed, worries have not settled into her brain yet. When she sleeps, she's safe in her own world and I'm terrified that when she's awake, her nightmare will begin.

I reach out my hand and caress her cheek. Her skin is soft. I notice that when she sleeps her skin seems softer than ever. Maybe because she isn't tense yet, her problems give her some respite.

My heart squeezes in my chest. What if I can't protect her like I promised? What if she'll be ripped from me like every woman in my life? In the past, it wasn't my fault. I couldn't do anything to stop it. But I brought this on her. I put her in danger, and I don't know if I'll survive it if something happens to her.

I strip of my clothes, slip into bed, kiss her on the head and wrap my arms tightly around her. She huffs in her sleep, then she puts her hand around my waist, her head against my chest, and the fear in my heart intensifies.

CHAPTER 22

Silver

"Are you fucking serious right now?" I storm into the bedroom and find Raphael putting on his shirt.

He turns around with a puzzled face and that innocent look makes my blood boil. He didn't come back until this early morning and now he has the guts to look like he did nothing wrong.

"About what?" His eyebrows knit together without the slightest sign of guilt.

"I don't know. Maybe about how it's been fifteen days since we've started fucking and you spent the night with a prostitute!"

He opens his mouth, but nothing comes out. There's pain in his eyes, and I didn't expect that.

"Don't even try to deny it. Lola saw you walking out of the club with the redhead. We all know she's an escort," I bark at him.

The way he lowers his head in defeat is confirmation enough to make my stomach roll in disgust. How stupid I was to believe him. I knew he paid to have sex. I saw him with my own eyes at the club. I feel so humiliated I want to cry.

"I can explain." He lets out a sigh.

"You promised you wouldn't humiliate me! I gave you everything, I slept with you, and you humiliate me in front of everyone who knows me." Rage drips from my words.

He rubs a couple of fingers over his eyes, and I notice the dark circles under them. He's tired, and yesterday I'd have been worried about him, but now I'm glad he's exhausted. It's a petty thought, but it makes me feel a bit better.

"I know I made a mistake but it's not what you think," he says, sitting on the bed.

"What a cliché," I spit.

He looks at me and I see regret in his eyes. It's too late to feel guilty now.

"It's really not what you think. Please sit down." He's so defeated that for a moment I hesitate.

I didn't anticipate an explanation. I don't even know what I was expecting, honestly. I've always thought men who pay for sex are lying bastards who don't deserve a second chance. But to tell the truth, since knowing Raphael, I've completely forgotten about this aspect of his life. I sit next to him as doubt creeps into my aching chest.

"So, you didn't meet with a prostitute last night?" I'm confused.

He shakes his head, and my hope dies a bit. "I met with her, but I didn't have sex with her."

I don't know what to think. "What does that mean?"

He takes a deep breath and stares in front of him for a long moment, then turns and pins me with an honest look. "She's Kelsey's little sister."

This is so unexpected I don't know what to feel. Disbelief and discomfort hit my gut in a painful blow. "You're fucking your dead ex's little sister? That is messed up!" I blurt out.

He shakes his head again and I'm tempted to slap him to stop it. I'm glad I sat down next to him. I don't know if my legs would keep me standing right now.

"I'm not fucking her. I never have. And I've never paid a woman to have sex with me. When Kelsey died, Jenny became restless. She was always a troublemaker, but she spiraled out of control after her sister died. A few months after Kelsey passed, her parents called me telling me she had become an escort. They were desperate and they asked me to talk to her." He clenches his jaw as though these memories are painful for him.

I can't even imagine what those parents went through and my chest aches for them. I keep silent, giving Raphael time to tell his story.

"I was never able to make her change her life, but I can't abandon her either," he whispers.

"Why did she do it? Fifteen years is a long time to rebel against what life throw at you. No matter how much pain you're in." It almost seems like she's not rebelling at all, but driven by something else.

"She says she likes it like this. I don't get what the appeal is to have sex with men that treat you like a piece of meat, but the more I prod her to open up, the more I find she's actually okay with what she does. I guess she just enjoys sex and doesn't care where it comes from." He's clearly come to terms with the fact that he won't ever understand her choices, but he's accepted them.

"Is that why you meet with her? To check if she's okay?"

"This is where this story gets messed up. God, this got so big I don't even know where to start." He rubs a hand over his face and a sense of dread invades my stomach.

Seeing him so vulnerable makes my body hum with fear. Raphael is never vulnerable, never defeated or struggling over something. He's the confident one who solves problems.

"After a few months into this life, she told me about a girl she knew who didn't want any part of being an escort, but who was beaten and raped and forced to become a prostitute. I asked about this girl, but I didn't know how to help her. I couldn't barge into a brothel and kidnap a woman I knew nothing about. So, I used my connections to contact an FBI agent who could attempt to break into the human trafficking organization and get the guys who were doing it. Jenny feeds me information about the girls she meets and I feed them to my contact. I never planned to become a snitch. I kind of drifted into it without realizing it, at first. Then I saw the results of the information I was getting: the people who were getting arrested for it and the girls who were returned to their families. So, I kept doing it."

Finally, this makes so much more sense than Raphael paying for sex. Of course, he's helping others to the maximum extent. Usually, when a man comes up with an elaborate excuse for his infidelity, I call bullshit and turn my back on him without thinking twice. This is the most surreal excuse someone has ever fed me for being caught with a prostitute, but knowing Raphael, his ethics, his wanting to do the right thing, help someone out, it makes more sense than anything.

"I know I fucked up by meeting her in that club, but she doesn't want to meet me anywhere else. I'm sorry I humiliated you. There's no excuse for that," he adds with a plea in his voice that melts my heart.

I say nothing. I stare into his honest eyes, raw with emotion, and anything I was going to say dies on my lips. How can you reproach a man for making you look like a fool in the eyes of a friend, when he's literally saving people's lives? My bruised ego is nothing compared to what he does. He made a mistake, but it was not entirely his fault.

The feeling of overwhelm rampaging in my chest is tearing me apart. I shouldn't care so much about him. I shouldn't let my heart get so close to his. It could catch feelings and I can't afford that. But I can't stay away from him either. He's tied to his past in a twisted fate I don't know if I'm comfortable with, but I am too, and I have no right to ask him to let it go.

I lean in and close the distance between us. I brush his lips with mine and sense the initial surprise that catches him. The small gasp from his lips is all I need to be drawn into his vulnerability, into the depth of the abyss he's hiding inside. He willingly carries the weight of the world, stubbornly trying to help everyone. But there is something underneath the strong surface, a fear that runs deep in his bones that no one else sees.

We're so alike in so many ways it's scary. Which is why, when I slip my tongue into his mouth, it's like coming home. And it's terrifying. It's been eight years since I had a home, someone to come back to, and the idea of losing it again is enough to tie my stomach in knots. A gut-wrenching feeling that almost makes me bolt.

Almost. Because there's something in Raphael that I don't want to let go of. His fierce resolution to keep me safe. For the first time in my life, I have someone else in my corner. I'm not alone, and the thought is irresistible.

He stays there, kissing me back with a slow, tantalizing passion that ignites my body. He is not taking charge of this moment. He's giving me his most valuable gift, his vulnerability. I slip my fingers under the fabric of the shirt he never buttoned, and I pull it off his shoulders, letting it fall to the floor.

I put my hands flat on his chest and push him on the bed, straddling his hips. He closes his eyes while I trace the arch of his eyebrows with the tip of my fingers. I move to his straight nose, the soft curves of his lips. I want to commit to memory the perfect features of his face.

I lower down to kiss him slowly and take my time to enjoy the feeling. His hands slide under my t-shirt and with a quick gesture I take it off. I turn back to lean against his body. Skin against skin, shivering when my naked breasts caress his defined chest.

I kiss every inch of his skin, enjoying his body quivering under my touch, and when I reach the waistband of his boxer briefs, I linger a bit, tantalizing the soft dark hair covering his lower belly down to his crotch. I lick and nip my way down, hooking a couple of fingers under the hem of the fabric and freeing his semi-hard shaft.

I skim his velvety, hot erection with feather-light kisses and seal my lips over the bead of precum leaking from his tip. He moans softly, never opening his eyes. He is letting me do whatever I want with his body, and I feel the weight of this moment. I take him in my mouth and suck, eliciting a deep groan from his chest.

His erection grows on my tongue, pulsing and leaking salty drops down my throat. I take him deep until he is on the verge of coming undone, then I stand, take off my panties and straddle him, slipping his shaft into my wet core. Slow and deep, connecting every part of me with every part of him. I lay on his chest, wrapping my fingers around the back of his neck.

I roll my hips in a crescendo of wetness, pleasure, sweat, and hot breath. I take him deep and slow, and when my pussy clenches around his cock, triggering his own orgasm, he wraps his arms around my body, coming undone in my arms.

It's the most powerful, raw connection I've ever had with a man. The lines are so blurred I don't know where the physical pleasure ends and the emotional connection starts. Because this moment doesn't taste just like sex; it has the bittersweetness of making love.

CHAPTER 23
Raphael

Silver is sleeping next to me, and watching the peaceful pout on her lips makes me want to kiss her until she wakes up and then kiss her a bit more. Yesterday's fight comes to my mind and a weird feeling stirs in my chest.

I can't stop thinking about the hurt in her eyes when she thought I'd been fucking Jenny. The raw emotions she shows only in the privacy of this home are something I'll never get used. It's like she feels safe enough with me to let down the walls she's built over the years. It's an honor I'm not sure I deserve.

Yesterday, I fell apart. Telling her about Jenny and the things I do with the FBI was like grabbing the weight on my shoulders and throwing it out the window. Apart from Dave, not even Matthew or Harrison knows the extent of what I do. They know I meet with Jenny from time to time, but they think I do it out of an obligation to check on her.

Telling Silver about the rest was as liberating as ripping a giant band-aid off my heart and I started to bleed. I let her see me vulnerable, something I've never done before with a woman, and it felt like discovering another world, a better one.

"Hey," her sleepy voice pulls me out of my thoughts.

"I think we should do something this morning," I blurt out with no warning.

She frowns and her puzzled expression is so adorable I don't know if I can resist kissing and making love to her.

"What?"

"Let's go have breakfast on the beach," I say, and she seems to relax.

A smile forms on her face and I'm glad she's in for it. "I'll put on my bikini," she answers with a yawn as she stretches and rubs her eyes. "And stop staring at me like a creep while I sleep."

I chuckle and jump out of bed to go to check if everything is ready while I wait for her to get dressed.

We reach the small beach near Malibu an hour later. It's deserted, especially during the week, It's a bit difficult to reach the sandy bottom through the thick low shrubs. Not even the surfers come to venture out and surf in these waters, with its hidden dangerous rocks. I discovered it a few years back when I needed to escape my father and didn't know where else to go.

As we settle on the blanket facing the ocean, I open the lid of the cooler we brought with us. Silver closes her eyes and inhales deeply. A contented smile appears on her face and I'm curious to know what's in her head.

"What are you thinking?" I ask, handing her some fruit and the yogurt we brought.

"I'm originally from the Midwest, so I was just gloating about how much I like the weather here."

I laugh. She never talks about her previous life and I'm sometimes curious. I don't press her but the longer we live together, the more she opens up.

"Do you miss anything besides the weather?" I half-tease her. I'm genuinely interested about what she went through.

She shrugs and turns toward me. "Not really. I was going to live in a big city anyway, I didn't have a lot of opportunities there. The only thing I went back for was to visit my family, but not having them there, I don't miss other things so much."

I nod and try to comprehend what it means to decide to part ways with the family you love. When Alba and Kelsey died, they were ripped away from my life. It was hard, but I knew I could do nothing to bring them back. I can't imagine surviving after willingly walking away from them. I would probably have taken the selfish route and kept them with me, even if that was the most dangerous option. I'm not as strong as Silver.

"Is that why you chose to study law? To escape your small town?" I'm curious about her studies.

She shakes her head. "I pursued it because I believe in justice. Ironic, considering that's the reason I screwed up my life, but I still believe in it."

I nod and she seems to study me. "What?" I ask.

"Maybe I can't be a lawyer, since I can't graduate, but I've studied and worked my ass off and I know things. I can help with what you're doing with Jenny, maybe even investigate it more thoroughly, professionally. If you'll let me. I don't want to force it if you don't feel comfortable with it."

I stay silent for a while, surprised and moved by her offer. It would be less painful to share this aspect of my life with her, but I don't know if I want to drag her into this mess.

"Thank you. I'll think about it," is the only promise I can give her, but it's honest and I think she appreciates that more than anything else.

She nods and turns back to the ocean and the breakfast she is nibbling on while deep in thought.

"How do you know about this place?" she asks.

"One time, I needed a break from my father, and I didn't know where to go. I was so desperate that I just walked down the trail without knowing what was here." I chuckle at the memory.

"Do you get along with him?" She studies me with an intensity I'm not used to.

I watch the waves slapping lazily on the shore and think about what to tell her. "For the most part, yes. Sometimes he pushes to the point of breaking, but if you know how to handle him, he's someone you want in your corner." Because otherwise you're dead, but I prefer not to tell her this.

"He seems…intense," she mumbles.

I scoff. "Understatement of the century. But you stood up to him. He probably admires you for that. He doesn't like weak people. He always pushes them to grow a backbone."

"Was he like that with you? Pushing you to be the best?"

"Does it show?" I smirk at her, she laughs, and I know she gets it.

"Shouldn't you be working right now, instead of slacking off here with your trophy wife?" She winks, teasing me, and I cand stop a laugh from bubbling up in my chest.

"From time to time, I need to relax too, especially after I met Jenny. Our encounters can be…draining, sometimes." I glance at her, gauging her reaction.

She smiles reassuringly and nods. There's something peaceful in the way she understands my needs; we're way more similar than we care to admit.

**

I drop Silver off at home and ask Dave to drive me to the old warehouse where I meet the agent. I don't know his real name;

he asked me to call him "Cop" and the irony is not missed on me. He likes to meet in secret, but I think it's more about protecting my privacy, considering the public reach I have, than needing to hide our meeting.

When he called me on our way home, my nerves started to get the best of me. He's never called me, I seek him out. And the fact that it took him only twenty-four hours to get back to me about the favor I asked can mean only two things: there's nothing to worry about, or there's a lot to be afraid of. I'm terrified it's the latter.

"Tell me you have good news," I say as soon as he reaches the car.

His face is unreadable, as usual, but his words make my stomach clench. "I have good news and bad news."

It's such a cliché I want to scream. The good news almost never compensates for the bad.

"Are you going to tell me or not?" I press impatiently, and he gives me a sideways smile.

"The good news is that the mob is not looking for her."

Relief expands my chest and I can almost breathe easily. This is really good. I thought they might be on some kind of manhunt. Mobilizing the entire city's crime organization just to take care of her, or worse, join forces with local criminals, would be a nightmare come to life.

"When she testified, she took out the head of the organization. Since then, there's been an internal civil war to take control. They're too focused on fighting each other to pay attention to her. To be honest, she did them a favor by opening up the playing field for other potential leaders to step up," he explains, and concern rises in my chest.

"But?" If this is the good news, I don't know what the bad could be.

"He has some connections outside prison. A few loyal people that still look up to him. The guys I was able to track down, the ones who followed her case, could account for everyone but two who disappeared. They started keeping an eye on all of his loyal cronies when she ended up in the newspapers, but lost track of two about a month back." He hands me an envelope with a couple of mug shots inside.

I curse under my breath. "There are two of these people on the loose and nobody told her?" I raise my voice and feel the blood simmer in my veins.

The thought of having put her in danger is driving me nuts. Consciously, I know this is no one's fault. She couldn't predict that stupid innocent kiss would blow up on social media, and I didn't know that saving her from that coffee shop creep would lead to this. But I can't stop thinking that if I had done something differently, she'd be safe now. Guilt builds in my chest and I can't keep it down.

"There is no reason to assume they're here in Los Angeles. For all we know, they could be dead. It happens all the time: criminals drop off the radar and you find them ten years later in a car in the middle of a lake."

"Yeah, but not two related to an old case who magically disappear after the main witness of a trial goes viral on social media!" I bark, and he has the decency to not laugh at my outburst.

"She's safer with you. You're a future senator, hurting her would be the same as attacking you personally. They're not that dumb to try something, especially publicly. And then there's your father. A lot of people are scared to piss him off."

"I don't know what you mean," I murmur, but we both know what he's talking about. The FBI knows about him. They've been trying to put their hands on him since forever, and I'm in the middle of this battle. My father always kept me out of his "secondary business" to keep me clean. Neither my opponents, the public, or even the FBI have anything against me. I've always played by the rules so as not to jeopardize my rise to the highest arena of politics.

He raises an eyebrow, challenging me to insult his intelligence again. I drop the subject and suck in a deep breath.

"Listen, we're keeping an eye on you anyway for the intel you're giving us. Adding those two to the list is not a big deal. If there's anything even slightly off, I'll personally warn you," he tries to reassure me. "Right now, there's no reason to be concerned. It's more likely they're buried in concrete somewhere for pissing off the wrong crowd."

I nod, appreciating the effort he's putting into this. He's probably doing it because I feed them information and they don't want to lose my help, but still, he's going out of his way to give me these tips.

"Thank you. I'll use this." I wave the folder.

"Good. Oh, and next time we should meet somewhere else. This warehouse is too exposed."

"Okay. Just out of curiosity, do we have to meet in secret like this?" I suggested a warehouse the first time because I was so scared, I didn't want to risk meeting anyone I know, but now it just seems silly.

"No, but it's fun to watch you pretend to be a secret agent meeting in creepy places." He chuckles, turning around and walking away.

"Asshole!"

He laughs and waves without even bothering to turn around. I watch him disappear silently, like he didn't just drop a bomb on my life.

I knock at Silver's home office, and she looks up with a smile. She's decorated this place nicely, with pastel furniture, plush carpet, and comfortable armchairs with coordinating cushions. One entire wall is covered in shelves where she keeps adding law books. I've never seen someone so passionate about a job she can't technically do.

"What are you working on?" I ask, walking to her desk when she waves me in.

"Doing some research on human trafficking." She turns her computer toward me.

I chuckle. "I'll have to tell the guys at the FBI not to freak out at your research history."

She grins. "They're your friends. You deal with them."

I kiss the crown of her head. She seems surprised by my sudden display of affection, but then leans into my touch. After my conversation this afternoon and the worries pounding in my chest, I crave contact with her. I need to know she's safe and sound in this house.

"Did you find anything interesting?" I scroll through some of her research. It's various deep analyses of human trafficking organizations and how they find ways to snatch girls from their everyday lives. How they brainwash them to not rebel against the life they're forced into.

"Not exactly. This is outside my area of expertise. I was just trying to get an overview, so I know what to dive into with my research. If I don't know the basics, I can't help you in all this," she explains and my chest caves in.

She's too good for this world, and too precious to be staying with me in a fake relationship.

"You're amazing, you know that?" I kiss her temple and she blushes; I don't know if it's the compliment or the kiss.

"Where have you been today? Not even Matthew knew where you were, and that guy knows how many times you go pee!" She giggles so innocently it makes her look almost younger.

"I went to meet my father for some stupid campaign thing," I lie, and my heart squeezes in my chest.

I hate not telling her the truth, but I don't want her to worry about what's happening. Maybe she'll be mad if she finds out, but I'd rather see her happy. I can take care of her safety.

I always had the dream to protect the world, I suppose I'm starting with her.

CHAPTER 24

Silver

He lied to me. Yesterday he came to my office and lied to my face about where he'd been. I know because Cindy called asking where he was, because his father was at his office. What are the chances that he used his father as an alibi at the same time the man was looking for him? Almost zero, but it happened, and I found out he lied.

And this makes me uncomfortable. How many times has he lied to me? How many secrets is he hiding? Many. I know that the circumstances that brought us together didn't spring from love, but I thought there was complicity. I thought he trusted me.

Was he with a woman? The grip of jealousy tightens my stomach, even if I have no right to feel it. We agreed to not have any other significant others while we're together, we're having sex, but you can't control who you fall in love with. What if he met someone? What if he found the love of his life? All the certainty I've been building during these last months crumbled yesterday in the face of that easy lie.

This morning I have to try on my wedding dress for the first time, for Pete's sake. Even if he does decide to go through with this plan until it's safe for me to disappear, if he's now found someone else, it doesn't feel right.

I stand up, change into something appropriate for my appointment this morning, and walk to the kitchen. The ghost staff—as I've come to call them, since they're so quiet I rarely see or hear them around the house—has already set up breakfast so I dig into it, brewing over what I'm feeling.

This relationship is fake and I shouldn't feel jealousy, but after I wrapped my mind around the possibility that it could work in the long term, having it jeopardized makes me uneasy.

"Here you are. I woke up alone and thought you ditched me." Raphael tightens his arms around my waist and kisses my neck.

Comforting feelings warm my chest. He's affectionate and treats me like I'm his partner. He feels at home with me, and my head is exploding with all these mixed feelings. But I don't dare ask him where he was. I'm not one to make a fuss about where my partner is, I refuse to check his phone out of jealousy or point fingers in accusation. If he lied to me, he had his reasons and I have to deal with that. And in reality, he's never disrespected me and I have no reason to think he's doing something behind my back.

That doesn't mean it hurts less.

"I need to be ready for my wedding dress fitting this morning," I say, turning around and kissing him and enjoying his soft lips on mine.

He tilts his head and studies me. "How are you feeling about that?"

I shrug. "Weird, I guess. I never thought this moment would come, and now it's not exactly real, so I have no idea how I feel. I'm happy, a bit excited, but weirded out about feeling butterflies for something that isn't necessarily love. Does that make any sense?"

He chuckles. "I think so. I'm still trying to wrap my head around it."

"By the way, Cindy sent me pictures of the centerpieces for the tables, and we have to choose one. Apparently, the florist plans months in advance, and we're already late. You don't have to do it, if you trust me, I'll just pick one," I suggest, not sure how much he wants to be involved in this.

He frowns. "No, I want to take a look with you. I'm not letting you do everything. I mean, how hard can it be to pick flowers?"

I'm touched by his determination to be involved. Which is why my heart skipped a beat yesterday when he lied. He seems genuinely happy with me, but at the same time, he doesn't trust me with everything. I know things not even his friends are aware of, yet he hides other parts of his life from me.

"You have no idea, do you?"

"Show me." He kisses my forehead.

We grab our breakfast from the kitchen counter and move to the living room table where I've laid out the wedding brochures Cindy sent me yesterday.

"Holy shit," he whispers at the sheer amount of material scattered on the table.

"Are you sure you still want to help?" I chuckle.

"Of course, I'm sure. I'm just surprised. It's a freaking centerpiece, for Pete's sake!" He barks out a disbelieving laugh.

And when he sits down and pulls me into his lap, I'm pleasantly surprised by the intimacy of this moment. Not in my wildest dreams did I imagine a man helping me plan our wedding, let alone enjoying it.

"So, how about we go through the pictures and make three piles: yes, maybe, and hell no—over my dead body," I suggest.

"Yeah, I like that plan." He tightens his grip on my waist and nods.

I grab the packet of brochures and place it in front of us. His eyes widen comically.

"How many photos are we talking about?"

"About a hundred and fifty," I snicker.

"What?" His head snaps in my direction.

"I had the same reaction. Don't worry, you'll get the hang of it."

He chuckles and shakes his head. "Go ahead, I'll text Matthew letting him know I'll be late."

I grab the first picture of an elaborate piece with iron spikes and white roses entwined with pearls.

"Hell no!" we both say, as I put the picture on the appropriate pile.

I grab the second one and indicate yes, but it's a no for Raphael. "Should we put it on the 'maybe' pile if we disagree?" I ask him.

"I'll never agree to tall centerpieces," he says in a firm tone that piques my curiosity.

"What's your problem with tall ones?" It's a peculiar thing to have such a strong opinion about.

"I've been to enough galas and formal events to know that a tall centerpiece blocks your view of the person in front of you. If you want to have a conversation you have to bend sideways or just talk to the person sitting next to you. You end up *not* wanting to be there," he explains and I'm mesmerized by his knowledge.

"Wow. I didn't think about that. Thank God you're the kind of guy who wants to be involved in these decisions." I kiss him on the lips, and he smiles.

"I'm glad I can help." He sweetly pecks my cheek and my stomach flutters with excitement.

Half an hour later, we've narrowed it down to three choices.

"Classic white roses, modern white roses with a hint of blue, or a bit more rustic with a variety of white flowers and splashes of lavender?" I ask him.

He frowns in concentration and looks adorable sweeping his gaze from one picture to another, trying to imagine what our wedding will look like.

"Dump the blue one. It's too modern for my taste," he says, and I have no doubt about his choice, considering he lives in a gorgeous mansion with stuccos and bright colors reminiscent of the Mediterranean.

"All white or lavender?" I wave the two pictures in front of his face.

"It depends on the wedding venue and style, I suppose. Do you want something fancy in a ballroom or something more casual outdoors?" he asks, and I'm surprised this is something he can envision. Usually, it's the woman who has her wedding planned to perfection on a Pinterest board. The groom normally just shows up for the ceremony.

"Outdoors. Not a fan of fancy and uptight." I chuckle.

"We have a winner." He cheers, picking up the lavender photo and studying it carefully.

"That was easier than I thought," I admit.

"We're a good team." He kisses my lips.

"Yeah," I agree, but the conviction in my chest wobbles thinking about the lie.

***

Lola follows me out of the car and lands her eyes on Sven. She smiles coyly at him, he smirks as he checks out her low-cut dress showing off her boobs, and I divert my gaze because I feel like I'm intruding in their flirty bubble.

I look around this upscale neighborhood, the street dotted with boutiques I'd never imagined before meeting Raphael. It's funny how my lifestyle has changed so dramatically in the last months just because of one man. I'm not complaining, but it makes me think about how many sharp turns your life can take.

Eight years ago, I had my life figured out with an exact career to pursue and lost everything overnight. Then when I thought I had regained my balance, this other overnight turn put me in a whole new level of craziness.

I look away from the luxury surrounding me and glance at a beaten-up pickup. That's something I'm more familiar with. It's such a contrast from the other nice cars parked along the curb that it stands out like a sore thumb. A man inside is staring at me and when he notices me staring back, he adjusts his baseball cap and fumbles with something on the dashboard.

It's just a fraction of a second, but a chilling feeling expands in my gut. There's nothing off about him, he wasn't holding my gaze or anything. I can't put my finger on why I react this way, and it unsettles me. Maybe catching Raphael lying to me undermined my sense of security more than I thought.

"Are we going in?" Lola's voice drags me out of my thoughts.

I turn toward her. She and Sven are finally done flirting. He's back to his professional demeanor, and he doesn't seem concerned by that pickup.

"Yes, sure." I smile at her, and turning around to go inside, I glance back at the man and discover he's not even in his car anymore.

I let out a small sigh of relief and relax my shoulders. I have to remind myself that Raphael took care of my safety and there's nothing to worry about. That guy just happened to be less rich than most people around here, and a sense of guilt creeps into my chest for judging him by his appearance.

The boutique is one of those high-class places where you can only get in by booking an appointment in advance. They offer a private room with floor-to-ceiling mirrors, white sofas for your guests, and a dais to stand on and admire yourself in the finest gowns on the market. Champagne and macarons are included in the experience.

The saleswoman greeting us is in her mid-thirties, her hair pinned back a tight brown bun and a high-collared dress that fits her perfectly running down to her lower mid-thighs. Her measured smile adds a bit of warmth to an otherwise way too uptight person.

"What's the vibe of the wedding? Formal or more relaxed?" she asks.

"Relaxed," I answer at the same time Lola says, "Formal."

I turn toward her, and she arches her brows while sipping champagne. "What? You're marrying a senator! I think your guests will expect black tie and all." She shrugs.

This is the difficult part of this charade. We don't even have guest list.

"We're going for a less lavish ceremony," I explain to the woman who just nods, her face unreadable. If she thinks it's odd marrying Los Angeles' most desirable bachelor in an intimate down-to-earth ceremony, she's not giving away anything.

"Is it an indoor or outdoor ceremony?"

"Outdoor," I say at the same time Lola says, "Indoor."

I turn to her again and she raises a hand, sealing her lips. The saleswoman's lips curve upward and it's the most noticeable reaction since we stepped foot in here.

"It will be an outdoor wedding and we'll have lavender, daisies, gerberas, and white roses in the centerpieces. Not exactly rustic, but a more casual feel," I finally explain.

She nods again and I start to wonder if she has any feelings whatsoever or if she packed her heart away in a box before coming into work this morning. "Do you want something with lavender color in it?"

"Oh, no. I prefer white with lace, but not too sophisticated," I answer in a rush.

The woman nods, again, then excuses herself and walks out of the room.

"You have no idea what you want, do you?" Lola smiles at me.

"Nope."

"Are you sure you want to go through with this? You should be happy to plan your wedding…" Her voice trails off like she's not sure what else to say.

I asked her to come with me because I thought it was sad to look for a wedding gown all alone, but the truth is that I dreamed about sharing this moment with my mom and sister. I imagined their squeals when I find *The One*, but that will never happen. Until I stepped inside this place, it didn't hit me how much I missed them.

When I was a bartender, the pain of missing my family was a dull ache in the background, but now that I've started to really live my life and not just survive it, I realize they'll miss every important milestone and I'll miss theirs.

"I am happy." And in part it's true. I'm getting something I didn't know I could have and I'm grateful to Raphael for that.

"Are you sure? Because he's sleeping with prostitutes, and if you want to call it off, you have every right to do so." There's bitterness in her voice.

I glance at her, seeing the hard edges of her expression. She's very protective when it comes to men. She hates when women forgive everything in their men and I'm sure she thinks I'm overlooking his infidelity for the sake of this wedding.

"He's not…" I murmur.

"I know you told me he has a good excuse. How convenient that he has a great explanation for being caught with an escort. A believable one, too." Her words drip sarcasm.

I can't even look her in the eye because the truth is that his excuse is so elaborate and straight out of a movie that no one in their right mind would believe him. But he seemed truthful. Last night when he lied to me, he seemed honest too.

The saleswoman chooses this moment to roll in a rack with about ten dresses. I stand up and browse the selection. They all have lace, there are a few shades of white, and they're a wide variety of styles. Flowy gowns, fitted ones, silky with a layer of lace or puffy with layers of tulle, and they all have one thing in common: they're gorgeous.

"This is just a start to narrow it down to meet your tastes. Then we'll start from there to find you the perfect dress," she explains with the same warm, composed smile.

I pick the one that catches my attention first. "I don't know, I think I may have found *The One*," I murmur, admiring the magnificent piece of art in my hands.

It's love at first sight. It's a simple silky dress with a deep V-cut in the front and the back almost completely uncovered. The silky part is sleeveless, but it's the lace covering the entirety of the dress that caught my eye. It's simple with a subtle pattern, and it covers the dress from neck to toe. It has long bell-shaped sleeves that let you see skin without being vulgar. Same in the back.

I've never felt a desire to wear something like I'm feeling about this dress right now. The saleswoman helps me to change into it, and when I look at myself in the mirror, tears spring from my eyes.

It's perfect.

It compliments my figure and skin tone so nicely it seems designed just for me. I know I have to try on other dresses to be sure, and I will. But nothing will change my mind: this is it. The tears begin to fall harder. If my mom and sister were here, they would have said that this is fate, that this marriage is blessed. But my mom and sister will never see this dress, and somehow that makes this wedding seem more like a curse.

"Did you hear what I said?" Matthew pulls my attention back to our meeting and I'm finally able to move my gaze from the street outside my office window to his face.

"Not a single word," I admit.

He studies me for a while and then shakes his head. "I can't work with you today."

I inhale deeply and rub my eyes, trying to focus on my job but finding it difficult to concentrate since my encounter with the agent. A series of gruesome scenarios keep replaying in my head and I don't know how to stop this downward mental spiral.

"Sorry, I promise I'll focus on this." I wave my hand toward the papers scattered on my desk. What the hell is this, anyway?

"No. We're both wasting time. This isn't urgent. Just solve your problems with Silver and come back when you can get your head in it."

"I don't have any problems with her!" I answer way too quickly for someone with a clean conscience.

Matthew raises his eyebrow, a silent challenge not to bullshit him.

"I'm just a bit tense," I admit.

"For the last ten days, it's been increasingly impossible to work with you. So, if it's not her, it means you have another problem I'm not aware of, even worse than your trouble in paradise." He pins me to my chair with a stern gaze.

I don't know what to tell him. Ever since the agent told me about Silver being in danger, I can't focus on anything but her. On top of that, I feel guilty for lying to her. And the more I worry about her, the less able I am to tell her the truth, and the deeper I'm digging myself into this pit. But I can't tell Matthew. He knows we need to increase the security because my father told me there is movement around Silver, but he doesn't know the details. He knows I prefer to deal with security personally, because most of them are mixed in with my father's men and Matthew wants to know as little as possible when it comes to him.

"It's nothing, really. Some bullshit about the wedding." Now I'm lying to him too. They say if you want to be a politician you have to be good at it, and I am. But they never tell you how to deal with your conscience afterwards with the people you care about.

"Go home, please. Go to her and don't come back until you've resolved this issue."

I feel so out of balance lately that I don't even try to come up with an excuse to stay. If this is how I feel for a woman I don't even love, I can't imagine having a career while hopelessly in love.

When I walk into the living room, I find Silver with fifty or more small boxes in front of her. Paper in hand, she is reading and putting them in an order I don't understand.

"What the heck are you doing?" I chuckle and she jumps, startled.

"Jesus. I didn't hear you come home." She puts a hand on her heart.

"My question still stands. What are you doing?" I don't get what she's up to this time.

Every time I come home there's some news, big or small, that awaits me. Ten days ago, it was that she found the perfect dress and was so excited about it, I felt confident enough to put that in the big news pile. Yesterday, it was that she finally managed to master a recipe she was trying for a while—small news information pile. Regardless, there's never a dull moment coming home to her and I'm getting used to it. All day, I anticipate this moment I walk through the door and find out if it's a big pile or a small pile day.

"The bakery I contacted for the wedding cake sent sixty-three samples of cake. I'm putting them in the order they suggest tasting them, to avoid screwing up the tasting," she explains, reading another line and putting a small white box with the logo next to a similar box, neatly positioned in a row.

"Sixty-three? That's more than our guest list!" I choke on the number.

She looks at me shyly, like a little girl caught doing something bad. "Yeah. It may be my fault. When they asked my preference, I told them I don't have a favorite, so they decided to send one sample for every flavor they make. In my defense, I didn't even know there were sixty-three different cake flavors."

"Jesus. That's a lot to taste!" I blurt out.

She smiles and my day feels a bit better. "When I drop your name, they tend to bend over backwards to please me. I think catering the cake for your wedding day is a big deal for them. You're famous enough to give their business a huge boost if you're happy with it. Hence, the sixty-three boxes."

I rub a hand over my face. "This is why I hate adding my name to anything. Too much pressure. For Pete's sake, it's a cake! If I don't happen to like how it tastes, the bakery shouldn't go out of business."

She smiles sympathetically and then points to the kitchen. "Grab a fork and a glass of water. You have a lot of tasting to do. I'm not risking a sugar coma alone," she jokes, and I follow her orders.

I sit next to her, helping her put the boxes in order and then grab the papers and throw them on the chair next to me.

"Hey! We need that. Those are the descriptions of the flavors!" she complains.

"No, we just need to taste them and see if we like what's in our mouth. Should we do a yes, maybe, and hell no, that's disgusting pile?" I ask.

"Of course. Is there another way to sort through this mess?" She laughs and I chuckle.

Inside the first box is a small, white cube on a golden paper disk, a couple of inches wide.

"It looks...plain. But I guess they'll decorate whichever one we choose." She seems unsure about how to go about this tasting, what we should look for in a cake.

I pick up my fork, plunge it into the small cube, and then feed her the bite. Her luscious lips wrap around the fork and I can't stop my imagination from going down a way dirtier path than cake tasting.

"So? What do you think?" I ask after I take a bite too.

"Meh. It's...plain." She crinkles her nose.

"I agree. Next!" I pick another box with a pink cube on a golden disk this time.

I repeat the same action as before and we both moan over the sweet vanilla flavor that explodes on our tastebuds.

"This is a yes for me!" she moans and I smile.

"I agree. Next!" I pick another box.

She giggles. I could spend hours listening to her giggle. The thought is heartwarming and terrifying at the same time.

Halfway through our testing, we've reached a state of sugar-induced coma.

"If I try one more bite I'll throw up," she whines as I take the fork from her hand and drag her onto my lap.

"I can't try any more tonight, but if you want we can continue tomorrow," I suggest, but she scrunches her face in disgust.

"No. No way. I'm not eating another piece of cake for the next ten years."

I can't stop a laugh from rising in my chest and squeeze her closer. She laughs too, but when she puts her eyes on mine, her smile fades a bit.

"Are you keeping secrets from me, Raphael?" she blurts out without a warning.

The dread invading my chest is hard to ignore. "No, I'm not keeping secrets from you." I hear the lie slip out from my lips, and my moral compass shifts a bit in my chest when I see the hurt cross her face, then disappear almost as suddenly.

***

"God, why are you always in this sauna? Are you still on a strict diet or do you just like to sweat?" I ask Harrison as soon as I join him in one of the small saunas of the Hunting Club.

After feeling like a coward for blatantly lying to Silver, I asked him to meet, more to get out of the house than a need to sweat with one of my best friends.

"I booked another role, and guess what? They want me ripped, without an ounce of fat. Surprise, surprise!" he sneers angrily.

I take him in for a long moment. I'm so caught up in my own shit I haven't noticed this underlying unhappiness in my best friend. He's always wanted to be an actor since I've known him, but lately he's become more angry about what he has to do. He hit stardom young, winning an Oscar early on in his career, but now he seems to struggle with getting roles that give him the chance to really act, roles he deserves. Instead, he gets stuck doing blockbuster movies that require more nudity and less acting.

"Do you really need that job? You can always turn it down and wait for something better." There's no easy way to say it without hurting his feelings.

"He's *the* director. You don't turn down his movies if you want to have a long career in Hollywood." His tone is almost resigned.

I open my mouth to speak, but what can I say? He knows what's best for his career. I'm in an arranged marriage to boost mine—not exactly a great position to judge his choices. I'm worried about him, though.

"So, I guess you have to suck it up and do it. Does it at least pay a lot?" I try to steer his feelings toward a more positive side to this mess he's getting into.

He frowns and thinks about it. "Yes, it's a very good deal. My agent wouldn't go for anything less."

"Of course, he wouldn't. He gets a percentage on your contracts." I can't stop from rolling my eyes.

I never liked that guy much. He's a shark, and not in a good way. He convinces people to do what makes the most money not what makes them happy or successful. Harrison is an excellent actor, and he can handle every role that falls in his lap, but that doesn't mean he couldn't do better.

Harrison smiles. "It's a good movie, don't get me wrong. It gives me the chance to star in a dramatic role and I'm glad for that. I'm just cranky because I want a cheeseburger and a huge piece of cake, but I can't have it. Sometimes I'm just tired of sacrificing every pleasure in life for the sake of my career. But then I remember I love my job, and that puts things back in perspective."

I nod, understanding where he's coming from. I know a thing or two about putting my career before anything else.

"Well, if you change your mind about the cake, I have sixty-three tasting samples of wedding cake at home." I chuckle.

"You what?" His eyes widen in disbelief.

"I swear. I came home today and found Silver buried in cake. If I eat something sweet right now, I'll throw up." Nausea crosses my stomach. It's a good bakery, it isn't that, but there is such a thing as too much of a good thing and today, I reached my limit.

He laughs, then goes quiet and puts on his best-friend-worried-face. "Is that why you're hiding in this sauna?"

"Because of the sugar rush? No, I can deal with that." I try to joke it off, not dive into the real reason I'm sweating like a pig with him.

"You know what I mean. Are you rethinking this wedding thing?" The worry in his tone is as clear as day.

"No, not for a second. It's honestly going great, and I can't complain about that. The funny thing is, I like planning it. Maybe because we don't have the pressure of the real thing, but we're having fun choosing the details for our wedding. The wedding planner presents all of the options and we just sit there, choosing what we like the most. It's refreshing, once in a while, to choose something because *I* like it and not because someone else likes my choices. Does that make sense?" I try to explain.

His expression softens and a small smile graces his lips. "It's called 'living your own life,' I'm glad you finally tried it."

"Idiot." I playfully kick his shin.

"So, you and Silver are doing great? I mean, you like living with her." He's like a proud dad enjoying his son attempting his first steps.

I've never seen him look at me like this. It's just a relationship, he shouldn't be beaming because I'm capable of one. Maybe almost fifteen years of avoiding anything resembling a romantic connection has worried my friends more than I thought.

"Yes, I actually like spending time with her. She's smart, funny, compassionate…sexy," I admit.

"Do you sleep with her?" There's no malice in his words. Just curiosity about the extent of my relationship with her.

I nod, not wanting to go into the detail I'm sure he doesn't want to know.

"So, what's the problem? Why are you here instead of at home with her?" He gets to the point of this conversation, making me uncomfortable.

"I lied to her. A massive lie that could compromise everything we've built together."

"Do I want to know the details?"

I shake my head. "No, you don't, trust me."

"Okay, so come clean with her."

I've thought about it a lot, and at this point I'm not sure it would lead to the best outcome. I fucked up, and there's not much I can do to control the consequences. Which makes me uncomfortable. I'm used to planning my life down to the smallest detail.

"It's not that straightforward."

"Why?"

"Because I fucked up and I could lose her." There, I said it out loud. I laid out my worst fear.

"Are you in love with her?"

I don't answer. I don't want to go down that path. Every time I cared for a woman in my life, every time I gave her my heart, she disappeared from my life. Kelsey, Alba, my mother, somehow even Jenny slipped between my fingers without anything I could do to prevent it.

I'm not setting myself up for another heartache. Not again. The thing is, I don't know if I have much of a choice in this particular situation.

CHAPTER 26

Silver

As the hot water runs down my back, I close my eyes and let the drops wash away the sleepiness from my skin. I'm tired and it has nothing to do with my new life. My new existence is great. I've never had a sense of purpose in life, not after the trial anyway. I was hiding and living day by day. Living with Raphael has given my life new meaning. I'm not just playing the role—a pretty face at his side. I'm doing good, like working with veterans to help to give them the medical assistance they need, visiting schools to assess what needs improvement.

I'm being useful. I'm needed. I'm helping people in ways I've always wanted to do. I have a re-energized focus and I couldn't be happier.

The exhaustion is Raphael's fault. I barely sleep, because every night he worships my body in so many ways there's not an inch of my flesh that isn't sore, tingling with pleasure, responding promptly to his touch. He ruined me. I'll never find anyone who could make me come alive inside like he does.

"Turn around." His low, raspy voice makes me shiver.

I slowly pivot and face the shower wall. He presses his chest against my back, and I put my hand on the tiles in front of me to balance his weight. He lathers my shoulders, slipping slowly down my skin, cupping my breasts and squeezing firmly. He pinches my nipples and I moan. He does it again and I push my butt against his raging erection.

He slowly drags his fingers down my stomach, my belly, until he slips them between my legs, and pinches my clit. A low groan comes out of my chest, and I can't do nothing to stop it. An animalistic sound revealing my arousal.

"Do you like that?" he utters in my ear.

"Yes," I breath as he releases it and the blood rushes to the spot, making me almost come.

"Good. Because I'm gonna fuck your pussy from behind, and I want you to squeeze my balls dry when you come around my cock."

Damn, he can talk dirty! "What are you waiting for?"

He pauses for a second with his fingers between my folds. A deep growl rises in his chest, and he bites my shoulder while he pushes my legs apart. He positions his erection at my entrance and with a long powerful stroke he buries himself deep inside me.

I moan at the fullness of his intrusion. He backtracks, almost slipping out of my wet entrance, and then pushes roughly inside me again. He fucks me slowly and vigorously, with every plunge rhythmically stroking and pinching my clit.

His hips slap against my ass and every blow pushes me closer and closer to the wall until my forehead is resting on it.

My orgasm mounts slowly but steadily and when I reach the peak, it's so shattering my legs give out. Raphael holds me tightly to his chest while I ride out my pleasure, wave after wave until he comes inside me, his cock twitching deep inside my core, filling me up with his seed.

"Damn, that was good," he pants, resting his forehead against my back.

"Agree. Amazing." I finally have the strength to stand up without him holding my waist. I turn around and kiss him. "You know, I could get used to those orgasms."

He raises his eyebrows. "Then I'll have to find new ways to pleasure you, or you'll get bored. My new personal challenge."

"Not complaining." I slip my fingers into his hair and drag him closer for another kiss.

His lips possess mine and when his tongue slips into my mouth, my world tips a bit, pushed by the hammering in my chest. It's sex. It's just sex. I have to convince myself that it can't ever be anything different, more. But while my head might be able stay on track with this logic, my heart is all over the place as I drown in Raphael's world.

"Can we go for round two?" he whispers against my lips.

I rest my hands on his perfectly sculpted chest, putting some distance between us. "No. I'm already late for my appointment at the bakery."

I reluctantly take a step back from his inviting semi-erection. The lust in his eyes almost makes me reconsider my decision, and his nakedness isn't helping my resolution one bit. He moves a little closer and sees me hesitate for a second. He's a true politician—good at reading people and taking advantage of their weaknesses.

"Damn it! Stay away," I squeal, laughing when he grabs my ass and squeezes it, dragging me against his cock.

"I'm not keeping you here!" he states innocently.

"Yes, that's exactly what you're doing!" I protest.

He finally lets me go then turns off the shower, and as soon as he opens the glass door to grab a towel, I already miss his embrace, the warmth of his body. He wraps the fluffy fabric around me and dries my naked skin. I love the attention he gives me.

"We're not together this morning, right?" he asks as we brush our teeth in front of the antique bathroom mirror. I never imagined doing something so mundane with a man and liking it.

"No, I have to go to the bakery to confirm the cake flavor we chose, plus decide on some other arrangements for the decorations." I shudder at the thought of tasting another sugary bite. It's been five days since our tasting, and I've only been able to eat salty foods.

"I hope they're not going to make you try anything while you're there." He gives me a sympathetic smile.

"I have a list of at least five excuses to turn them down," I assure him.

He chuckles and comes closer after rinsing his mouth. "Do you want me to come with you?" he offers, hugging me from behind and kissing my cheek.

"Don't you have something more important to do, like save the world?" I tease.

He smiles and turns me around, trapping me between the sink and his body. In moments like these, I wish I could spend the day rolling around naked between the sheets with him.

"The world is spinning just fine without me helping it. If you feel overwhelmed by the wedding stuff, I can help you." He seems concerned, and I don't get it. It's just a matter of dropping by with the name of the cake and nothing else.

"I'm fine, Raphael. There's really nothing to worry about. It's just a matter of telling them what we decided and going over some details for the decorations. They'll probably give me a bunch of pictures to choose from and that's it. We can do our yes, maybe, hell no! list and we're good."

He seems worried, and I can't shake the feeling that it's related to the secret he's keeping. He's become more protective since lying to me, and I can't put my finger on what's making him want to be around me all the time.

"Okay, but if you need help, just call me and I'll drop everything and come." He pins me with an intense gaze.

"Is working with Matthew so boring you need an excuse to bolt?" I joke.

"Sometimes he makes me want to choke him," he admits with a laugh.

It takes me forty-five minutes to get ready and then another insane amount of time to reach the place. When I finally walk into the bakery, I'm feeling flustered.

"Sorry, I'm a bit late," I tell the blond woman behind the counter, Kelly, whom I recognize from when she delivered the samples.

She smiles and waves her hand, dismissing my concerns. "Los Angeles traffic is a nightmare. Ten minutes is considered early around here."

I smile because it's true. I'll never get used to factoring in extra time to get anywhere in this city.

"Have you decided which flavor you want?" she asks, guiding me toward a small room in the back. There's a desk scattered with papers and dozens of boxes are stacked against the three walls. The sugary smell is even more intense in here, since we're right next to the room with the big ovens where she does the baking.

"We want the orange cake with the chocolate chips in it," I say, sitting down on the chair in front of the desk.

Kelly seems to lighten up at the choice. "One of my favorites!"

"It's pretty good," I admit. "And Raphael loved it too."

She widens her eyes at the mention of him. "He tasted it too?"

"Of course, he did! We went through all sixty-three samples."
I don't have the heart to tell her we got through about half of them and then gave up.

"I didn't think he had time for that kind of thing. I'm sorry, it's none of my business, but I thought that important people like the two of you have a wedding planner doing all this stuff." She babbles on a bit nervously. It's the first time someone is fidgeting in my presence and it's a bit of a surprise.

"We have someone doing all the booking and organizing of details, but we do most of the decision making. It's our wedding, and this is the fun part."

She chuckles and picks up an iPad with a pen and starts to take notes. "So, what's the theme of the wedding?"

"The what?"

"The theme. You know, how you're coordinating everything to look consistent?" She tries and fails to hide an amused smile at my shocked face.

"It's a wedding, isn't that enough of a theme?"

She giggles and I relax a bit. I haven't put much effort into thinking about my wedding because I never considered it a real possibility. Now I regret not creating a Pinterest board with a bunch of ideas for my special day.

"I suppose it's a start." She tries to comfort me with a smile.

"We have white roses, gerberas, and lavender centerpieces," I blurt out like a kid in school caught not having their homework done.

"See? That's a theme." She nods, jotting down lavender and white on her iPad.

I didn't think choosing a cake for a wedding was so complicated. "Thank God I have one," I murmur and she chuckles.

"No worries. I'll guide you with questions and you'll be fine."

Two hours and a billion question later, I don't feel fine. I'm exhausted and had no idea you have to decide on so many details for a cake. And the cupcakes. And the dessert buffet. Apparently, we're also going to have a candy cart.

"Sorry for making you wait so long. I didn't think there was so much to do for a freaking wedding cake," I mumble to Sven as we step out of the bakery.

"No problem. They gave me plenty of cookies to keep me entertained." He winks at me, making me chuckle.

He's not one to talk a lot, but I've discovered he has a good sense of humor. I don't know how he doesn't go nuts sticking so close to me, doing basically nothing but looking around and keeping others from coming too close. I would be bored out of my mind.

I walk next to him toward the SUV that's became part of my daily routine. A car honks, startling me, and when I turn around to possibly flip them off, my heart plummets into my stomach. On the other side of the street sits the same beat-up pickup I noticed outside the wedding dress shop. Same rusty patches, same muddy plates, same pine tree air freshener hanging from the rearview mirror. The only thing missing is the guy with the baseball cap. I wouldn't think twice about it if we weren't on the opposite side of a city with almost four million residents. What are the chances of someone hitting the same two places less than two weeks apart in neighborhoods fifteen miles away?

I grab Sven's arm and his eyes dart to my face. "I think someone is following me." My voice trembles as the fear slips down into my gut and clenches it tight.

He looks around, taking in every face. "Are you sure?" His gaze never leaves the street and the parked cars surrounding us.

"See the pickup parked on the other side? The beat-up one?"
He nods.

"It was outside the shop where I tried on wedding dresses. I didn't give it much thought at the time, but I noticed it," I explain in a rush, stumbling on my words. "There was a guy with a baseball cap inside."

He grabs my arm and nudges me quickly toward the SUV. He unlocks it, opens the door, and helps me inside.

"Stay here and don't move. It's probably nothing, but I'd rather check to be sure. I'll lock the doors. Don't freak out, okay?" He smiles at me, but I can see the tension in his every movement.

From the car I watch him cross the street, phone on his ear, to look inside the pickup while he talks. He finishes the conversation, and before turning around, he scrapes the mud from the license plate and takes a picture. It all takes less than two minutes, but my heart never stops hammering in my chest. Something is wrong. Something is very wrong.

Sven jumps into the car and turns around with a smile. Sven rarely smiles, especially if you don't crack a joke.

"There's nothing strange about the pickup. I don't think it's anything to worry about it, but I want to bring you home and check on the plates, if that's okay with you?" He asks me with way too much nonchalance to *not* worry me.

I try to smile and nod. "Yes, please, bring me home." The feeling is so surreal that all I want is to go home and lock myself inside my office.

Today, Raphael should be working from home, and I can't wait to see his reassuring smile and know I'm safe.

Sven starts the car and dives into the traffic with a bit more urgency than before. We travel at a steady pace for a few blocks, his eyes on the road in front of him for half the time, in the rearview mirror the other half. He's not looking at me. He's checking the cars behind us and the feeling we're being watched is overwhelming.

My stomach clenches in fear and when I see him pick up speed, I almost throw up. "What's going on?" I ask, leaning between the two front seats.

Sven doesn't answer immediately, speeding through traffic and checking regularly behind us. I turn around but I don't see anything but a lot of cars stuck in Los Angeles traffic. But when Sven suddenly cuts into the lane on the left, I see the pickup behind us.

I can feel the blood draining from my face and my heart beating erratically in my chest. I'm sure I can't breathe.

"Get down on the floor and don't move," Sven orders in a firm voice.

I'm so stunned by his command I sit frozen in place, staring at him in the rearview mirror.

"Now!" he barks and I jump in my seat.

I fumble with the seatbelt, finding it difficult to remove. It takes me three tries before getting it right and dropping to the floor of the car. Hiding between the front and the back seats, I can't see the street or other cars, but I can feel Sven picking up speed and cursing under his breath.

The next few minutes pass in a blur. I'm so frightened trying to figure out where we're going and what's happening that I don't realize Sven has slowed down and come to a stop until someone opens the back door near my feet, and I squeal in terror when he touches my leg.

"It's me. It's Raphael." His sweet voice penetrates the fog of fear and confusion.

I crawl over to him and wrap my arms around his neck. He grabs my waist and pulls me out of the car, and when I put my feet on the ground, I realize we're home.

As soon as I can find my voice, I blurt out, "Someone's following me! Someone's been following me for weeks."

"I know. I'm sorry. I know," he whispers in my ear, tightening his grip around my body.

I push away from him. "You know?" My strained voice comes out like a squeal. I look at Raphael's face and see the guilt filling his eyes to the brim. His words sink in.

He knows.

This is the secret he's been keeping from me. He lied to me. He looked me in the eye and lied about the one thing he promised he would do. All the trust and faith I put in this relationship, along with my heart, crumbles.

CHAPTER 27
Raphael

"You knew they were following me, and you said nothing?" she shouts furiously.

A few feet from me, Matthew looks like he's trying to decide whether to jump between us or not. I wouldn't let him. I deserve everything she's hurling at me. I deserve her rage because I caused her fear. I should have told her.

"I didn't know they were following you," I admit in a calm voice that doesn't match how I'm feeling right now.

"But you knew something was going on," she points out.

Dave stares at me with a blank expression, but I can see his jaw twitching a bit. He knows we screwed up by keeping it quiet. He helped me set up more security with my father's men, but it wasn't enough.

"Yes. I was tipped off about the possibility that two men related to your case had gone dark. Just two people, not the entire organization. They're not *all* after you," I try to explain, realizing that this is not reassuring at all. Two men or a hundred, it's still a threat.

She scoffs and shakes her head. I can see the terror building in her eyes as this information sinks in. She paces between the couches in the living room while biting her nails. I've never seen her lose control like this. She's always so calm, but this is too much even for someone as strong and rational as her.

She stops in the middle of the room and shoots her gaze at me. "Where is the second one?" Her voice is shaky.

"What?"

"You said there was two men. Only one is following me. Where's the second one?" She puts her hand on her stomach like she's about to faint.

"We don't know yet. I've got people coming to help us determine what's going on and which of the two is following you."

"What's going on? You put me and my family in danger, that's what's going on!" she hollers angrily.

An icy chill expands in my chest, and I lower my gaze. She's right. She is freaking right, and I don't know if I can do anything to fix this mess at this point. As usual, I put my career first and this time I fucked up.

"Silver, please," Matthew's stern voice of warning annoys me.

"Shut up, Matthew! Shut the fuck up, or I swear to God I'll kill you," Silver hisses, pointing a finger at him. My best friend has the decency to close his mouth. "You're the one who suggested this. You put me in this situation and now I have to deal with it. You don't give a shit about me or my family. We're just collateral damage in his run for presidency. So, please, do me a favor: Shut. The. Fuck. Up."

The silence that follows is almost deafening. She's right. We all thought we could handle this, but we had no idea how big of a deal this is. We don't even know what they want with her. Scare her? Kill her? It's insane to think they could get away with it. She became a public figure like me when she showed up at my side. Her death wouldn't go unnoticed, not even if it looked like an accident.

The door swings open and Sven comes in, followed by five other leaders from the security team. They glance around the room and look worried, either because they have more information already, or because Silver looks like she's ready to kill someone.

"We have some question for you," Sebastian, the head of the team, says to Silver.

He's in charge now. That's clear from his confidence, his tone, and the way he invites Silver to sit down and she indulges him.

"We have a couple of pictures of the guys we suspect are following you. Can you take a look and point out which one you saw?" he asks, sitting on the couch next to her.

She looks at him, then at me, then at him again. Disbelief and fury morph her face. "You have pictures? You have fucking pictures of them and said nothing? How much do you know and when did you plan on telling me?" She spits this last part at me.

Sebastian doesn't flinch at her outburst. He just stares at her for a while, assessing her, and then opens the folder in his hand. "There was no reason to suspect they're here in Los Angeles. They just disappeared from New Jersey. People like that vanish all the time. They're criminals, they get killed, or they just want to fly under the radar because they fucked up," he explains so matter-of-factly I want to punch him in the face.

He's used to these kinds of situations. He *has* to be cool and collected when tensions are running high. But I can't stop being protective around Silver. Matthew looks at me like he knows what's crossing my mind. He shakes his head in a subtle plea to not make things worse.

"Or, you just missed all the red flags about this case and fucked up." Silver's cold remark hits Sebastian square in the face.

His lips curve in a small smile and he nods stiffly. "Or we fucked up," he confirms. "Do you recognize which one followed you?" He shows Silver the mugshots.

She glances at the pictures and frowns. "Neither."

We're all a bit shocked. We expected she would at least hesitate or second-guess herself.

"Please, look again," he insists. "Sometimes it's difficult to recognize a person from a picture but try and isolate some feature of his face and tell me if it's the same person."

Silver pins him to the couch with a stern look. "I did isolate some feature of his face, and unless he got a nose job, he is neither of those two."

Sebastian looks at the other four security men standing in a corner of the room.

"Get someone here who can do a sketch based on her description," he orders, and one of the men nods and walks away with Sven.

"Is my family okay?" Silver's broken voice brings our attention back to her.

She's looking at Sebastian but I feel the weight of her fear. It's raw and palpable and suffocating. What have I done? What have I done?

"As of the last time we checked with the people following your case, they're okay," Sebastian confirms. It's a non-answer, the kind I give when I don't know, or don't want to tell someone what's going on. My stomach clenches in a painful grip.

"So, you have no idea," she states.

"We have no reason to think they're in danger."

I want to punch him in the face. He can't use these mind games on her. She's way too smart and way too involved for him to underestimate her and treat her like a pain in the ass. She technically *is* a thorn in his side, given that I could have chosen one of the women my father suggested and nothing like this would have happened. But I don't regret my decision for one minute. Silver is the best thing that ever happened to me.

"Just like you had no reason to think there was someone here in Los Angeles following me," she points out.

"Considering you just confirmed that he isn't one of the two people we suspected, no, we have no reason to think someone is after your family." Sebastian's answer is stern, making my blood boil.

"Enough!" I snap and everyone looks at me. "I want to know who this man is, how he's related to those two, and if her family is in danger or not. I want a report every hour until we get to the bottom of this shit. Do you understand me?"

Sebastian just nods, stands up, and goes to talk to his men. Silver stands up too and I reach out a hand to try to touch her, but she dodges me.

"It's better if we stay home until we know if it's safe to go out. I'll cancel every appointment and ask Cindy to reschedule yours too," I say to her, but she's not meeting my gaze. "Silver, you're safe in this house," I add, and she just nods.

Everything I say right now is like water skimming over her but not soaking in.

"I'll be in my office if you need me," is all she says, turning around and walking toward the other room.

I follow her. She may not want me here, but I need to know she's okay, or at least will be. "Silver," I whisper, closing the door behind me.

"You promised to keep me and my family safe." There is no accusation in her voice, she's just stating a fact.

Yes, I promised and failed to deliver. Her back is turned, but I can feel her hurt. She trusted me and I let her down. The emptiness in my chest is suffocating.

When I speak, my voice sounds insecure. "You're safe. I promise, you're safe."

She turns around and pins me to the spot with a severe look. "Am I? For how long? And what about my family? Do we have to spend our lives locked in a room because we'll get shot otherwise? You promised to keep me safe, Raphael, but I am not safe. Not by a long shot."

I open my mouth to reassure her, but there's nothing I can say to fix this situation. I failed, just like I failed to protect Kelsey and my sister.

It's a curse I can't break. I deserve to spend my life alone.

CHAPTER 28
Silver

Sitting on the bed, I stare at a picture of my family. It's an ordinary picture of us in our backyard in the summertime, laughing at something someone said. My mother, my father, and my little sister and I are sitting around a table. I don't remember who took the picture.

"Is that your family?" Raphael asks, sitting next to me.

I didn't hear him come into the bedroom. I nod without looking away from my phone.

"This is the last picture I have of them. After that summer, I moved back to college and then I never saw them again."

He says nothing. I know he's hurting over this situation. Fear made me take my anger out on him, but rationally I know he really did try to protect me. It's just that my heart can't seem to accept what my mind knows. He wants to be the hero, to save everyone, but he can't. Some things are bigger than he can handle, and he needs to understand that he can't fix everything.

"I was trying to remember who took this photo or what we were laughing at, but I can't remember anything about that day. At least nothing important. That's what makes me so angry. I took those moments for granted and I can't have them back.

Why were we laughing? What was the occasion? Someone else took the picture, who was it? A relative? Friend?"

He finds his voice. "You look happy. Does it matter why?"

"Yes. Because I want to relive that memory and I can't. Because we're so busy doing everything else that we forget to celebrate the moments we spend with the people we love. It matters because you might not see them again for the rest of your life and you lost the opportunity to be happy with them." I find the courage to look at him in the eyes and I can see the pain he's going through.

"They're not dead, Silver. You'll see them again," he whispers.

I shake my head with a sad smile. "In the beginning I hoped so. God knows I tried to figure out a way to resolve the situation and reunite with my family. But there is no happy ending for me. Not even a normal life apart from them. See what happens when I try to have a normal existence with you?"

"You can be happy. Don't doubt that. You can't give up now," he pleads.

"Stop, Raphael. Stop it right now. Don't give me false hope. Don't do that to me, please." A hiccup shakes my chest and I realize I'm crying.

Raphael wraps his arms around me and holds me tight. I'm falling apart and nothing, nobody can keep me together, not even Raphael with his promises and good intentions.

A knock on the door startles both of us.

"Sorry to interrupt. The sketch artist arrived a few minutes ago." Matthew's low voice makes us turn toward the door.

"Give us a minute." It's more an order from Raphael than a request.

I don't know if they got into a fight or if they're both just stressed, but the tension between them is palpable. It's increased almost daily since I started living here.

"No, I'm fine. Really, I don't need a minute. The sooner we get that sketch, the better." I stand up and open the bedroom door, tired of this day, of all the people inside this house, of the crazy criminals out there. I'm just tired and I want this to be over.

"Are you sure? You don't have to do anything you're not comfortable with," Raphael reassures me, but with one glance at his best friend I see that he doesn't agree.

"I'm sure. Don't worry about me."

I can see he wants to protest, but thinks better of it and follows me out of the bedroom without a word. The living room is bustling with people. Some I know, others are completely new faces. They all turn when we walk in, staring for a few heartbeats, and then turn back to whatever they were doing before we interrupted. It's like they're trying hard not to make me feel uncomfortable, which actually makes me feel even more, well, uncomfortable. I'm not used to all this attention and I'd rather disappear than be on the receiving end of their stares.

"The sketch artist is in Raphael's office." Matthew guides me through the living room.

I follow him inside the office, noticing that Raphael is not right behind us. The head of the security is talking to him, but when he feels my gaze on him, he snaps his eyes toward me and gives me a warm smile. It's a small gesture, but it sustains me long enough to enter the room and not feel trapped.

The woman in front of me shakes my hand and invites me to sit next to her on the couch. Sven, who was with her in the room, gives me a nod and walks out with Matthew on his heels, reassuring me they are just outside if I need anything. When they close the door, I let out a sigh.

"Long day, huh?" she asks gently.

I don't remember her name. It's an odd thing to notice, but I just realize she told me her name and I don't recall what it is.

"You can say that again," I murmur, rubbing a couple of fingers over my eyes.

"We'll do this as fast as we can. Okay?" Her voice is calm, but her look tells me she's assessing me. Probably to see if I'm going to cry, freak out, or have any some other kind reaction to this situation.

"And then what?" I ask, because it's been bothering me since everything started to crumble around me. What am I going to do? I'm trapped in this house with a man who doesn't love me, not in the romantic way. He cares about me, sure, but love is a completely different thing altogether.

"And then we wait." She gives me a compassionate smile.

We wait. The one thing I don't want to do. It's being eight years. I've waited eight years for the other shoe to drop and now I have to wait longer. It's like waiting for your death sentence to be carried out. You're terrified, but at some point you just can't stand to wait anymore, and you'd rather just get it over with than be tortured with the idea of death.

"Are you a cop?" I ask, not sure where she comes from. I have no idea where most of the men in this house today are coming from. They're scary looking enough to be Raphael's father's entourage, but I can't be sure about that.

"I work for the police department but today I'm here because I'm Sebastian's friend," she explains and I realize they didn't involve the police.

I don't know if this scares me or not. Sometimes I wonder what Raphael's father does for a living, other times I decide I don't want to know. From what I've gathered living here, he doesn't question his father's business practices. As though he doesn't want to get involved in shady things. And maybe this is what I need right now. The people that should have had my back, the official channels that got me into the protection program, failed to follow those two people. Maybe this is the only hope I have to survive this.

Describing and drawing the man who followed me took longer than I expected. A couple of hours later, I walk out of the office with a million doubts about my description and the woman's reassurance that it's normal to feel like you described a completely different person.

The living room is quieter now, but people are just spread out around the house, they didn't leave the premises. Some of the security team is on the patio, others in the kitchen. Sebastian is setting up computers and other gear on the dining table. They're all busy doing something. Even Matthew is frowning at his computer and doesn't even notice me. A small victory for me, I couldn't stand his judgmental face right now.

The only one who seems lost is Raphael. He is sitting on the couch, rubbing a hand over his face. His shoulders are hunched like he's carrying the weight of the world. It's heartbreaking to see him like this. He's always so put together; my heart aches to see him so defeated. I walk to him and without saying a word I reach out my hand. He looks up at me and says nothing. He just stares into my eyes, looking for answers I can't give him. I grab his hand and guide him out of the room, away from the problems and into the safe bubble of our bedroom.

He stops in the middle of the room, studying me, waiting for my next move. He seems powerless, defeated, a bit scared, maybe. I don't want to see him like this. This is not the Raphael I know, the man who swore to protect me.

I walk to the bathroom, turn on the hot water in the bathtub and go back into the bedroom. He doesn't move an inch, but is following my every move. I close the distance between us and reach out to caress his cheek. He leans into the touch and briefly closes his eyes. He returns his eyes to me when I grab the hem of his jacket and slowly pull it down off his shoulders, placing it on the bed. I do the same with his tie, his shirt. I kneel in front of him and remove his shoes, gently peeling off his socks. I unbuckle his belt and unzip his trousers, then slowly drag them down his legs along with his boxers.

Every layer I peel from him shows me more of the raw feelings bleeding from his heart. Raphael has trained himself to be strong for those who are vulnerable, but nobody stayed around long enough to be strong *for him*. I'm not that person. I can't carry the weight for both of us. But in the privacy of this room, we can be vulnerable together. We can share this weakness without anyone judging us, without having to be strong for anyone else.

Naked in front of me, he watches me drop my clothes to the floor and show him my vulnerability.

I grab his hand and guide him into the bathroom where the tub is now full of hot water. He slips into it first and I follow him, nestling between his legs. His semi-erection presses against my lower back and when he wraps his arms around me and rests his forehead on my shoulder, he lets out a long sigh.

I feel him relax against my back. Skin against skin, we let our fear slip away into the water.

"I don't know what to do," he confesses in a whisper.

"I don't know either, but I don't want to think about it right now. I want to be here, with you, and chase away this emptiness inside my chest," I answer after a long silence.

He grabs my chin and turns my head enough to look him in the eye. He doesn't say a word, but he crushes his lips on mine and sinks his tongue inside my mouth. He keeps me firmly in place as he slips his fingers between my legs. I moan and he swallows every sound with this kiss.

He is rough, frantic, stroking my tongue with his and biting my lips when I try to pull away. He pushes a couple of fingers inside me and cups my pussy, keeping me firmly against his growing erection. He grinds against my back, hard and demanding.

"I need you inside me," I whimper when he pinches my clit.

He slips his hands on my inner thighs, forcing my legs apart, then pushes one knee over the edge of the tub. I'm open for him, for his cock, his fingers, his exploring. He reaches down and fondles me, putting his hard, long shaft up against my entrance. He grabs my hips in a painful grip and pushes me down on his cock in a rough powerful lounge.

I cry out but I don't stop him. I need to feel him deep inside me, fucking me with his powerful strokes. He pumps into me in a frantic rhythm. The water sloshes on the floor and I have to grip the tub to brace against his pushes. But it's not enough. It's not enough to fill the emptiness inside me.

"I need more," I breathe. "I need to feel more. I need to feel the pain. I need to feel alive," I confess without a bit of shame.

We are alone, the two of us, vulnerable and honest. Skin to skin, without walls or filters muffling the naked, human need of our souls.

He slips out of me, leaving me empty and alone as he steps out of the tub in all his naked glory. He rips open my makeup drawer and grabs the coconut oil and the black velvet pouch I brought when I moved in with him. He slips back into the tub behind me and without saying a word he coats a couple of his finger with oil and reaches for my back door. He pushes a couple of times until I relax enough to let his finger invade me. It's uncomfortable but not painful. He plunges in and out, preparing me, and when he slips his fingers away to push his erection in, I'm ready for the invasion.

He fucks me up my ass as he rubs my clit, slowly coaxing my orgasm. I rest my head on his shoulder and closes my eyes enjoying the fullness, with my legs spread open and my heart fluttering in my chest. He hammers me, grunting and biting my shoulder.

"Do you trust me?" he growls into my ear.

"Yes," I breathe, and I feel something pressing against my pussy.

I snap my eyes open and look down between my legs. With the pink dildo I sometimes used before I met him, he's entering my pussy. It's a bit cold and foreign, but I'm so wet it meets no resistance slipping deep into my core.

"Fuck." I let out a low, guttural moan.

He cautiously plunges it into me and I arch my back, pushing against his hand to accommodate more.

"Yes, please. Fuck me," I whine when he goes painfully slow.

He doesn't let me say it twice, he starts pounding my ass again as he fucks my pussy with the dildo and rubs my clit. I come so hard my body tenses and arches, squeezing his cock inside me.

"Fuck," he growls while he empties himself inside me.

He slowly withdraws the sex toy and puts it on the stool where he grabbed it. He tightens his arms around my body and keeps me flush against his chest while his erection softens and slips out of me.

We stay there in silence for a long time, until the water turns cold, and Raphael pulls me into the shower to warm up again. He washes my body, my hair, taking care of me like it's the only way he can feel useful.

***

We walk out of the bedroom and see the sun has already set.

Security is still here, and I doubt they'll go away anytime soon. Even Matthew seems like he hasn't moved from the spot we left him.

Sebastian approaches as soon as he sees us, his expression unreadable as usual. "We have news," he says, beckoning toward the couch where I gladly sit down.

I'm so spent after our afternoon in the bedroom I don't have the strength to worry. I don't know if they heard us or if I look thoroughly fucked, but I don't even care enough to feel embarrassed about it.

"We have the name of the guy who was following her," he proceeds when we sit down. "He's a local criminal."

"So, he has nothing to do with the New Jersey guys?" Raphael frowns.

"That's the problem. We were able to track his movements, he wasn't careful, and we discovered he met up with one of the guys we're looking for in a gas station in Nevada."

"What does that mean?" I blurt out.

Sebastian looks at me and for the first time I see compassion in his eyes, and it chills me more than his unreadable face. "It means they knew we'd be looking for them and they were smart enough to plan this carefully. They never stepped foot in Los Angeles. Which means they're a step ahead of us."

I can't even process his words. It's like someone slapped me in the face and my ears are ringing. It's happening and I can't stop it.

"You'll be fine. *We* will be fine," Raphael whispers in my ear. I didn't even realize he had put his arm around my shoulder.

"No. I will not be fine. *We* are not going to be fine!" I snap at him, standing up and walking back to the bedroom.

The world is spinning so fast the only thing I want is to disappear from it.

CHAPTER 29
Raphael

"I need your help."

My father's face is a mask of fury. I've never seen him lose control like this and I almost regret choosing his home office for this discussion. A more public place would have probably saved my life because I'm pretty sure he's going to hit me.

"I told you to dump her!" he growls.

"Well, I didn't so now I need your help," I snap, taking him by surprise.

I've never rebelled against him, not even as a teenager, but I'm so desperate I'd do anything right now.

I didn't sleep last night. After Sebastian confirmed that the person following Silver was most likely sent by The Hangman of New Jersey, I was on such high alert I couldn't close my eyes. So, if my father expects to have a civil political conversation with me right now, he's in for a big surprise.

"I'm not helping you. I'm not doing anything for that bitch. So, dump her ass end get your head in this campaign or I'll cut your funds!" he shouts back.

I stand up from the couch and storm to the desk, slapping his laptop shut. I'm so furious his eyes widen in shock and, maybe, he sees me as I am for the first time. I'm done with him and his threats. Done with being held by the balls in order to do his bidding. Done being his puppet.

"I don't give a shit about what you want!" I shout in his face. "Cut my funds, do whatever you want. Because if you don't help me get rid of the people who want her gone, I swear to God I'll retire from politics!"

He is still for a second, surprise covering his face. But then he snaps out of it and grabs me by the collar. "I will kill you! I will fucking kill you!" he hollers.

"Go ahead. Kill me and then explain it to everyone. You think the FBI won't know it? I work with the FBI! They're keeping an eye on me, and they'll be right on your ass if anything happens to me. Everything you've worked for will crumble around you," I hiss, and he releases my shirt.

I don't know if it's the confession about working with the FBI or that my threat sounds more serious than a crazy rant, but my request seems to sink in.

He points a finger in my face. "You are an ungrateful son of a bitch."

"Well, it takes one to know one."

"And what are you paying me for my services?" He smirks defiantly at me.

I stare him down, done feeling guilty or inferior to him. He needs me as much as I need him.

"Nothing. Because you need me in the White House. And when I'm there, you'll come crawling to me and show your true colors," I spit back in his face.

He takes a while to study me, his face void of emotion. It's unnerving how he can switch from fury to…nothing, in a split second.

"Be careful when you threaten me because I could decide to get rid of the origin of the problem." His voice is low and menacing.

Silver. He's saying if I take things too far, he'll kill Silver. I never thought I was capable of killing someone, but right now, I wouldn't hesitate to take him down.

"If you do anything like that, if you hurt Silver in any way, I will tear your empire down one crime at a time." My tone is equally menacing.

The door behind me opens and Marianne steps in looking serious. "Help your son," is all she says in the puzzled silence that follows her appearance.

"This is none of your business. Stay out of it," my father barks at her.

She takes another step inside, and I don't know whether to tackle her and push her out before my father takes out his fury on her, or step aside and let her chew him out for a bit. She doesn't look like a defenseless woman who needs my help.

"For God's sake! You both want the same thing, ultimately, but you're such stubborn asses you don't know how to help each other."

"Marianne," I start, but she silences me with a raise of her hand.

Looking at my father, she says, "The girl isn't going away, and you can't do anything about it without making it worse. So, just help him and get over it. He didn't listen to you, so what? He's a grown man who makes his own decisions, and if that hurts your ego, then you're not man enough to be his father. A real man would deal with the problem and get it over with." She rolls her words out without missing a beat.

I always thought of her as a meek woman who followed her father's directions first and then her husband's. But I think I greatly underestimated her. She's quiet but not meek, and from the way my father looks at her, he has huge respect for her opinion.

"It may take a while," he finally says.

I can't believe the way she made him change his mind, but I'm not going to belabor the point.

"I don't care, I just want it to be final. I don't want to have to deal with this in the future."

Marianne's eyes widen at the implication of my words. I know I'm crossing a line I've never crossed in the past, and I'll deal with my conscience when the time comes, but this is Silver's safety and I don't want any chance that this thing could haunt us in the future.

My father just nods, and I read understanding in his eyes.

I walk out of the office with Marianne, and when I close the door us, I breathe out a low sigh. She looks at me as we walk to the front door, and puts a hand on my arm before I leave.

"You found the right one, huh?" She smiles sweetly at me.

I lower my gaze a bit, embarrassed. "I don't know if she's the right one, but I know I would do anything to keep her safe."

A knowing smile curves her lips. "Isn't that love?"

"I don't know, it didn't start in the most conventional way," I admit.

"So what? Sometimes you give up too quickly on someone when things don't go as planned. But when you're forced together, you have to stick it out, and sometimes that's what it takes for a deep connection to form." She winks at me and I realize that my father and I have a lot more in common than I thought.

***

When I walk through the front door, I'm exhausted. After the conversation with my father and a night without sleep, I'm so drained I just want to crawl under the sheets and sleep until this shitstorm is over. But one look at Matthew and Sebastian's faces over their computer screens tells me we're just getting started.

"What happened?" My voice comes out barely more than a whisper.

"She's gone. Silver is gone!" Matthew blurts out, his face strained by worry and fear.

"What do you mean 'gone'?"

"She took off when you were out. She left everything, her phone, credit cards, everything. She just ran away," Sebastian explains.

I put my hands on the entrance table because I'm not sure my legs will bear my weight. I open my mouth to ask a million questions that cross my mind, but nothing comes out. Only one thought remains: *she's gone*.

And just like that, another woman I love disappears from my life.

CHAPTER 30

Silver

The sun filtering through the stained-glass windows gives this place an almost fairy-tale quality, welcoming me into an otherwise empty space with its warm light. The white walls and flooring match the pews, and a light breeze carries a faint rosemary scent inside. I didn't notice rosemary shrubs when I walked in, but maybe I was just crying too much to take in my surroundings.

It's been hours since I sat down in this little church. The tears have dried on my cheeks and my hiccups faded a long time ago. All that's left for me to do now is watch the rays of sunlight dancing across the floor of this place. Because when I left the house this morning with every intention to disappear, I had no idea what my next step would be.

I walked out and kept on walking until I found the hiking trail that leads here. I kept going for what seemed like hours, avoiding the main streets, and it wasn't the best decision. Under the late June sun, with no water or head covering, I risked fainting or worse. Possibly even dying of heat stroke, if it took too long to wake up or be rescued. But in that moment, I wasn't thinking about the consequences.

I just needed to disappear. To go back to the anonymous life I had until almost five months ago. Before I screwed up everything. I followed my gut, but my gut seemed to stop leading me when I got here.

It's like the farther I am from Raphael, the more lost I feel. And I hate being lost. I can't control my life when I don't know where I'm going, and not knowing is more terrifying than the thought of those men following me.

"It's peaceful here, isn't it?" A male voice startles me.

I turn around and find a priest standing behind me, one hand on the back of a bench and the other gripping a walking cane. He's old, in his late seventies maybe, with white hair, a face wrinkled with age, and dressed all in black. The only colored part of his clothing is the white collar peeking out in the center of his neck.

"Sorry, I didn't mean to startle you. I thought you heard me come in." He raises the cane a bit in explanation.

"No. I'm sorry. I was lost in thought and didn't notice you come in." My voice is hoarse from crying.

"May I?" he asks, pointing to the space next to me on the bench.

"Sure."

He sits down next to me and rests both of his crinkled hands on the cane in front of him. We stay like this for a while. I don't know if he expects me to say something, but I don't even know where to start if I have to confess my sins.

"Rough day?" he asks, without wavering his gaze from the small altar in front of us.

"Yes. Rough day," I confirm.

"Do you want to talk about it? Sometimes talking about the problems that pester us helps us to slay the demons behind that problem."

I turn toward him more curios than before. "Are you allowed to talk about demons in a church?"

"Where should we talk about demons if not in a place where God can protect us?" He finally turns around and smiles kindly at me. The first warm human contact I've had all day.

"Fair enough," I murmur.

I turn toward the altar and consider saying something. I don't know if he recognizes me or not—he is a man of God—but he probably watches TV, and my face is all over the political news these days.

"Is it possible that God would punish you for something you don't even know you did?" I ask.

He takes a deep breath and seems to contemplate my question. "God is not one to take revenge. He doesn't point fingers and punish you. When your life comes to an end, your good and bad actions will be put on a scale and that will decide where you spend the afterlife."

"So, if someone kills another person but does a lot of good things to balance it out, he'll end up in heaven?" The idea is terrifying.

He smiles at me and shakes his head. "There are mortal sins that can't be atoned. When you cross that line, nothing can save your soul."

At least I don't have to deal with The Hangman in the afterlife. Unless I go to hell and meet him there.

"Good." I nod.

"Sometimes our conscience punishes us more than God does," he continues after a long silence.

"That's what I don't understand. Why is that? I did the right thing. I helped people. I decided to sacrifice my life to bring justice to someone who couldn't get it for themself. I gave a mother the justice she deserved after losing her son. And I'm paying for it. Every single day I'm paying for that decision." I can't keep this bottled up anymore. I need to get it off my chest.

"Some would say this is God's way of testing your faith, but I think that sometimes life is just cruel and unfair. You shouldn't carry the weight of something you didn't do."

I look down at my hands fidgeting with the hem of my t-shirt. The problem is, I can't drop that weight because my decision ruined my family's future. I can live with not having a happy ending for me, but I can't endure the idea that they'll never have one either. Sometimes I feel selfish because I chose what my conscience told me to do, but I didn't consider other people's lives.

"I'll leave you for a few more minutes before I come back to close everything up," he tells me after a while.

I snap my head toward his angelic face. "I thought churches were always open for people who need shelter," I blurt out, not sure what to do if he kicks me out.

He looks at me for a long moment, like he's searching my soul to see if I deserve to sit here or not. The thought of what I did in the tub with Raphael yesterday makes me want to stand up and bolt out of here.

"A long time ago churches were always open. These days, we need to keep them safe from thieves and people who don't respect the sanctity of these places."

"Oh." It's the only word I can manage without bursting into tears.

"Do you have somewhere to go?" His soft voice is reassuring. I shake my head no.

"Do you see that door?" He points to a small door on the right wall. "There is a sacristy and a small bathroom. You can lie down on the bench in there and sleep a bit. You look like you need it. It's not much, but it's all I can offer."

"Thank you. It's perfect."

He smiles and slowly walks out of the church with a steady thump of his cane on the floor. I don't know how I missed him coming in.

After he closes the door and the click of the key resonates in the silence of this place, I'm left alone with my thoughts again, the only demons I'll never be able to escape.

CHAPTER 31
Raphael

"Okay, but let's put aside politics now and talk about something more personal. Shall we?" asks Sean Hardin, the journalist from one of the most influential economic newspapers in the country.

I don't have a choice, do I? He gave us the questions in advance, and would have interviewed Silver too, but she's not here. Matthew thought it would be worse to cancel, so I put on my grown-up pants and showed up for the interview.

I was polite, I answered all the questions without being harsh, even though at times I just wanted to stand up and walk out of this room. The only thing stopping me is the fact that we're filming it for the website, and having proof of my diva complex on video would be the end of my run for senator.

"Go ahead, I'm ready." I put a smile on my face and hope it looks real. Today Cindy had to work extra hard on my makeup to cover the dark circles under my eyes.

Silver disappeared yesterday, we have no idea where she is, and it's driving me crazy. Quite literally, to be honest. It's all I can do to focus on anything but finding her. I have the best men on the case, my private investigator is working overtime to find her, but the terror gripping me isn't waning. Every hour that passes is worse.

"When we scheduled this interview, we requested that Silver Argent join us. She agreed to come but today you showed up alone. What happened?"

This question was planned, but it's still painful to hear.

"She ate something that gave her food poisoning last night. She wanted to come anyway, but the shape she's in right now… let's just say it would scare us all." I force a chuckle that almost chokes me.

Sean chuckles too. "She'll be thrilled to hear your description of her."

I scratch my head to feign embarrassment. "Well, that won't be a pleasant conversation for me."

He lets out a composed laugh while I pretend to be shy about talking about my better half like she's possessed and throwing up everywhere. It's all so phony that my skin is crawling under my suit.

"So, no trouble in paradise?" He cracks a smug smile.

I smile too, but I want to punch him in the face. "No trouble in paradise."

"So, should we be anticipating some big personal news? You know? Morning sickness can take you down for real." He beams, no doubt thinking his question will lead to the biggest news story of the year.

Thinking about Silver pregnant with my child is something that warms my chest. For the first time since Kelsey, I could have something to look forward to. The idea of losing her makes me feel sick.

"Don't start those rumors. She's not pregnant, write it down carefully on that iPad." I laugh but I want to cry.

The realization of what I could lose hits me hard in the chest and the rest of the interview is a blur I can hardly handle.

When I finally stand up from the armchair and exchange the usual pleasantries with the journalist before walking away, I feel my legs almost give out under me. It's hard to stand here, exchanging small talk with him while his assistant takes the microphone off, and we quickly agree to another interview if I get elected. With Silver this time. I'm running on nerves and caffeine this morning, and smiling is as painful as getting my teeth pulled.

The moment I sit in my car and Matthew takes his place next to me, I allow myself to relax and let out a sigh.

"You should consider preparing a press release where you announce that you split up," he says as if it's some small inconvenience we have to take care of. He doesn't even look up from his phone as he trashes my relationship with Silver.

"What the hell is your problem?" I snap.

He turns toward me with an annoyed face. "Has it ever occurred to you that she took the money and bolted at the first chance she got?"

"She didn't even grab her credit or debit cards. Are you insane?"

"She can always say she lost them and have new ones made. It's not rocket science," he spits, and for the first time I don't recognize my best friend. He's mean and angry, and it has nothing to do with my campaign.

"Stop the car!" I shout at Dave who looks puzzled but finds a spot to safely park.

"What are you doing?" Matthew asks as I bend over him, struggling to reach the door handle and open it.

"Get out of my car. I don't know what your problem is, but I don't want you here," I hiss, and he looks at me wide-eyed.

"We're miles away from the office! Are you crazy?"

"If you keep talking like that about Silver, I don't want you near me, or her."

"It's fake, Raphael. Did you forget that this is all a fake relationship, a fake wedding? Did you miss that memo?" he hisses angrily in my face as Dave turns around, unbuckling his seatbelt, ready to intervene if this fight escalates to something more physical. He has no idea how close I am to punching Matthew in the face right now.

"It doesn't feel fake to me!" I shout in confession, and this shuts him up.

We stay silent for a long moment and Matthew lower his gaze to his lap. "I know," he whispers. "Trust me, that I know."

"So, why are you fighting it so much? Why are you pushing her away?" My voice comes out broken.

He takes a deep, long breath and then raises his face to the ceiling, resting his head on the headrest. "Because I loved Kelsey and Alba, and you're forgetting them," he confesses, breaking my heart.

"It's been fifteen years, Matthew. Fifteen years. You can't stop living for that long. At some point, you have to move on." The pleading in my voice is loud and clear.

"It hurts. It hurts to move on. It seems like everything we worked for these fifteen years, all the plans we made to do good, are losing their meaning. We had a purpose, we wanted justice for Kelsey and Alba, and we wanted it on a completely other level. We wanted to change the world," he says quietly.

"The plan hasn't changed. We still want to change the world."

"Now you have Silver." He looks at me for the first time and I see the defeat in his eyes.

"So what? That doesn't change the fact that we're going forward with our plan. If anything, she can help us carry it out. She has pretty strong motivation to give us a hand," I point out.

He nods and smiles sadly. "Yeah, she's pretty cool," he admits, and I finally understand where his anger is coming from.

Matthew, like Harrison and me, is still hung up on a past that haunts us after fifteen years. We were a tight group; we grew up together, and when Kelsey and Alba died, they took a little part of us that never came back. Every one of us copes in our own way. Matthew doesn't like the fact that things are changing. We've been so stuck in this loop of chasing our dream, we didn't notice life was going on around us.

Silver did this for me. She forced me to look outside that loop and find other ways to reach my goal. But Matthew is still there, stuck in that reality, running in circles like a hamster unable to jump out of that wheel he's comfortable with. And when he didn't see me on that wheel next to him, he lost his balance and stumbled out into a world that's different, and in some aspects, scary.

I failed Matthew. I failed to save him in the ways I'm trying to save everyone else, and my heart bleeds for him.

***

I enter the Hunting Club and head to the cigar room. It's noon, but when I called Harrison, Aaron, and Leonard, they immediately dropped everything they were doing and booked the room for a private event. I don't often ask to meet them in the middle of the day, not wanting to take advantage of their time and friendship.

I sit down on the leather armchair under their worried scrutiny.

"Silver disappeared yesterday," I blurt out.

They stare at me in silence, like I just told them I killed someone. No one talks for several minutes and I'm almost worried they didn't hear me or I didn't say it out loud.

"What do you mean she disappeared? How? Why?" Harrison is the first to break the silence.

"Yesterday morning she walked out of our home and didn't come back," I announce, and then I explain everything that's happened since the beginning. How I met her, the proposal, the sex, everything I've hidden from them.

They suspected something was going on but say nothing. Besides Harrison, who already knew most of the details of the situation, they listen to my story, eyes wide and perfectly still, gripping their glasses of liquor and taking in every crazy detail.

"Fuck," Leonard breathes out after I finish. "Fuck," he repeats without adding anything else.

It's rare when he has much to say. But very few things render him completely speechless, and apparently this is one of them. He's always calm and collected, accustomed to functioning in high levels of stress and nothing unsettles him.

"Why didn't you tell us? We could have helped." Aaron frowns at my secrecy.

"It was...I honestly don't know," I admit. "You don't flaunt something like this, and I honestly didn't realize how much I was caught up in the relationship until I lost her. I mean, I care about her but..." I don't even have the courage to finish the sentence.

"It doesn't feel fake anymore, does it?" Harrison says.

"No, it doesn't. It feels pretty fucking real," I admit.

I've already told Matthew that my feelings for Silver go way beyond "pretending," but I blurted it out in the heat of the moment. Admitting it to my friends a second time makes it really sink in. I don't know if I can live without her.

"There's no reason to think they got her, right?" Leonard asks, going back to his usual pragmatism after his initial shock.

"No, there's not. We dug deep into this, and she walked out on her own will, and we assume she's hiding somewhere. Probably scared." I'm certain of it. I would have torn the city apart if I had the slightest doubt that she's been taken.

"Why walk out? She's safer with you," Aaron murmurs and I can't argue his logic.

"When you've been running from your past your entire life, it's hard to know what's the right thing to do. You just get stuck in your own head, and you're not objective enough to know what's best for you," Harrison explains, and I totally get it. We're all running from that damned day in one way or another.

"So, what will you do if she doesn't want to come home? If she disappears and leaves the city entirely. You can't force her to come back." Leonard voices my worst fear.

I've thought about it a lot since yesterday, and the terror that grips me every time I imagine that outcome is physically painful.

"I don't know. I'll die inside, I guess."

CHAPTER 32
Silver

I wake up to the sound of gentle knocking at the door. Every single part of my body hurts from spending the night on a wooden bench, but at least my exhaustion made me sleep. In the split second between opening my eyes and reality sinking in, I feel at peace. A real, deep peace that lightens my chest despite my aching muscles. It's fleeting, but I cling to it as long as I can. I can't explain where it comes from, but it's probably my mind giving me a bit of relief from the turmoil of the last few days.

A second knock on the door pulls me away from the comfortable feeling once and for all.

"Coming," I answer groggily as I sit up.

I open the door to find the old priest smiling and raising a paper bag from Starbucks. The image is so unexpected that I don't even know what to say.

"I thought you might be hungry, so I sent one of my catechists to get you something," he explains at my puzzlement.

"Thank you. You didn't have to…" I take the paper bag and look inside. My stomach growls at the sight of the muffin and the smell of coffee. I blush in gratitude.

"I know, but it's my pleasure to feed a woman in need."

I nod and dive into the bag, tearing a piece of muffin and putting it in my mouth. I almost moan when the sweet flavor hits my tastebuds.

"How are you feeling this morning?" he asks and my heart skips a bit.

Can I lie to a priest? No, I can't. "Trapped?" It comes out as a question because I don't know what I really feel.

I want to disappear, to go back in time to when things were easier, but I realize I can't. I'm not delusional enough to believe that's a real option, but I take a minute to bask in the comfortable feeling this thought gives me.

"Why don't we take a walk outside? The sun isn't scorching hot yet."

"What time is it?" I ask when I realize I left everything back at the house, including my phone.

"Seven-thirty."

It's a mundane detail that somehow puts my mind at ease. At least I know it's been almost twenty-four hours since I walked out of the house. Not that I'm counting the minutes I'm separated from Raphael, but I'm aware of time passing. It's a small thing that gives me a sense of control over my life.

I follow the priest through a small door behind the altar, and my breath catches in my throat when I take in the view outside. The small church is perched on top of a hill that looks out over one of Malibu's many canyons, with its sturdy trees and shrubs accustomed to the drought of this area. The ground is dry and dusty, dotted with rocks of every size that give this place a wild, uninhabited look.

The church is something right out of the movies, painted white with a small bell tower, and has the look of the last refuge for someone on the run.

I take a bite of the muffin and sip at the coffee, walking slowly next to the priest.

"Is all of this church property?" I point at our surroundings.

He nods. "This hillside down to the main road. There's a small cottage over there where I live." He points his cane toward the west.

"It must be peaceful living up here," I mumble more to myself than to him.

He smiles. "Others call it lonely and crazy, given my age, but yes, you could call it peaceful too."

"I'd like to live in a place like this."

As soon as the words slip out of my mouth, I realize I just left a place like this. Raphael's house is not so different from this church. It's on the top of a hill with acres of vineyards and olive trees surrounding it. It's true, there's a lot of staff coming and going, but the place is mostly peaceful.

"Don't you like where you live?" His question is harmless, but I know his intention is not small talk.

He's probably wondering why a woman needs to sleep on a wooden bench in his sacristy and is nudging for answers. He's a priest, not an idiot. He knows people don't run away for no reason, especially with no money, phone, or any kind of baggage.

"Yes, I like where I live," I admit.

"So, why are you running away?"

I think about it. There are a million reasons why I don't want to stay in that house, and not one of them makes sense right now.

"Sometimes things get overwhelming, and you just need to disappear," I murmur.

He doesn't stop or look at me. He just nods and proceeds along the small path that leads into the taller shrubs. The silence goes on for so long that I think that he's completely forgotten about our conversation until he speaks again.

"Disappear or just take some time alone to think?"

I wish it was just a matter of thinking my way to a solution. This situation is so tangled it's no longer in my power to fix it. The only thing that would actually help everyone would be taking me out of the equation. Leaving Los Angeles is something I can control and would at least keep Raphael safe. I don't know if it would help my parents, but I refuse to drag yet another person I care about into this mess.

"Thinking will not solve the problem. Relocating far from Los Angeles will be more effective."

He nods again and takes his time to weigh my words or weigh his. I've known him less than twelve hours, but he strikes me as someone who thinks carefully before saying anything.

"And what about people you leave here in Los Angeles?"

"What about them?"

"Would they be happy if you…relocate?" For the first time he glances at me and there is some worry in his eyes.

"They'll be fine. Maybe a bit sad at first, but they'll understand I did it for them."

He stops, surprising me, and turns completely toward me to look into my eyes with his pale blue irises. I'm pretty sure he's staring straight into my soul and sees all my sins.

"Are you certain that taking away their freedom of choice is best for them? Or is it best for you?" His calm demeanor does nothing to soften the punch in the gut that his words deliver.

"What if they don't understand the danger?" I ask.

"What if they do and decide that you're worth the risk?"

I open my mouth to find a response, but nothing comes out. People often say, "I would die for you." It's a powerful thought, but when it comes to actually facing the possibility of dying for someone else, you realize how stupid that idea is. What happens when you die for someone? What good is it to leave the other person dealing with the consequences of your actions? Is it a blessing or a curse to survive the person you love? The decision to die for someone else affects both lives, not just the one who sacrifices theirs.

The priest resumes his walk, and I follow with more questions in my head than before.

"If you decide the best choice is to find a new life far from Los Angeles, I can ask around for help," he suggests after a long silence.

"Thank you for your help, but I don't have money. I can't pay to leave here." Also one of the reasons why I'm still stuck at this church.

"Money. Money. You all think about money, but what if people do good things out of generosity?"

"I would say maybe they don't want money but something else for their services," I blurt out.
I didn't mean to disrespect his offer, but I've never met anyone who helped others out of the goodness of their heart.

"What happened to you that you decided to build such thick walls around your heart?"

"Life, I guess."

"Well, it's time for you to find out that life can be forgiving and good too."

I want to believe him—I need to—but I can't. Every time I let my guard down, something happens to rip the happiness from under my feet. Raphael is just the latest in a long list of people I love who suffer because they're close to me. It's time to break this cycle once and for all.

CHAPTER 33
Raphael

"I can't do this anymore," I blurt out, interrupting Matthew mid-sentence.

He sighs and rubs his face. This is hard for him too, I know, but I can't think about the campaign knowing Silver is out there. They didn't see her in any of the security camera footage surrounding the house. She avoided the main roads and the cameras installed on the gates of the neighbors' houses. She didn't call a taxi or an Uber. She just vanished in the middle of this neighborhood. It's Malibu, for Pete's sake. How is it even possible that nobody saw her?

"Raphael, please." Matthew voice is a mixture of desperation and resignation.

"She's been gone for two days; I can't stay here and do nothing." I stand and pace my home office.

"You have the best men on this case. Just let them do their job and you do yours," he pleads.

"I can't. I can't focus on my career when I know nothing about where she is. I spent the last fifteen years wondering what would have happened if I'd gone for a run with Alba and Kelsey that day. I refuse to stay here and wait for someone to show up at my door and say they've found her body."

He groans. "And what do you want to do? Search every street and house in the city? You don't even know if she's still in the Los Angeles area."

The idea alone that she's left the city without us noticing is enough to make me sick.

"Yes. If necessary, I'll do exactly that."

"Do you even know where to start?" It's more of a curious question than a rebuke.

"No. She's not at Lola's, they already checked. She's obviously not at the club," I repeat out loud and feel the desperation sink in. This is Los Angeles, not a small town in the middle of nowhere. She could be anywhere. I flop into the armchair behind my desk.

"Okay. We need help," Matthew says before standing up.

"What do you mean?"

"We can't work like this. If you're going to stay here moping and worrying all day, I might as well help you find her."

A small smile forms on my lips. "What do you have in mind?"

"Let me figure out something," he murmurs, walking out of the room.

Half an hour later, Matthew, Harrison, Aaron, and Leonard are in my living room, waiting for my instructions.

"You know I don't have a plan, right?" I openly confess.

Leonard gives Matthew the stink eye. "No, we didn't know," he growls.

"Well, he's your friend and he needs your help. Just go with the flow," Matthew rebukes.

"Go with the flow? Jesus Crist, you're his campaign manager, don't you plan things years in advance?" Leonard counters and Aaron and Harrison chuckle at their banter.

"Seriously? This whole fucking week I've been trying to work with him, but he's out of his mind. At this point I'd do anything to find her and just get back to normal," Matthew spews.

"It was a spur-of-the-moment decision. It's not his fault," I chime in before they tear each other's eyes out.

Leonard scowls at me, and I smile. I know he's not angry; he just hates to be interrupted on a work day.

"So, where do we start?" Aaron asks.

"The security team already checked all the places I thought she'd be. So, scratch those."

"Should we go through her things to see if there's anything useful?" Harrison suggests.

The idea of poking around in her things is creepy, but maybe he has a point. Maybe there's something that can lead us to her. She must be someplace she feels safe and confident that nobody will find her. I need to remind myself she's not hiding from me. She's running away from the ones who are after her. For all we know, they still think she's holed up in this house.

"My team already checked her phone and computer, but we can take a look at her office," I suggest, guiding them into her space.

"Wow, she's really into law," Aaron murmurs, taking in the shelves full of textbooks.

"Yeah. She's pretty smart. She has a passion for criminal law," I confirm, starting to go through all the wedding flyers. My heart aches. I want to marry this woman.

"It's ironic that a trial prevented her from pursuing her dream," Harrison considers and I can only nod.

"Can't she graduate anyway and practice? I mean, you could pull some strings to help her," Leonard suggests as he flips through some papers in a drawer.

I snort. "She'd probably rip my balls off."

Matthew chuckles, nodding and agreeing with me. "And she can probably do more if she sticks with Raphael. She has a good eye for spotting problems and a good heart when it comes to people."

Surprised, I turn toward him. It's the first time he's said something nice about her. He doesn't look at me, but he's wearing a small smile—he knows I'm staring at him. After the conversation we had in the car the other day, this is probably his way of telling me that he's okay with her. Not that I need his approval to have a relationship with Silver, but having him by my side is a huge deal for me.

"Jesus Crist, this woman is more organized than Leonard," Aaron sighs and we all chuckle.

"Shut up," Leonard murmurs.

It takes about fifteen minutes to go through Silver's office and we find no clues to help us find her.

"We suck," Harrison states, plopping down on the couch in the living room. We all follow his example and sit with him.

"We're not going to search the bedroom, right? I don't want to find something *personal* I don't want to know about Raphael," Leonard says with a smug smile directed at me.

"Idiot," I say, but immediately my mind goes to the dildo in the bathroom, and I feel my cheeks heat up like a teenage girl. "But you're right. There's nothing interesting in there."

"Thank God we're not private investigators for a living, or we'd be starving to death," Aaron mumbles disappointedly.

I don't know what they expected from this search, but probably not getting stuck after fifteen minutes.

"Where the fuck is she?" I rub a hand over my face. "She's driving me crazy. I'm terrified someone's going to knock on that door and tell me she's dead."

My friends say nothing, they just look at me with gloomy expressions and worry in their eyes. The fact that she hasn't come home is probably sinking in.

As if on cue, Dave steps into the living room and everybody turns toward him, wide-eyed. In a split-second, my heart hammers in my chest. *Please, not like this. Please, not like this.*

"Sorry to interrupt, but a priest this morning dropped this at the front door. One of my men just told me." He hands me a pamphlet.

"What is it?" Harrison asks.

"Did he say anything?" I frown at the picture of the small church.

"He said you should check it out for your wedding," Dave explains.

I open the pamphlet and find a picture of the inside of the church. It's small, simple, and decorated with flowers. It would be perfect for a wedding. *Our* wedding.

"Since when do priests go door-to-door advertising their churches?" Aaron asks, as puzzled as everyone else in this room.

"Maybe since they're losing followers yearly, they thought a highly visible wedding at one of their churches would help as a publicity stunt," Leonard suggests.

"Jesus! You're more cynical than usual today." Harrison frowns at him.

I stare at the pamphlet in my hands, feeling like I'm missing something. "This is weird. I've lived here for years, and I've never gotten something like this. Especially not dropped off by the priest in person."

"Well, this is the first time you're get married, so…" Matthew points out.

He's right. Still, this is just weird.

"Where is it?" Aaron asks.

"What?"

"The church, where is it?"

I turn the pamphlet over and search for an address. My blood freezes in my veins. "It's literally up the hill behind us."

"Are you kidding me?" Matthew asks, dumbfounded.

"Am I the only one who thinks we should check that church?" Harrison suggests.

In a matter of seconds, we're on our feet and rushing to the front door. I have no idea what I'll find there, but at this point, I'm not taking any chances.

"You're sure he was a priest?" I check with Dave.

"He said so," he confirms. "But I'll take some men with us, just in case. I don't trust letting you go alone."

"He's not alone. There are five of us," Harrison complains.

"Yeah, five dumbasses who have no idea how to carry a gun," Dave points out.

"Oh. Maybe you're right," Harrison murmurs, looking away and blushing.

Leonard Chuckles as Dave rolls his eyes.

Five minutes later, we're packed into three different cars driving to a church like maniacs following a flimsy clue. But if someone gave me a flyer advertising the moon, and that's the only place I hadn't checked for Silver, I'd buy a ticket for the next trip in a heartbeat.

CHAPTER 34
Silver

I plunge into the dry ground with the shovel and force my way under the weed's roots. I lean on a rock and pull it out of the ground with dull snap. I'm covered in sweat, my hair is plastered to my head, but I keep digging my way around the small patch near the church.

"How is it going?" Father George's voice startles me.

I turn to find him holding out a bottle of water. I take a big gulp and dry my face with the sleeve of my t-shirt.

"How long has it been since anyone's helped you with these weeds?"

He smiles. "A while."

This morning he came into the church asking if I had decided yet what to do. He wanted to know if I needed his help getting out of the city. I think he's a bit worried, but I don't know if it's about me or the fact that I'm living in his church.

The problem is that I don't know what to do. The rational part of me thinks I should just rip the band-aid off, leave the city and start over. It's what I did years ago, and it worked then because my parents and sister were already in the program and out of my life. I had nothing to lose.

This time it's different. I have Raphael, and while I keep telling myself that this relationship isn't real, my heart knows that's ridiculous. The proof is that I could have left by now, but I'm still here waiting to find the strength to walk away.

Father George suggested some manual labor to clear my head. He says physical exertion helps you think more clearly. I think he's old and just needs someone to clear weeds out of this herb garden.

"I made some calls and found someone who's driving out of the city next week. Are you still interested?" he asks after a long silence as I finish the water. I didn't expect this conversation. I asked for it, but in my heart, I hoped he'd never find a way to help me. It's like telling you to toss a coin to decide something you're in doubt about. It's not the result that counts, but what you hope for right before the coin lands. That's your answer. I guess mine is that I don't want to go.

I lean on the shovel and look down, feeling a bit embarrassed. I'm a twenty-nine-year-old independent woman, I should know what I want. The truth is that I'm lost. I have been for a long time, but I can't run away anymore. Now I have a reason to stay.

"It seems like you've decided," he smiles.

"I'm sorry I gave you all this trouble for nothing," I blurt out.

He pats my arm and smiles. "Everything happens for a reason. Maybe you walked up this hill to stumble on the church where you'll one day be married."

I bark out a half-laugh. "That's the most elaborate method I've ever heard of for finding a wedding venue."

"Well, at least you'd have a good story to tell your grandchildren," he says, lacing his arm with mine and guiding me to the small door that leads into the church from behind the altar.

"That's for sure," I agree.

We walk into the church, and I feel immediate relief. The sun was roasting me alive, and I didn't even notice. I take a few step in and have to brace myself against the altar. In the middle of the aisle stands Raphael. I blink a couple of times, sure I'm having a heat stroke and hallucinating.

He takes a step toward me, hesitantly at first. Then another and another until he is a few feet from where I stand. His hair is disheveled, and he has bags under his eyes. He's wearing sweatpants and a t-shirt outside the house, and this worries me most.

"What? How?" I want to say so many things but nothing intelligent comes out of my mouth.

"I love you," he blurts out and my heart skips a beat. "I should have told you sooner. I love you and I can't live without you. I don't care if it's here in Los Angeles or anywhere you want to go. The only thing I know is that I want to spend my life with you."

He doesn't touch me; he doesn't come closer. He pours his heart out and waits for me to say something. I feel the lump growing in my throat and the tears pressing at the corner of my eyes. This is what I was waiting for. I was scared to put my heart on the line and be the only one to do it. I was scared I was going to get my heart broken and decided to run away to keep it from happening. But no matter how far I go, my heart without him is destined to be broken. It can't survive away from him.

"I love you too," I whisper.

He doesn't wait for one more word from me. It's as though this single sentence is everything he needs to hear. He closes the distance and holds me tight.

"Raphael, I'm sweaty, dirty, and I stink." I giggle, tightening my arms around his waist.

"I don't care. You could be covered in manure, and I still wouldn't let go," he whispers.

"Gross."

"Don't run away from me again, please." He tightens his grip around my body. It's like he can't stop holding me, like he's terrified I'll disappear again.

"I'm not going anywhere," I whisper back.

"Good."

He detaches just enough to grab my face in his hands and kiss me like his life depends on it. He slips his tongue into my mouth and moans at the pleasure of it. He takes my hair in his hand and bites my lips, taking every single breath away from me.

"Oh, come on! You're in a church, have some respect." A voice comes from the back of the church.

I just now realize we're indeed in a church, and we are not alone. Raphael detaches himself with a disappointed groan and I turn to see Father George chuckling and walking toward what looks like a dozen people staring at us.

Matthew, Harrison, Leonard, and Aaron stand with smug smiles on their faces, looking like they knew it all along. Behind them, a bunch of bodyguards that look very relieved at this outcome.

I look down, ashamed that I caused so much trouble. I realize that Raphael was not the only one affected by my disappearance. A lot of people in this church are breathing a sigh of relief, and I didn't understand just how many people cared about Raphael's happiness until this moment.

"Let's go home," he whispers, pulling me toward the entrance.

Those words never felt so true as in this moment. I feel like I've finally found a place in this world where I am safe and loved.

CHAPTER 35
Raphael

I walk into the bedroom with Silver in my arms, wrapped up in a towel, and I put her on the bed. After coming home from the church, we spent an hour in the shower, washing away the dirt, the sweat, and the fears that covered her body and soul. I found her. I finally brought her back home and my world stopped spinning.

I never thought I'd find someone after Kelsey, but Silver tiptoed into my life and carved out a space for herself. When she left me, I realized how big that space was. Enough to make me miss her desperately and crave her presence.

I lower myself over her body and brush her lips with mine. She smiles and looks up at me, curving her lips just for me. I could spend the rest of my life looking at her like this.

I kiss her again and get lost in the perfection of this moment. I take in her taste, the softness of her skin, the warmth of her body. I commit to memory everything about her because I don't want to spend a single day in my life forgetting how she feels in my arms.

Her fingers slip down my naked body, from my shoulder to my butt, exploring every muscle and every inch of my skin. She feathers her fingertips across my lower back and a shiver of pleasure runs down my spine.

I taste her lips, her jaw, her neck. I unfasten the towel knot and let it fall on the bed, then brush the tip of my tongue over her shoulder and lower, over her breast. I take my time kissing and licking the skin of her perfect mounds and then I suck in the peak, making her back arch, pushing her breast against my mouth. I tease her nipple with soft bites and slow licks, then I turn my head and focus on the other one. I repeat the torture and she arches and moans and drags her nails down my spine.

I kiss my way down to her navel and then farther down between her legs. I sink my tongue between her wet warm folds, making her groan. She grabs my hair in a firm grip and guides me to her clit. I lap, suck, bite her most sensitive part, until she comes on my tongue. I let her ride the waves of her orgasm, grinding my face until she comes down from her high.

I'm not done. To be honest, I'm just getting started, because I have every intention of making love to her all night long. I kneel between her legs and bury myself deep inside her. She catches her breath, biting down on my shoulder. She wraps her legs around my waist, and I slowly pump into her.

I wrap my arms around her and hold her tight while lunging into her core, making her moan and whimper and squeeze her pussy around my cock as she comes again. I bury myself deep inside her and empty not only my seed but all my feelings for her inside her womb.

I kiss her again before lying beside her and wrapping her in my arms. We stay there for a long time, without saying a word, just wrapped in our own feelings.

"Marry me," I whisper after a while.

Silver turns around and frowns at me. "What?"

"Marry me," I repeat, kissing her nose.

"I'm already marrying you. Have you forgotten?" she giggles.

"For real. I want to marry you for real. Nothing fake, no pretending, nothing. Just me and you."

"Really?" She seems surprised by my proposal.

I sit up and slip out of the bed. Naked as the day I was born, I kneel in front of her stunned face. She looks at me wide-eyed and I can't understand why. Isn't it clear that I love her?

"Will you marry me?" I ask again, and this time my proposal sinks in.

She smiles sweetly. "Yes. I want to spend the rest of my life with you."

She bends down and kisses me with a slowness and a passion I can't describe. It's like she is trying to convey all her love in this kiss and I'm drinking it all in. I want everything about her. Her love, her passion, her loyalty, her fears. I want all she has to give, and I want to give her all I have.

I crawl into bed and lie down, taking her in my arms. Tomorrow we'll think about our problems, but right now? This is the time to make her mine.

***

We wake up in the morning a bit more rested than yesterday, but not by much. We spent the night discovering every inch of our bodies and every part of our souls. But unlike yesterday, my chest is loads lighter and my mood brighter. When I sit next to Silver at the kitchen counter for breakfast, I take a moment to admire the glow on her face. She looks even younger with that dreamy smile on her face.

"Am I crazy to be happy this morning? I mean, with everything going on, the people after me, the mess that is our life right now, shouldn't I be a bit more worried?" She shares her thoughts.

"It's not crazy. Our lives are a mess, true. But we're here in this house, we have people working to solve these problems and most importantly, we're planning to spend our lives together. Is it difficult? Yes. Is it a reason to not be happy? Hell, no!" I kiss her.

She chuckles. "You make everything seem so easy. You seem so in control of your life that sometimes I envy you."

I scoff. "*Seem* is the key word here. The reality is there's a big team of people that have my back. If I'm not able to juggle something, I have someone else who can do it for me. And you have that too. My team is your team."

"Does Matthew know about that?" she jokes.

"We had a good chat about it. He knows now."

She seems surprised, but I don't want to go any deeper in a conversation that involves my best friend. I'm not sure how much he wants to share it with her.

"So, what's the plan now?"

"We eat breakfast, then we have an appointment here with the private investigator I have on your case."

"I'm *your case* now, am I?" She playfully pushes my shoulder.

"As far as your safety is concerned, yes, you are my case." I grab her hand and drag her toward me.

She slips her arms around my neck, while I hug and kiss her.

"Sorry to interrupt." Dave's voice comes from the living room.

We turn around to find him staring awkwardly at our feet. I smile and want to make a joke, but he seems embarrassed enough so I don't.

"Sebastian is here for the update," he explains.

"Let him in."

I grab Silver's hand and guide her to the couch while Dave lets Sebastian in. She seems tense, but I flag it as normal behavior considering the circumstances. The head of security walks in and casts a glance at Silver, a mixture of relief and wariness in his eyes.

"Do you have any news?" I ask when he sits down across from us.

"Not about the man following her. We have the guy under watch, but he hasn't done much since he followed her here, and we expected that. We don't want to scare him away, so we're waiting for his next move."

I nod. "We just wait?" I ask.

"Yes. You're safe in here." He gives Silver a meaningful look. She lowers her gaze, blushing. "Sorry about that."

He softens his tone. "It's okay, but don't do that again. We need all our resources on those sons of bitches. We can't waste precious men searching for you. This is the safest place you can be."

"I know, it won't happen again. I apologize for what I did. I realize it was stupid." She raises her head and owns her actions.

"Don't worry, we know you're smart, but I'd run away from him too sometimes. He's a pain in the ass," Sebastian jokes, and we all laugh. It breaks the tension looming over us.

"I briefed your staff about the changes I made to security, considering the other matter that we talked about," Sebastian continues.

"What other matter?" Silver frowns and my stomach clenches in excitement.

"Are they here?" I ask.

Sebastian nods. "In the car."

I turn toward Silver and grip her hands. She's pale, clearly nervous about more bad news shaking her life, but I hope this is good news for her.

Suddenly, I'm more nervous than I've ever been. "Listen, I wanted to surprise you and wait until the wedding. It was going to be my gift to you…sort of. But I think you need it more now than in a few months, so I'll stick with a more traditional gift for the bride."

I'm used to dealing with every kind of problem, solving them head-on. But this time her happiness is at stake, and I feel the pressure to get it right.

"What's going on? Seriously, I don't need any more surprises right now. I'm good with what I already have," she complains.

I chuckle and Sebastian does too. I take her face between my hands and kiss her on the nose. "This is not a bad thing, I promise," I whisper.

She bites her lip but relaxes a bit. I nod at Sebastian who stands up and walks out the front door. He comes back a few minutes later with two women and a man following him.

Silver freezes on the spot. I'm not even sure she's breathing. Her eyes widen, her mouth hangs open as she grabs my hand and squeezes it like she's on the edge of a cliff, terrified she'll fall.

"How?" she whispers while the three people, her family, walk hesitantly toward her.

It's like time has stopped and everyone in the room is frozen in place. The first hiccup shakes Silver out of her shock, and she turns to me as though asking for confirmation that she's not crazy, that I see her family too. Then she stands up and runs toward her parents and sister, hugging them tightly, one arm around her mother and the other around her father. Her sister joins the hug from her mother's side.

Sobbing, she lets out a low guttural sound that cracks my heart open. I've never heard anything more painful than the cry of this person I love. Her mother, father and sister cry too, but nothing compared to the agony coming from Silver.

I move closer and as her legs give out with emotion, I'm there to help her stand. Her face is contorted in a heartbreaking grimace. Too much. This is too much for her and I kneel besides her, holding her tight, trying to soothe her pain. I expected this to be an emotional moment for her, but not so much she can hardly breathe.

Her parents kneel in front of her, trying to comfort her. Her sister stands a step behind, weeping and clutching the t-shirt at her chest.

"It's okay, Silver. I got you," I whisper. "I got you, babe."

But in all honesty, I don't know what to do.

"Am I going crazy, or is Dad feeding the birds?" I ask my mom while I watch my father in the garden throwing seeds at a bunch of Scrub Jay.

It's been ten days since Raphael surprised me with their arrival. I cried, went into shock, and cried some more before I believed they're real, physically in this house. I made peace a long time ago with the fact that I wouldn't ever see them again. Watching them walk through that door was more overwhelming than anything I've experienced in my entire life.

"Your *fiancé* bought a huge bag of seed yesterday because Dad was going nuts," my sister answers, walking into the room.

"Your father isn't used to staying inside all day. He wants to go hiking and fishing," my mom explains as she chops some vegetables.

My heart squeezes in my chest. There are so many things that I don't know anymore about my family. My sister, for example. I left her when she was a scrawny fourteen-year-old and now she's a twenty-two-year-old woman who just graduated from the University of Washington. She's smart and funny, and she's done a lot of things I know nothing about. Like, she was a cheerleader in high school and chose to major in Computer Science and Engineering. She likes to hike with Dad but also cook with Mom.

Three entire lives I've missed, and nobody will ever give them back.

"I'm sorry to drag you into this mess. Again," I murmur, and my mom looks up and smiles.

"Sweetheart, you didn't drag us into anything. We supported you eight years ago; we'll support you now. You didn't ruin our lives. We were well aware about what we were going to face, and we decided to do it without any regrets." She tries to reassure me, but I still feel the guilt in my chest.

"And now you're engaged to a hot, rich senator. I mean, that alone erases anything you've done or will do in your life," my sister chimes in and my mother chuckles, shaking her head.

"So, I just became the hall pass?" Raphael asks, entering the room.

I turn around and watch him stroll toward me in sweatpants and a t-shirt, barefoot and sexy as sin. I didn't realize how much sexiness he exudes until I've spent time in this house with him and my family. I live in constant fear that my parents will see on my face all the filthy things he does to me.

He grabs my chin, tips my head up, and kisses me. It's just a peck on the lips, but it's enough to make me hot. "Hello, gorgeous," he whispers.

"Oh, come on! You can't be all mushy in front of a single woman. Not fair!" my sister whines and we all laugh at her expenses.

"You'll find someone too, I promise," I reassure her.

She turns toward Raphael and puts on a sweet smile. "Do you have a friend you can introduce me to?"

Raphael pretends to think about it. "Nope, they're way too old for you." He gives her a meaningful look and my mom nods in approval.

"Oh, come on. How old can they be?"

"Like thirty-five?" I point out.

"You've met them? Who are they?"

"I don't know. Harrison Bates?" I play dumb and enjoy her reaction.

Her mouth hangs open, eyes wide, as disbelief covers her entire face. "Are you freaking kidding me? *The* Harrison Bates? The hottest man in Hollywood?"

"Hey! Five minutes ago, I was the hot guy here!" Raphael jokes.

"You're taken, you don't count," she fires back.

"He's still way too old for you," my mom points out.

My sister crosses her arms over her chest and pouts. "You're not making my life easy. We're stuck here; you could at least call some of your friends."

Raphael raises an eyebrow. "Who do you think I am? Tinder?" He laughs.

"Okay, enough!" my mom interrupts. "You're still my daughters. I don't want to hear about hookups or Tinder or friends with benefits. I'm openminded but not *that* open. I don't want to hear about your shenanigans."

"Yes ma'am," Raphael stiffens next to me. I turn to find him blushing a bit.

Is he afraid of my mother? He looks almost...cute. I thought I'd seen every facet of him, but I guess you never stop finding new ones.

"Okay, but if we don't do something, we're going to go insane and start feeding the birds with Dad," my sister points out.

Raphael relaxes a bit and smiles at her. "I promise I'll find a way to take you out to dinner. Even if I have to rent out the entire restaurant to keep you safe."

My mom smiles sweetly at him. "That's not necessary, Raphael. You've already done more than enough for us. You don't have to do anything. We'll be just fine in this mansion with a swimming pool and theatre room." She ends her sentence with a scolding glance toward my sister.

"It's not a problem. If you're happy, Silver's happy, and I can't ask for anything more in life." He kisses me on the temple, and I melt a little in his arms.

"Those birds are savage!" My father's voice thunders from behind us, walking into the room.

"You've been feeding them since this morning, they're probably high on seeds or something," my sister points out.

Another booming voice comes from the direction of the front door. "They'll come back every morning and bring their friends. They're smart and know where to find easy food."

We all turn around and see the imposing figure of Raphael's father. Well, this morning is becoming more interesting by the minute.

"What are you doing here? I wasn't expecting you." Raphael frowns and I can't tell what he's feeling. He seems tense, but he also looks taller in front of him. More confident, almost. I'm not sure, but I'm guessing something happened since the last time I saw the man.

"I have news," he says simply, sitting on the couch in the living room.

I motion to my family to follow us into the living space where we find places to sit. We're all quite puzzled by the turns of the events, and I'm even more suspicious because Raphael's father seems to be the only one who knows what is going on.

"You're free to live your lives without anyone threatening you." He drops the bomb with such casual nonchalance that no one says a word.

"What does that mean? I don't understand," I blurt out when I feel Raphael relax next to me.

His father softens his gaze when he looks at me. It's the first time I've received that look from him, and somehow it's more nerve-wracking than his scowl.

"You'll be getting a phone call from the agent following your case," he explains. "He'll tell you that, unfortunately, The Hangman of New Jersey had a terrible peanut allergic reaction and died in his cell a few hours ago. Someone screwed up on his meal and they couldn't reach his solitary confinement cell in time to save him."

We let out a collective sigh. "Are you serious?" My voice trembles and my heart hammers in my chest.

He nods.

"What about the others following her?" Raphael asks.

"Do you really want to know?" His father nails him to the couch with a look and Raphael closes his mouth.

"You *killed* him?" My father speaks for the first time and a mixture of disbelief and discomfort covers his face.

"Do I look like a peanut to you? I don't kill people. I just deliver the news," he answers with a firmness that shuts my father up.

I don't know what to feel. I'm relieved because this nightmare is finally over. For good this time. But I also feel guilty that a man is dead because of me. It doesn't matter that he was a bad man.

"He deserved it." My mom's quivering voice breaks the silence. "He killed a fifteen-year-old boy in cold blood. Ripped him from his family, from his mother. He made our life a living hell for eight years. He ripped our daughter from our family, from me. He deserved everything that came to him. He ruined lives, he didn't deserve to have one."

Her words are so full of bottled-up pain that nobody says a word to her. I grip her hand while my father puts an arm around her shoulder. My guilt subsides a bit until it becomes a background noise in my heart. She is my mother. She suffered because of him; he shouldn't be more important than her.

"Does that mean that we can live our lives like normal people now, seeing each other like a real family?" my sister asks excitedly.

"I guess that's what we can do now." I can hear the relief in my voice.

"I can't believe this is real. I just can't wrap my mind around it," my mom murmurs.

I turn toward Raphael, who's been particularly quiet during this conversation. He's staring at his father with an unreadable expression.

"Are you okay?" I whisper to him.

He turns around and smiles. A genuine one, full of many unspoken feelings. "I'm fine."

He doesn't say anything else, and I understand that he asked his father to take care of the problem. From what I know, he's never before been involved in his father's shady business, but this time he crossed a line. I don't need to ask him about it. His smile is happy, but it also carries a weight that is heavy on his heart. He did it for me, for my family, for our life together. I can never thank him enough for taking this on his shoulders.

I kiss him on the lips, on the cheek, and then just below his ear. "Thank you. This means a lot to me. I promise we will carry this burden together," I whisper.

He stills for a moment and when I look in his eyes, I see gratitude radiating from them. He nods slightly before putting a hand around my neck and pulling me in for a kiss that leaves me breathless. He puts every emotion into it, every fear, every burden, every tear, but also every happy memory we will build together, every year we will spend making this dysfunctional agreement into a real family. There are promises hidden in this kiss, unspoken words that taste like love and caring.

"I can't wait to spend my life with you," he whispers against my lips.

And I smile and then laugh outright at the happiness bubbling in my chest.

CHAPTER 37
Raphael

"Are you in there?" I whisper.

"Of course, I'm in here. Where else would I be?" Silver whispers back.

"I don't know, I was scared that this night apart would make you reconsider."

"Raphael, it's literally one night," she whisper-shouts.

"I know, but you can never be too sure. Can you open the door?"

She sighs loudly enough to hear through the wooden door. I smile imagining her, hands on her hips, scolding me.

"The whole point of sleeping in separate rooms is so you can't see the bride until she walks to the altar, which is fifteen minutes from now. Shouldn't you be there already?"

"Yes, I should," I admit.

"So, why are you here?"

Good question. "I don't know. Maybe because I want to say that I love you before we're overwhelmed by this day?"

There's a long pause and I'm almost sure she'll open the door, but she doesn't. "I love you too," she whispers.

"Oh, for God's sake, you two. Can we get on with this wedding? You can see each other in fifteen freaking minutes." Silver's sister, Roxanne, shouts from behind the door.

There are giggles and shushing noises, and I can't stifle a laugh.

"How many are in there listening to this conversation?"

"Five! Five women dying of envy listening to you two love-birds," Lola chimes in.

"Where the hell have you been? We're waiting for you at the altar!" I turn around and see I'm surrounded by my friends in tuxedos.

"Harrison! Can you drag him away so we can walk out of this cottage?" shouts Lola.

"Is that Harrison Bates? How do I look?" Roxanne whis-per-shouts but we all hear her.

Harrison's ego puffs out his chest until his shirt is almost busting open as a grin spreads across his face.

"Don't even think about it. She's twenty-two." I point a fin-ger at his face.

He opens his mouth to protest but Leonard gives him his ter-rifying scowl. It works every time.

"We're going!" Aaron shouts through the door and then they drag me away from Father George's cottage.

When we told the priest we were getting married in his church, he offered his home for Silver to change in, since the church is too small to have a separate room for the bride. They walk me through the trail that leads to the small white building. Matthew, Aaron, Harrison, and Leonard, all surround me to the point that I almost trip on their feet.

"If I rip my pants because you trip me, you'll have to answer to Silver," I complain, and they all take a step away from me.

"We thought you bolted. We were making sure you'd be at the altar on time," Matthew explains.

"Why would you think that?"

"Maybe because it's five minutes before your wedding and you disappeared?"

"I... You know what? Never mind." I honestly don't know why I felt the need to check on her. Maybe because I needed to know she's still here, that she didn't disappear out of the blue. When someone you love dies suddenly, you don't have time to say goodbye. You don't have time to say anything at all, and you live in a limbo where it's hard to find closure. When something like that happens to you, it leaves a mark you can't erase from your heart. I needed to know she hadn't left.

We pause for a minute outside the church to take a deep breath and compose ourselves, then we walk down the aisle surrounded by the guests we invited to the ceremony. It's an intimate one, thirty people total, but we only wanted the people we care about. This is a moment for families, not politics.

The church is decorated in white roses, gerberas, and lavender. Simple bouquets that don't overwhelm the simplicity of this place. We opted for a simple ceremony too, just exchanging vows and rings, nothing more. Father George is officiating it.

When I arrive at the altar and turn around to see Harrison, my best man, and the rest of the groomsmen, a lump forms in my throat.

"Don't start crying now, or you won't be able to stop when you see her. Keep it together until she's here, then you can cry," Harrison whispers to me.

"Is it that obvious?" I force the words out of my throat.

"Yeah, man." He smiles, and it's a genuine expression of happiness, not a joke.

As soon as the violinist we hired starts to play, I look at the entrance and see the simple lavender dress Silver chose for Roxanne, her maid of honor, and the other bridesmaids. They look stunning in their long gowns and hairdos. First to walk down the aisle is Roxanne, followed by Dakota, and I glance at Aaron's adoring look when he sees her. Then Lola, and last, Cindy. I was surprised when Silver chose her as a bridesmaid, but she said they'd become quite close while working together on my campaign.

Cindy's entrance becomes a blur when Silver steps through the door, accompanied by her father. Her white lace and silk dress looks painted on her, the soft gown flaring at her hips and falling delicately on her long legs down to the floor. The veil covering her face and chest gives her an angelic look. She's breathtaking and I can't take my eyes away from her.

"Breathe," Harrison whispers to me.

"I can't," I answer and hear a soft chuckle from Father George.

Tears start to stream down my face, and I'm not one bit ashamed of it. She walks slowly toward me, her gaze never leaving mine. When she's a few feet from me, I want to rush to her, pull her next to me and make her my wife, but I can't. This is her moment with her father. He removes the veil from her face and a cascade of red curls peeks out from under it. He kisses her cheek and turns toward me.

"Take care of her," he murmurs with a smile, and the only thing that my stupid emotional brain can manage right now is a nod. No words leave my lips.

My eyes return to Silver when she steps next to me. "You look gorgeous," I whisper to her ear.

"You look handsome too," she whispers back.

And we stand there in our little bubble, not caring about anything else happening around us until it's time to exchange our vows. Harrison has to nudge me when it's my turn to speak, making the guests chuckle.

I clear my throat and pray not to mess up this moment. "You have made me the happiest man in the world today, choosing to become my wife. You are the strength I didn't know I needed and the joy I didn't know I lacked. I'm proud to be your husband and join my life with yours. I will be there to cherish your successes and to be your partner in everything that life throws at us. I will catch you when you stumble, and I will carry you when you are too tired to walk. I promise to nurture your dreams and help you reach them. I promise to love you fiercely when the sun is shining and when the storms shake our lives. With this ring, I promise you will never have to face the world alone." My voice breaks with emotion as I stare into Silver's eyes filling with tears.

I put the ring on her finger and grip her hand until she's ready for her vows.

She takes a deep breath and giggles nervously. "Okay, this is going to sound a lot like Cyndi Lauper, but I promise my words are in there too."

I chuckle and the guests do too, but I can't help falling more in love with this woman.

"If you're lost, you can look and you will find me, time after time. If you fall, I will catch you, I'll be waiting, time after time. If you are weak, you can rest and lean on me, time after time. If you are sad and your heart aches, you can confide in me, time after time. If you are worried and awake all night, I will hold you until you fall asleep, time after time. If you are afraid and can't take a leap in the dark, I will hold your hand and jump with you, time after time."

She takes a deep breath.

"Raphael, I put you through this bad poem not to torture you, but to tell you that there is nothing I wouldn't do for you. I will be at your side every step of our journey and I'm happy and proud to have you as my husband. In putting this ring on your finger, I give you my life, my love, my forever."

There is not a single dry eye in the room and mine are full of tears too. I never thought I could love again, but this fierce, strong woman in front of me taught me that there is more to life than surviving.

"In the name of the Father, the Son, and the Holy Spirit, I now declare you husband and wife. You may now kiss the bride," Father George chimes in.

I cradle her face in my hands and lower to kiss her. Silver. My wife.

Six months ago, I walked into a café in desperate need of a wife and reluctant about finding one. Today, I'll walk out of this church thrilled that my wife found me and taught me that you can fall in love twice in your life.

EPILOGUE
Raphael

November Midterms

The room is full of staff and the closest—and most influential—supporters. It's almost two in the morning and I can see the exhaustion on their faces. It was a long run, a tight battle with our opponents, but we're still in it, and we have a fair chance at winning.

The results are not official yet, we have a bit of a margin on our opponents, but there are still votes to count and percentages to gain.

Silver approaches me with a smile but her slow pace reveals her exhaustion. "Dave told me there's a man in the back waiting for you. He says his name is Cop, but I don't know if I heard it right," she whispers in my ear and my blood runs cold.

The one and only time Cop came to me it was to give me the worst news I've ever heard. It's been months since I saw Jenny, and fear that something has happened to her grips my stomach.

Matthew, as if on cue, turns to me and frowns. I smile, hoping to be convincing.

"I have to go talk to him. I'll be right back," I whisper in response.

"I'm coming with you," she says firmly, and I stop, looking her straight in the eye.

I've never brought anyone with me when meeting with him, but she knows what I do, and I promised her to not keep any secrets. She's smart, she deserves my full honesty, and I'll probably need her more than she needs me.

I grab her hand and walk toward the back door. When I step into the hall leading to the front entrance on one side, and to the conference room of the hotel on the other, I spot Dave in front of one of the small conference rooms doors. I make my way to him quickly, suddenly less tired and more nervous. Silver follows close behind me.

Dave opens the door into the well-lit room and I spot Cop in a suit staring at an art piece on the far wall. This is the first time I've seen him all cleaned up, and without his beard and ever-present hoodie, I struggle to recognize him.

"Sorry to interrupt your big night." He smiles at me and nods at Silver, not even questioning her presence here.

"Not a problem. Is there news? It's been months since I saw her." I can hear the nervousness in my voice and Silver squeezes my hand tightly.

"Big news, something that can't wait," he confirms and my stomach drops.

"Can you cut to the chase? I have something going on in the other room that requires my attention." And I want to know what happened to Jenny.

He chuckles and shakes his head. "Okay, okay. I'll cut the bullshit. Tonight, we are conducting the biggest sting against the organization to date. At this moment, they're arresting fifty-six persons involved in human trafficking exploitation. It's a high-profile operation, involving politicians and many well-known faces in the US." As he explains, my heart starts pumping faster in my chest.

"This is fantastic! This is absolutely amazing," I blurt out, happiness and excitement filling my chest.

He smiles and nods. "It is. And if you try to contact Jenny, she won't answer," he adds, and my heart stops dead as fast as it started to run.

"What do you mean? You know Jenny?"

Again, he nods. "We always knew about her, and we kept an eye on her. We let you talk to her because she trusted and spoke with you. But the place she was in wasn't safe anymore. They would have guessed there was a mole and found her. We took her out and put her in a safe place. She's fine, heathy and starting a new life," he reassures me.

I sigh out loud. So many emotions overwhelm me in this exact moment, but the only one I focus on is relief. She is safe. She is heathy and safe, and that's the only thing that counts.

"Thank you."

"Good. I'll let you go back to your night."

"Wait. Is there a reason you choose the midterms to take them down?"

He smirks. "They're so focused on the big news in politics they weren't paying attention to what was going on around them. They didn't even realize something was off."

He doesn't wait for my reply, he just walks out the door and disappears in the same ghostly way he did all these years I've known him.

"If you ask your father, maybe you can find out where she is." Silver's voice makes me turn around.

She's worried and seems surprised when I smile. "No. She's fine; she's starting a new life. I helped her as much as I could, now it's time for someone else to take care of her. I can't save every woman on this earth, at least not one at a time. I need to focus on winning the elections and saving women one law at time. That's my plan, my grand scheme, to create a safer world for women."

She looks at me like I'm the most important person on the planet and that is all I need to walk out of the room and go back to claim my victory.

When I step inside, Matthew runs to me. "Where the hell have you been? They just gave us the results—you won! You won, Raphael! You're California's new senator!"

I did it. I fucking did it! I stepped into the big tank. Now it's time to swim and fight and chew my way up to the top.

I grab Silver's hand, walk to the podium, and take in the brightness of my future next to the woman who will walk with me in the halls of the White House. Because, next to someone like Silver, anything is possible.

BONUS EPILOGUE
Silver

Fifteen years later

"So, they're kicking us out, huh?" I grab Raphael's hand and lean against his shoulder.

"It looks like it, yes," he chuckles.

"After all you did for this country. They're just kicking us out."

"That's kind of how it works. After the end of the second term, they change tenants in the White House."

Senator, and two terms as president of the United States. It's been quite an adventure.

"What do we do now?" I can't hide the sadness in my voice.

"We keep saving the world, just in a different way." He kisses my head as we stare at the massive white building in front of us.

"We could enjoy our family. Go on vacations without worrying about avoiding a war," I suggest.

"That would be lovely. Do you think you can stay away from your organization for a while?"

"I think we have built a solid foundation for that. I can take a couple weeks' vacation."

"A couple weeks? How generous!" he teases.

"Are *you* able to step away from politics?"

He shrugs. "Probably not, but for the first month, we should be safe."

"Good. Are you still planning to save the world?"

He kisses my head. "Of course."

"So, we really have to go now." I turn toward him and peck him on the lips.

"Yes, the car is waiting."

"Alba, Christopher, go fetch Jupiter, he's barking at the photographers again."

I watch my kids run toward the fence that separates the White House grounds from the street. Raphael tugs my hand and we turn around, turning our backs on the most famous house in the world that was our home for eight years, and walk away.

When I met Raphael, I was afraid of the world and running from myself. Fifteen years later, that fear never completely disappeared. I'm afraid about what the world could become, but I've learned to use that fear to change things, not for me alone, but for my husband, for my children, and for the future generations that will receive this world from us.

We promised to change the world, and we won't fail to deliver on those promises.

***

Thank you for reading Raphael and Silver's story.
I have a special surprise if you want to read more of my
books. You can read the first book of the rock star romance
Roadies Series, Backstage, for FREE!

Yes, you heard it right! If you subscribe to my newsletter by following the link below, you can download the standalone novel for free!

https://hello.erikavanzin.com/welcome/

***

As an indie author, I sincerely appreciate you reading and helping spread the word!

If you loved The Senator: Raphael, please consider leaving a quick review. Reviews help readers like you find books they'll love.

BOOKS BY ERIKA VANZIN

ROADIES SERIES (Complete)

Backstage

Paparazzi

Faith

Showtime

Betrayal

LOS ANGELES BILLIONAIRES

The producer: Aaron

The senator: Raphael

About the author

Erika Vanzin is the Italian Amazon bestselling author of the rock star romance Roadies Series.

After traveling around the world with her husband, she settled down in Seattle, enjoying the marvelous Pacific Northwest. She brought from Italy a couple of suitcases, fifteen boxes full of books, and her most successful novels translated into English.

While she is not writing, she enjoys reading books, watching the Kraken hockey games, and working on DIY projects.

Keep in touch with Erika via the web:

Website: https://www.erikavanzin.com/

BookBub: https://www.bookbub.com/authors/erika-vanzin

Goodreads: https://www.goodreads.com/author/
show/14437720.Erika_Vanzin

Facebook: https://www.facebook.com/erikavanzinauthor

Instagram: https://www.instagram.com/clumsyeki/

TikTok: https://www.tiktok.com/@authorerikavanzin

Twitter: https://twitter.com/ErikaVanzin

Newsletter: https://hello.erikavanzin.com/welcome/

Acknowledgements

Writing a book is a journey, and I couldn't have reached this destination without the unwavering support and love from the incredible people in my life. Their encouragement, understanding, and belief in my dreams have fueled my passion for storytelling, making this book a reality.

My beloved husband, Dario. You are my rock, my inspiration, and my biggest cheerleader. Your unwavering belief in me and your constant encouragement pushed me to pursue my writing dreams. Thank you for your patience during the countless late nights and for being my sounding board whenever I needed it. Your love and support are the foundation of my success.

My wonderful family who instilled in me the love for literature and the importance of following my heart, thank you for fostering my creativity and for always being there to lift me up. I am grateful for each and every one of you.

Staci, my incredible line editor. Your keen eye for detail and your deep understanding of the genre have transformed my words into a captivating story. Your invaluable feedback and constructive criticism have pushed me to become a better writer. Thank you for your dedication, patience, and for believing in the potential of this manuscript.

Annalisa, my talented proofreader. Your meticulousness and sharp eye have ensured that my words flow seamlessly. Thank you for your meticulous attention to detail and for meticulously combing through the manuscript to catch even the smallest errors. Your contribution has made this book shine.

Chiara and Annalisa, my dearest friends. You have been my rocks, my sounding boards, and my source of endless support. Your unwavering belief in me and your constant encouragement have been the fuel that kept me going during the challenging moments. Thank you for your honesty, your inspiration, and for always being there to cheer me on. I am forever grateful for your friendship.

To my readers. Without you, this book would be mere words on a page. Your passion for romance and your unwavering support of my work have been a constant motivation. Your messages, reviews, and words of encouragement have touched my heart in ways I cannot fully express. I write for you, and it is an honor to share my stories with you.

To all the friends, mentors, and fellow authors who have touched my life along this writing journey, thank you for your wisdom, guidance, and camaraderie. Your presence has been instrumental in shaping my career, and I am grateful for every interaction and shared experience.

To everyone who has played a part, big or small, in the creation of this book, I thank you from the bottom of my heart. Your support and belief in me have made all the difference.